LAST EXIT TO MURDER

EDITED BY
DARRELL JAMES, LINDA O. JOHNSTON
& TAMMY KAEHLER

Down and Out Books, LLC
3959 Van Dyke Rd, Ste. 265
Lutz, FL 33558
www.DownAndOutBooks.com

Cover design by JT Lindroos

ISBN: 1937495566

ISBN-13: 978-1-937495-56-5

LAST EXIT
TO MURDER

This anthology is dedicated to the memory of Diana James, former Chapter President, for her untiring work in furthering the mission and interests of Sisters in Crime/Los Angeles and for her love and support of mystery writers everywhere.
She is dearly missed.

CONTENTS

Introduction — 1
Gary Phillips

Cam the Man — 3
L.H. Dillman

Rocket 88 — 17
Donna May

Shikata Ga Nai — 25
Beverly Graf

Dance Man — 41
Andrew Jetarski

Dead Man's Curve — 57
Paul D. Marks

Identity Crisis — 77
Lynn Allyson

The Last of the Recycled Cyclads — 87
Bonnie J. Cardone

Not My Day — 101
Stephen Buehler

CONTENTS

By Anonymous — 105
Miko Johnston

Road to Revenge — 111
Nena Jover Kelty

Traffic Control — 121
Eric Stone

The Lowriders — 135
Avril Adams

Driving Dead Daisy — 145
Laura Brennan

The Last Joy Ride — 157
Julie G. Beers

Kill Joy — 165
Laurie Stevens

Dark Nights at the Deluxe Drive-In — 181
Sally Carpenter

About the Contributors — 201

Introduction

Gary Phillips

There's something about the car.

It's where you sat against the warm tuck and roll leather back seat of the Chevy Nomad, your lips whispering against the cheerleader's luscious perfumed breasts after the big game. It was you and your dad putting the finishing touches on that four-barrel carb installed in the Pontiac Judge GTO. Or it was the metalflake emerald green Boss 302 Mustang matching your best hit-the-clubs outfit, ragtop down, wind against your knockoff Gucci shades.

Those cars were born Detroit Iron, but they were baptized on the West Coast.

Cars fuel our fictions: Jim Sallis' Driver, a sometime Hollywood stunt car handler and always robbery getaway man cruising Pico Boulevard, his mind slotted in neutral. Dominic Toretto racing that midnight dark Dodge Charger over the Vincent Thomas bridge in the original *Fast and Furious.* Michael Connelly's Mickey Haller, an ambulance chaser maintaining a rolling office in his chauffeured cherry Lincoln that eddies back and forth across the vast Southland sprawl.

The car is cool.

What better way than to examine the allure of the car and where it takes you but in this muscular collection of sixteen original stories, *Last Exit to Murder.* For this city wasn't built on rock & roll, though it blares from many a dashboard speaker of vehicles traveling miles upon miles of freeways and byways.

This city was built to be connected by those ribbons of concrete with last exits into tough neighborhoods, tony enclaves, and all points in between. This is where you can be cocooned in your car and drift by bodegas, nail parlors, psychic readers, dog groomers, auto parts suppliers and cut rate tax preparers, where the alleys behind those storefronts occasionally have bodies dumped in them.

In these pages you'll take joyrides through the darker streets. There are tales herein that capture the essence of our car-centered culture in the context of crime—those who commit it and those who might find themselves in the trunk, duct tape on their mouth, kicking at the lock to get out.

Buckle up. You got shotgun.

Cam the Man

L. H. Dillman

Mini-vans are wuss-mobiles, and this used Honda Odyssey my mom is checking out today is totally lame. Boring alloy wheels and paint the color of pigeon crap. No iPod hook-up or DVD player. If it were up to me, we'd be down the street looking at SUVs, but my mom says even the used SUVs are too expensive. Plus, she says, Nita is only seven and it's hard for her to climb into a tall car, and Troy is only three and it's easier to get his car seat in and out of a van. All I can say is, when I get my license in three years, I'm not going to be driving a stupid Honda Odyssey.

So we're here at Valley Vans on Van Nuys Boulevard on the hottest freaking Sunday of the summer, waves of heat shimmying up from the blacktop. The three of us kids have just about had it with car shopping. Mom's trying to read how many miles this Odyssey's got, and Nita's skipping in circles, and I'd rather be reading the new book in the *Doom Star Chronicles*, which is a graphic novel series, but I'm holding Troy's hand so he doesn't run off.

And this guy comes out of nowhere, just pops up and says to my mom, "Hel-lo gorgeous!" He's about the same age as her, which is thirty-six, and he's got blond hair, like my mom, but he's wearing a long-sleeved white shirt with buttons and a collar and black slacks, like a geek, while we're all in shorts and tank-tops because it's freakin' a hundred degrees out here.

Mom giggles a little bit. Because he called her "gorgeous" I guess. She thinks she's overweight.

"You like Hondas? Fantastic. We're running a special on 'em." He smiles, and his front teeth are different shades of white.

"How many owners has this one had?" my mom asks.

"I'm Cam," he says, shoving his hand out to shake hers. "And you are?" He's asking all of us.

"Angie Foster," she says. "And this is Scotty and Nita and Troy."

"Fantastic!" He pumps my hand like a jack hammer, then he squats down to eye-level with Nita and Troy, and I can see the roots of his hair are brown, just like Mom's. He shakes their little hands then stands up and winks at Mom. "Are there any more Fosters, or is this it?"

"It's just the four of us," she says, smiling. She's pretty when she smiles.

"Great! So you've decided on a mini-van?"

She nods. "For safety, for the kids."

I roll my eyes. We had an argument about this. I read that SUVs with electronic stability control are just as safe as mini-vans, but Mom never listens to me.

"Well, you picked the right place," he says. "We specialize in mini-vans, as you can see."

Yeah, we can see. Rows and rows of them. Loser-ville.

He pats the Odyssey. "You like this one?"

I start to say, "No," but Mom says, "Sure," and she's louder.

"How 'bout a test drive?" He bends down to look my brother and sister straight on. "Wudja like that?" When they don't answer, he offers to buy sodas from the machine inside and let us drink them on the way. "Only, you can't tell my boss," he says with a wink.

"Sounds good, right?" Mom says to us.

Nita and Troy giggle. They love their soda.

Cam asks my mom for her driver's license so he can photocopy it. Insurance requirement, he says. While he's off copying her license, I move Troy's car seat into the Odyssey for the test drive. Then, we all climb in, and Cam brings out the sodas and the keys and off we go. Mom is at the wheel and Cam is riding shotgun.

"You from LA?" he asks. "I mean, like, born and raised?"

Mom shakes her head. "Visalia. Came down here a month ago for a job."

She explains how she's a hair stylist and her friend in Burbank supposedly had a spot for her in the make-up and hair department at Warner Brothers, but a week after we moved the television show was canceled. In the meantime, Mom says, back in Visalia her sister Josie rented out our rooms. So now we're here and my mom had to find a totally different job. Blah, blah, blah.

Cam's shaking his head slowly the whole time, like he feels sorry for us.

"How about you?" she says to him. "Are you from here?"

He snorts. "No one's from here."

He turns to face the back and asks us what we're doing this summer and what school we go to and what grade we're in and what music we like. Nita's a total chatterbox, answering for all of us. Mom is listening with a happy look I haven't seen in a long time.

"What do you think?" Cam asks when we're back at the Valley Van lot. "Should we go inside and write up an offer?"

"I don't know," my mom says and sort of freezes up. She does that when she's put on the spot.

"Special's only on this weekend," he says. He's got perspiration stains under his arms. I wonder why he's not wearing short sleeves.

"I'm not ready to decide yet," she says. "And the kids are tired and hot. I've got to get them home."

I see his jaw muscles flex and his eyebrows narrow and his mouth twitch, and I wonder if he's going to explode because she won't buy the stupid van. But suddenly he relaxes. "I completely understand," he says. "These kids have been super patient." He squats down to shake hands with Nita and Troy, saying it's very nice to make their acquaintance, which makes them both giggle. Gag me.

I think we're done with the mini-van and Cam, but four days later, while Mom is at work and I'm babysitting Troy, who's taking a nap, and Nita, who's watching TV, there's a knock on the front door. We rent a two-bedroom house behind Manuel's Auto Repair in a cruddy part of the Valley, mostly stone yards and plumbing supplies and metal works, so it's not like there's neighbors who come visiting. No one ever walks all the way down the alley to knock on our door except bill collectors. So at first I don't even bother to get up.

But there's another knock and I hear a man's voice: "Hello? Anyone home?"

Nita stands on the couch to look through the front window. "It's the man from the mini-vans, and he's got a present for us!"

I check it out. Cam is on the stoop holding a big blue cardboard box with a yellow bow on top. What the heck? Nita runs to the door, and I barely get there before she opens it.

"Hey, Nita, remember me?" he says through the screen with a big smile. He's got those mis-matched teeth and the long-sleeved shirt. "And Scotty, dude, how's it going? You grew since last time I saw you. What are you, like five-foot ten? One-fifty?"

"Five-eight, I think. Maybe one-thirty."

"Not bad for thirteen." He peers through the screen. "Your mom home?"

"No..." I say, like what did he expect at two o'clock on a Thursday afternoon? "She gets off at five. And we're not supposed to open—"

"Oh well, what I've got here is really for you kids anyway." He spins the box to show us the front. It's a picture of an inflatable pool, the kind you fill with a hose, with two dorky kids splashing around in it. Nita squeals and Cam chuckles.

I start to ask him how he found us, and then I remember Mom's driver's license has our address. I guess he heard enough during the test drive to know this isn't our best summer ever. He probably figured we need some fun.

"You don't have one of these already, do you?" he asks.

"No!" Nita is jumping up and down and clapping.

All the noise wakes Troy, and he wobbles out of the bedroom still half asleep with his nap-time diaper on and his skin all pink and his hair plastered to the side of his head. His eyes go big like beach balls when he sees the box.

"Troy, my man!" Cam calls out, and before I can say anything, Nita opens the screen and he's inside. "Okay, sugar, let's set this up."

She leads him through the living room and the kitchen to the back door. Our yard is hotter and uglier than the planet Zog, with grass that's mostly dead and no shade and the freeway roaring a block away. I wish I had a helicopter, so I could land and load up Nita and Troy and fly us off to the beach or the mountains. Anywhere. Even Visalia.

Cam looks around, sets the box down and puts on his aviator sunglasses. "Perfect." Then he pulls a Leatherman tool from his pocket and flips out the blade. He cuts the cardboard box, splits it open with a loud pop like when you hack into a watermelon.

He and Nita take turns blowing up the plastic pool while Troy runs around in his diaper. Then Nita gets the hose and turns on the faucet, but instead of pointing the stupid thing into the pool she sprays me and Troy and Cam, and now it's a water fight—which is kind of funny, actually. Pretty soon, everyone is soaked. Nita strips down to her underwear and Troy kicks off his soggy diaper so he's running around bare-butt naked, which is okay, I guess, 'cause it's like an oven out here and he's only three. I keep my shirt and shorts on even though they're wet. Cam only takes his shirt and shoes off, which is when I see the tattoos. On the inner side of his right arm, close to the wrist, there's a heart and some kind of Greek lettering I can't read. On the inner side of his left arm I see *F2L-LB.*

Finally the plastic pool is filled. Cam sits on the brick step watching my brother and sister flop around in the water. With the sun reflecting off his aviators, he looks like one of the Troopers from *Doom Star II.*

"You too grown up for the pool, Scotty?"

I shrug. "Just don't feel like it."

"Sit with me then." He pats the brick next to him.

"We're supposed to go to the grocery store pretty soon. My mom's counting on us to do the shopping." This is only a little lie. There's a market three blocks away, more of a liquor store with an aisle for food. I buy peanut butter and bread and potato chips there a couple of times a week, but today my mom didn't leave me any cash.

"Need a ride? I got the manager's Camaro this afternoon."

"Supercharged?" I can't help asking. I'm learning about car engines working for Manny. I help him clean the auto shop on Wednesday nights and Saturdays.

"Yeah. Six-point-two, V-8, pushing five-eighty horsepower."

"How fast?"

"Zero to sixty in four."

"Sweeeet."

Cam grins. "You got that right, Scotty. Hey, maybe I'll let you take the wheel, like down the alley. ' S 'bout time you learn to drive, dude."

That would be cool, but there's no way I'm leaving my sister and brother alone in a pool. I tell him no thanks. He loses the grin. Turns serious. Like, snap. Like when Mom didn't buy the Odyssey. He reminds me of the shape-shifter in *Doom Star* or the cop from the old *Terminator II* movie.

We don't talk for a few minutes, and then he says, "Hey, you got something to drink? Like a beer? You drink beer yet, my man?"

"No."

"Okay, how 'bout a pop?"

When I come back with a glass of water, my sister and brother are still splashing around, and Cam's holding his cell phone like he's been using it as a camera.

"Had to make a call," he says.

I wish I could see behind those aviators. Something about this guy bugs me. I tell Nita and Troy to go get some dry clothes on, and I start to tell Cam it's time for him to leave when he stands up. He's a lot bigger than me.

"Gotta hit the road. Boss wants his wheels." He puts on his shirt and slips into his shoes. "Tell your mom 'hi,' okay? Hope you like the pool."

"Yeah, thanks a lot."

I walk him to the door, watch him get into a red Camaro ZL1, hear the rumble as he drives away. Then I go back out to the yard. I bail the water out of the pool and open the air spigot and press until it's a plastic blue pancake.

"Wasn't that thoughtful," Mom says that night when I tell her about Cam. She's in the kitchen pouring her usual after-work drink, Captain Morgan's Rum over ice.

I follow her to the living room. "Isn't it weird he just showed up here?"

"I think it's great," she says, plopping onto the couch. "Most men wouldn't bother with kids, you know." She kicks off her shoes and clicks on the TV. *Wheel of Fortune* or some crap.

"Yeah, but—"

"Don't you like having a man around, Scotty? And for him to bring a present? Jeez. I hope you were nice to him."

She hunts in her purse for Cam's phone number so she can call and thank him. I grab the new *Doom Star* and head to my room.

"Hey," she calls after me. "Wish you'd get your nose outta that comic book. You've got enough imagination as it is."

It's Thursday, two weeks later. Mom just got home from work, and she's all stressed out. She pours an extra-large Captain Morgan's and sits us down. Aunt Josie's in the hospital. They don't know what it is yet. Mom has to make a trip to Visalia to see her.

"I'm leaving tomorrow after work," she says. "Be back Monday morning, early. You guys are staying here."

Nita and Troy begin to whine. I tell Mom there's no way I'm taking care of the rug rat and the brat for a whole weekend. Watching them while she's at work is bad enough.

"Don't worry," Mom says. "Cam is going to stay with you guys. Isn't that nice?"

Nita squeals, "Yea!"

"We hardly even know him," I say.

"We know him enough, smarty," Mom says.

Cam's been over three times since he gave us the pool. On Mom's day off he picked her up in his boss's Camaro and took her out to lunch, and one night he took us all to the movies at the Galleria. Last Friday, he took me and Nita and Troy to Universal City Walk, and we each got a T-shirt. I have to admit, that was totally awesome. A couple of days ago, he ordered a pizza to be delivered to the house at lunchtime as a surprise, which was kinda funny because the delivery guy went to Manny's auto shop first. Anyway, I guess Mom and Cam are dating. She likes him, but I don't.

"He's got tattoos," I tell her.

"Lots of people do."

"There's something weird about him."

She rolls her eyes. "You've got an over-active imagination."

Nita is chanting, "Soda pop, swimming, one-two-three!" Troy starts spinning like a rotor blade, repeating, "Soda pop, swim, pop." That kid would follow Nita into a house fire.

Mom says, "Looks like you're out-numbered, Scotty." She hugs me, then pushes back to look into my eyes. "Go with me on this one, okay? It's not like I've got a lot of options."

On Friday afternoon, as my mom finishes packing, Cam pulls up in a Dodge Caravan blaring the sound-track to that Disney movie *Cars*, like he's Mr. Mom or something. He's got on a long-sleeved white shirt as usual. I wonder if he wears it to hide the tattoos from the customers at Valley Vans. He's carrying a laptop case in one hand and a large box of pizza in the other. I imagine him morphing into an alien droid carrying a couple of big guns.

"Cheese and pepperoni," he says, handing Nita the box and me the computer. He squats down to my little brother's level. "How's it going, Troy?"

Troy shouts, "Cam the man!"

And everyone cracks up like it's the cutest thing ever. Except me.

Mom gives Cam the house keys and shows him how to use the microwave.

"Keep your cell phone charged up," she reminds me. "Be good and do what Cam says," she tells us. Then she does the whole hugs and kisses thing. I follow her out to her car. "Be nice to Cam," she says to me as she starts the engine. "We're lucky to have him."

After dinner, Nita and Troy and I sit on the couch to watch a DVD of *Despicable Me*. Cam spends the whole time at the table next to the kitchen working on his laptop. Must be really interesting because he hardly looks up. When it's time to put Troy to bed, Cam offers to help, but I do it. Then my sister and I watch *Fast and Furious 3*, which she isn't supposed to see 'cause it's PG-13, but Cam doesn't even notice. When the movie is over, Nita starts whining 'cause she doesn't want to sleep alone. So I let her take my place in the back bedroom with Troy and I let Cam have the bed in Mom's room because he says he has a bad back. I get the couch in the living room.

It's, like, midnight and I'm awake 'cause the couch is so freakin' uncomfortable. I've finished my book, so I decide to check out Cam's laptop. We haven't had a computer since we left Visalia. I'm in luck because it hasn't shut itself down, which means I don't need a password to log on. I go to his Internet, curious about what he's been surfing, but the history has been erased.

So I'm Googling around, looking stuff up, and I get the idea to search his name. Cam Groff. Cameron Groff. There's like ten thousand of them. I can't find anything about this one, so I look up "F2L - LB," his tattoo.

It stands for "Free To Love, Lost Boys."

WTF?

The home page has a photo of an old guy—like fifty or something—and a kid about ten holding hands and smiling at each other as they walk down a sidewalk under some big trees. I'm thinking the man is the boy's grandpa. Then I read more. This F2L-LB is like a club for freakazoids who believe that little boys and men should be able to love each other. They say it's natural and society is too narrow-minded and the government should butt out.

Holy shit.

Why does Cam have that tattoo?

Across the top of the Free to Love—Lost Boys webpage, there's a bunch of tabs. *Gallery*—which you need a password for—*Advocacy*, *Chapters* and *Helpful Hints.* I click on *Helpful Hints.*

> *What if we told you that you can get your own kids in an instant without making any? Well it is true. So here we come to single parents and moms with kids. Ideally, these will be impoverished or broken homes. The cost per boy ratio is cheapest. The usual guy doesn't like single moms with a lot of kids running around, so these moms are therefore suffering from a lack of men, love and self-confidence. This is especially the case with overweight ladies. We apologize in advance for saying this, but the uglier and fatter the moms, the easier it will be for you to get into that family.*

I start to feel sick.

> *The first thing to do is to get access. Be creative here. Check a website or a magazine or a paper with dating ads and search for single parents, women seeking men. Better yet, find a job where you are likely to meet these females and / or their families.*

Oh my God. Valley Vans.

> *Next you win the trust and confidence of the mother and the kids. Give them gifts. Offer to help out at home. Take the child(ren) on fun outings. How bad can it be to spend a day at the amusement park?*

The pool and the pizza and the car rides and the Galleria and City Walk. I want to puke. Cam's been using my mom to get to us, and she fell for it. Big time. I bet he thinks he's hit the jackpot. Three kids for the weekend. Yeah, Mom, we sure are lucky to have Cam.

I run to the kitchen counter for my cell phone, but it's gone. Is that part of his plan? He knows we don't have a landline. He knows Manny's shop is closed. He knows there's not another house within two miles. And he's sleeping ten feet from Nita and Troy.

I've got to get rid of him.

Mom doesn't own a gun. There's nothing sharper than a kitchen knife around here. I start to panic, and then I remember Manny has a gazillion tools. I grab a flashlight, slip out the back door and head to the hole in the chain link fence that separates our house from the auto shop. It takes less than a minute to undo the rusted padlock on the back door. I shine the flashlight on the shelves and the racks, looking for something gnarly.

I find it. Totally wicked! I watched Manny use it once. I make sure it's loaded, undo the safety and press down really hard to try it. Perfect. *Thank you, Manny.*

Back in our kitchen, my heart's pounding like crazy, and I'm trembling all over. I need to chill. I take a deep breath, close my eyes, exhale. Then I hear a weird noise coming from the back of the house. I tip-toe down the hallway to the bedroom where Troy and Nita are sleeping—my room. The door is open an inch, and light is coming through the crack.

I can hear Cam whispering, "There you go, baby...quiet."

I push the door open a few inches.

Troy is lying on the bed on top of the covers, face down. He's totally naked and his legs are spread wide. *What the?* I see Nita's head poking out from under the blanket on the far side of the mattress. She's asleep. Cam's standing at the foot of the bed, wearing pants and no shirt. The light is coming from the video camera he's pointing at my brother.

I ignite the Blazer Spitfire. The portable torch is putting out twenty-five hundred degrees Fahrenheit, but the blue jet is only four inches long. I point it at Cam.

"Get away from him!"

Cam swings around. "Whoa, whoa, calm down." He's grinning like a jack-o-lantern with those mis-matched teeth. "We're only havin' a little fun here, Scotty. Makin' a documentary." He sets the camera on the floor. It's a hi-definition Handycam.

"Yeah, right, you perv."

Troy rolls over, sits up half way and looks around. He doesn't know what's happening. Cam reaches to stroke my brother's arm.

"Don't touch him, you freakazoid!"

He reaches for my brother, pulls him by the legs. Troy twists and wiggles, but he can't break free. Behind them, Nita sits up. She blinks, rubs her eyes and turns white.

I want to roast the creep, but he's got Troy pinned in front of him.

"Drop the flame-thrower!" Cam hisses.

"Drop my brother!" I move in with the Spitfire, but Cam dodges, still using Troy as a shield. Nita stands up slowly on the bed behind Cam. There's a kinda fierce look in her eyes. She knows.

Cam pulls a knife from his pocket and flicks it open. It's the Leatherman. He pushes the shiny tip of it against Troy's tummy. "Shut the fucking thing off or I'll gut him like a fish."

I don't want to give in, but my whole hand aches from pressing the trigger down so long. I can't keep this up forever. Maybe I should do what he says.

Out of nowhere, Nita hauls off and slugs Cam on the side of the head. It's not enough to hurt him, but it's enough to make him flinch. He spins around to Nita. I move in, using all my strength to keep the Blazer Spitfire flame on high. In a split second, the blue jet touches the left side of his back and makes a little red circle that glows like a coal on a barbeque.

He screams, drops Troy on the bed, swings back around. He calls me a goddamn fucking little shit and comes at me with the knife, but he's half bent-over and not moving at full speed. I leap out of his way.

"You're gonna be sorry," he hisses.

I've got both hands on the Spitfire, both thumbs on the trigger, and I'm shaking. I can't hold the trigger down, just can't. My thumbs give out. The butane jet turns into a soft flame, like a candle, then goes out.

I say, "Leave us alone," and it sounds like a prayer.

He jabs with the knife, and I jump back. He misses me by an inch, but I'm in a corner now, stuck between the dresser on one side and the closet on the other. Nita and Troy are crying.

Cam's holding the Leatherman like a dagger. "I'm gonna make you hurt, and I'm gonna make them watch."

I've got to get the Spitfire going. It's my only chance.

He starts to lunge, but his back goes spaz. He groans and stops and winces in pain.

Somehow, I make my thumbs work again. I press down on the trigger, but the torch isn't igniting. *WTF?* Is it broken?

Cam has his strength back too. He twists the knife back and forth like he's practicing what he's going to do to me. I squeeze the trigger as hard as I can. The blue jet shoots out and almost gets his face. He springs backward and stumbles to the side.

I escape from the corner. The Handycam is lying on the carpet, green light blinking. I want to destroy whatever the freakazoid has in there. By the time Cam figures out what's happening, the twenty-five hundred degrees have melted the lens and part of the body. He dives for the camera, like he wants the pictures so much he doesn't care that I've got the Spitfire right there. The blue jet draws a stripe along his arm and hits the side of his stomach and catches the knee of his pants. He cries out, falls back flat on the floor. He sees his arm, which looks like a rocket used it as a launch pad. Glowing, bubbling, turning black. His side is even worse. Then his eyes flutter closed, and he's not moving. I think he's fainted or something.

"Get out!" I whisper-yell at Nita and Troy. "Wait for me at Manny's."

They jump off the bed and run.

I use the last of my finger power to finish off Handycam. The Spitfire slips out of my hands. I look back at Cam and notice the fabric of his pants is burning. It's a weird fire. The flame isn't big, but it's spreading like its hungry for the material. He wakes up and tries to roll over to suffocate the fire. But he can't. He's hurt too bad.

"Help me," he says with a moan.

I watch the fire as it burns his crotch. A tear rolls down his cheek.

"Help me," he whispers.

Maybe I will. Later. After those nuts are roasted into moon rocks. Cam the Man is not going to be Free to Love anymore.

Rocket 88

Donna May

"Beautiful, ain't she? Crying shame what we're about to do here."

"Yeah, Sal, it is."

Freddy the Fish and Long Sal stood at the lip of a canyon southwest of Palm Springs. The car in front of them, a nearly brand new 1954 Oldsmobile Rocket 88, had its "Futuramic" nose pointed right over the edge. The tortured landscape below held yucca, sage brush and a lot of jagged rocks.

A breeze kicked up and Freddy's eyes were drawn to the long strands of brunette hair dancing out the driver's side window. "Didn't think she was your type," Freddy said.

Sal's wife and girlfriend were blondes. It was the boss who liked the look of dark hair against pale skin and who had a bad habit of playing a little too rough. The body they'd retrieved from his pool house and stuffed into the trunk of the Oldsmobile earlier that morning had ugly bruises all over.

They'd propped the girl up in the driver's seat. That way, if anybody ever found the wreck, it would look like an accident.

Freddy pulled off his fedora and scratched the stubble on his cheek that his straight razor had missed. He didn't want to think about what the brunette's body would look like after the coyotes got hold of her. "Think we's far enough off the road, Sal?"

"Why would anybody come out here if they didn't have to?" Sal ran one of his fingers along the protruding taillights of the 88 and across the chrome logo of the rocket launching into space. "Damn."

"I know. Poor kid was only twenty-one. Car was a birthday present." Freddy planted his feet in the dirt and started to get into his pushing stance. "Let's get this over with."

But Sal pulled him back.

"What choice do we got, Sal? Boss was very clear about what we gotta do here."

"Can't go pushing her over a cliff. I don't care what the boss says."

There was no reasoning with Sal once he'd made his mind up.

Ten minutes later, after they eased the car back away from the edge, Long Sal and Freddy the Fish lugged the girl's body out of the driver's seat and Sal gently wrapped her in his cashmere coat. Then, as Freddy wiped his brow, Sal rolled the body over the edge and watched it ricochet down toward the bottom of the ravine.

"What in blazes? I thought you said..."

"Goodbye," Sal said in a soft voice.

Freddy looked down. The coat was the same color as the rocks so it was hard to see where it landed. "Yeah, goodbye, uh...What was her name again?"

"I was talking to my coat." Sal turned and looked at the car. "Like I said. Beautiful, ain't she?"

Freddy shrugged. "Boss'll kill you if he sees this thing coming down the street."

"Don't worry. Got it all figured." Sal got into the driver's seat and pulled out the keychain with the little chrome rocket ship. He eased the car back to the access road and let Freddy out next to his Dodge Dart.

"Tell the boss you dropped me off to visit my mother." Then Sal made a left and headed out toward Idyllwild, hugging the curves along the way.

He'd let his mother make him some waffles. And, after he put the 88 up on blocks in the shed behind her house, he'd get his uncle to drive him back to town. As long as Freddy didn't squeal, nobody would ever be the wiser.

But someday, Sal thought, after the boss was dead or in jail, he'd drive that gorgeous specimen of American automaking right down the streets of Palm Springs with his beautiful blonde wife in the passenger seat holding his baby girl, Clarabell, on her lap. And they'd look mighty swell.

"Man, that was righteous. White boy throwin' his guitar out into the crowd? Never seen nothin' like it. Got Deep Purple still ringing in my ears." LeRoy Gillis tucked the pick into his giant afro and stretched his legs out on the back seat. "First time I ever been around that many white people and ain't had no hassles. No Po-lice, nothing."

"That's what Cal Jam '74's all about. Luuuuv, you dig?" Michael started the engine, then swung his right arm over his sleeping girlfriend's shoulder and pulled her close. "Now you're glad Clarabell talked us into coming, huh?" Slowly, he maneuvered the big, vintage car out of the Ontario Motor Speedway. "Shit. This is like driving a yacht."

"When you two pulled up in this crazy thing, Mike, I thought the fuzz'd come down on us right quick. But this Rebel-Without-A-Cause-mobile made everybody smile." LeRoy shoved his hand inside the pocket of his fringed suede vest and felt the big wad of bills. "Yeah, they were real happy to see us."

"How much'd you clear anyway?"

"'Nuff to keep you in that college a little while longer, baby." LeRoy leaned back. "So Cousin Michael got hisself a cheerleader. A blonde one, too. This her Daddy's ride, huh? What'd he say when you showed up?"

"Bella hasn't even told her best friend about me. And she better never tell anyone." Though she was out cold, Michael slipped into a whisper. "Her father, man, turns out he's in the Mob."

"Damn, Mike. You kidding me? Gotta have balls of steel on you."

"Hell, I wouldn't have gone near her if I knew. Just found out today. I asked where this car came from and she started telling all kind of stories. Some serious shit."

"The look on your face, Mike. Did I say balls of steel? More like pudding."

"What do I do, LeRoy?" Michael lowered his voice even more. "Her Pops finds out, he could come after me like Dillinger or something." Michael slowed the car at a three-way fork in the road. "Remember which way we came?"

"Nah, man. This cactus look the same as that cactus to me."

Michael stroked the top of Clarabell's blonde head. "Great concert, though. Too bad Bella slept through everything after Seals and Crofts. What'd you give her, anyway?"

"She's your girl. I gave her the good stuff."

"Hey, Bella. We're lost." Michael shook her shoulder gently. "Need you to wake up. Come on, sugar." He shook her harder, then shot LeRoy a panicked look in the rearview mirror. "Clarabell? Come on, baby. Don't do this!"

He swerved the car onto the shoulder. They lay her down on the back seat and LeRoy started slapping her cheeks, hard.

Ten minutes later, after they'd tried everything they could think of, it was Michael's face LeRoy was slapping. "Calm down, man! Stop asking me what I gave her. She dead. Ain't nothin' we do gonna bring her back."

"Oh Jesus. What am I gonna do?" Michael pressed his hands to his temples. "We gotta set this car on fire. Burn it all. That's the only way. Give me your lighter."

"Can't be burning nothing here, fool. Look. Headlights. Soon as that concert lets out, we gonna have a whole army raining down on us. Be cool." He ran around to the driver's seat just as a yellow VW van pulled up.

"Heyyyy, it's the dude! Slow down." A straw-haired, sunburned surfer pointed out the window at LeRoy. "That was some radical shit, man. Got any more?"

"Nah, tapped out, sorry." LeRoy kept his voice light. "Hey, man, which way the city at?"

"We're going to Pasadena which is, like, straight, and," the surfer pointed left, "that way's the 10."

"And where that one go?" LeRoy pointed at the third road.

"I don't know. Mount Baldy, Victorville maybe?"

"Cool. Look, could you take my man, Mike, here back to Pasadena?" LeRoy slipped twenty dollars to the surfer. "Just take him to a bus stop. I gotta go another way."

"Okay, I guess."

"Bella," Michael clutched LeRoy's arm.

"I'll take care of everything, Mike. Don't you fret."

After serpentining for miles way up into the mountains, Leroy finally stopped where the access road had eroded away, near a deep crevasse. He started to gather dried brush and place it around the tires. When he thought he had enough, he glanced around. From one direction, he could see the orange glow of the city. In the other direction, he could see the car; the rounded lights, the chrome details, the perfect paint job and the little rocket ship logo glistening in the moonlight.

And after a few seconds of tracing his fingers along the curves, he put his lighter back into his pocket. Then he edged up as close as he could to see how deep the crevasse was.

So deep the body took twelve bounces on the way down.

"Sorry 'bout that, Clarabell," he said as he backed the Olds down the dirt path to the main road.

He'd tell Michael to forget all about her. Forget the whole thing. And he'd find a real out-of-the-way place to store the car for a while.

Someday, after Michael graduated and started living the good life in some suburb somewhere, LeRoy would pull that car out and drive his little nephews, Quenton and Garcel, all around Compton. And they'd look fine.

Victor Gonzales took the radio call and followed the flashing red and blue lights all the way to the end of the pier at Dockweiler Beach. He nodded to the other officer already on the scene.

"Ever seen either of these two before, Gonzo?" McKinley asked.

Victor shook his head.

Two young punks were splayed across the hood of McKinley's squad car with cuffs on. "How old d'you think this one is? Eleven?"

"Twelve."

"Shut up, Garcel," the older boy snapped.

A black man in a leather jacket walked up. Victor instinctively put his hand on his holster, but then he realized the man was holding up a badge.

"It's alright, officer. I'm Detective Jefferson, Anti-Gang Unit." The man pulled the taller hoodlum up by the hood of his Run-DMC sweatshirt. "I know these two. Wanna-bes. Call themselves Q-Dog and G-Money. What'd they do now?"

"Believe this? I come across these mopes throwin' whole garbage bags into the ocean. Guess what's in 'em?" McKinley held the last of the bags at arm's length, his face an unpleasant grimace. "Meat. What the hell these idiots doin' throwin' away bags of meat?"

"Well, these little idiots run with the D-Boys," the detective said. "Got a lot of bodies disappearing lately. So, I'm willing to bet you, officer, that bag does not hold top sirloin. Does it, Quenton?"

McKinley set the bag down and took a giant step away from it.

"Thing is, D-Boys M.O. is always the same. They put the bodies inside the trunk of a stolen car and drive them off the end of a pier, usually up in Malibu."

McKinley cocked his head at the boys. "What, you couldn't jack a car? Didn't know where Malibu was?"

"No, we had a—"

"Shut up, G."

Garcel threw an elbow into his brother. "I told you, Quenton. But no, you just couldn't let go of—"

"Garcel! Shut the fuck. UP. We want a lawyer. Call my uncle Michael."

"Yeah, we'll get you a lawyer. Don't worry. Hey, what's that?" The detective reached into the older boy's pockets and rifled around until he found a small silver object. "Look, Officer Gonzales. Seems you just found a car key lying on the pier."

Victor squinted at it. "House key more like."

"No, I think we're looking for a real classic." He held up the keychain shaped like a little silver rocket ship which reflected the flashing red and blue lights of the squad car.

It took Victor an hour and ten minutes of searching to find where the kids had stashed the vintage car behind the power plant. "What were you two vatos doin' with this cherry ride, eh? Looks brand new."

He made a slow circle of the car, looking at it inside and out, letting his hands rest on the chrome tail lights. The moment he touched it, he knew that car was never going to see an evidence tag.

After his shift was over, he'd sneak back and drive it out to his boyfriend's place in Palm Springs. And, in a few years, as soon as he figured the heat was off, they'd drive it all over town.

And they'd look Fab-U-Lous!

Shikata Ga Nai

Beverly Graf

It was a good night for Homicide Detective Eddie Piedmont until his Porsche started to argue with him. Eddie and his partner, Detective Shinsuke Miyaguchi, wrapped a murder investigation that had consumed the first six months of 2020 and tucked the suspect into a black and white for the ride downtown to Verizon, Ciudad LA's central police station, for booking.

The detectives felt good, riding the glow, but sleep deprivation started to kick in. Shin tucked his portly middle-aged frame into the patrol car and rode back to Verizon, planning to sleep in the bachelor pods tonight. Thirty-one-year-old Eddie just wanted his nice soft bed in Venice. With luck his girlfriend Jo would already be home with open arms and an open bottle of Grey Goose.

"I'm sorry, Eddie," the sultry tones of Sofia, his Porsche 911-S, said when he punched the starter button. "You're in no condition to drive. Please wait point-five hours until attempting to restart ignition."

"I haven't been drinking," Eddie told the car's computer. "Not yet."

Eddie blew a breath into his cupped palm and sniffed. He could use an Altoid, but stale breath shouldn't cock up the breathalyzer. The sleeve of his second favorite Armani suit, however, was a different story. It reeked of dirty socks with that familiar acetone underlay: green ice. Because the murder suspect had been cooking up some of the drug when they arrested him, his house had been filled with the fumes. While Eddies' nose had been temporarily desensitized to the stink, the fibers of his grey suit must have soaked them up like a sponge.

Eddie got out of the car, peeling the steel grey suit jacket and tie off his six two frame and unbuttoning the hand-tailored shirt of robin's egg blue Jo had given him because *it would bring out the color of his eyes.* Eddie shook the suit jacket hard in the hopes of airing out the fabric, and laid it in the trunk of his car. Shirtless, he climbed back into his Porsche, opened all the windows and punched the starter again.

But the car repeated its mantra, refusing to start for another point-five hours.

Eddie let out a string of obscenities. He glanced at the clock on the dash: 1:55 A.M. June 12, 2020. It was already tomorrow.

"Be patient," Jo would advise.

"Good excuse for a nap," Shin would say. "Just wait it out."

But Jo was a lawyer and patience was Shin's way. Not Eddie's. He knew car breathalyzers, standard on all vehicles since 2018, were supposed to shut down ignition and keep the drunks off the road. They weren't supposed to ground cops who reeked of fumes from drugs they hadn't even used.

Eddie reached over to the glove compartment and pulled out an aluminum can of Starbucks Java Jolt tucked inside. He popped the top on the inhaler and sprayed a sharp blast of the caffeine aerosol at the sensor as he punched the starter button again, simultaneously slamming the clock mechanism with his knee. The Porsche engine roared to life. Eddie grinned and pulled away from the curb.

Traffic on the residential streets of North Hollywood was pretty sparse at this hour. The drunks, at least those with programming skills or older cars, would just be starting to pour out of the bars and onto the roads.

"Sofia," Eddie said to the voice-activated phone as he passed Colfax, driving west on Riverside, "call Jo."

Jo picked up in two rings. The shimmering holo-image of her tapered fingers holding up a bottle of Crystal to the phone's camera floated in front of the dash.

"I thought we should break out the bubbly," she said. Eddie heard the rattle of ice cubes from the sweating silver bucket he glimpsed next to the bed as the camera shifted.

"Yeah?" he replied. "Special occasion?"

"Didn't you close a case today?" Jo said.

Eddie could see she was sitting in bed, cocooned in a white duvet.

"I did," he said grinning, "but that's not a special occasion. It's just the way I roll."

"Well, Mr. Wonderful, I'm in the mood to celebrate," Jo said, running a hand through her pale blonde hair. She told him about her triumph with a patent case that even a boring client dinner hadn't tarnished. Patent cases and boring client dinners—not for the first time Eddie was glad he was a cop.

"Are you driving naked?" Jo asked. "Where's your shirt?"

"What are *you* wearing?" he replied.

"Less than I was this morning," she replied with a teasing lilt. "Hurry." She hung up.

The light at the intersection of Riverside and Laurel Canyon changed from red to green. There was one car ahead of Eddie, a 2011 silver Prius that inched its way into the intersection to turn left. Eddie moved up behind it, willing the old lady, whose fluffy white hair made her look like a dandelion huddled behind the wheel, to hurry up and turn. Eddie could have turned twice by the time she'd crawled to the middle of the intersection.

That's when the new model Zhang Skorpian-Z sport coupe driving south on Laurel Canyon ran the red light. Eddie just had time to note the black and yellow flames running along the Skorpian-Z's crimson sides, the illegally blackened windows and tricked-out chromed twenty-inch rims, before the car slammed into the nose of the silver Prius. The old lady's car jerked counterclockwise, the skin of her Prius crumpling.

But the fire-engine red Skorpian-Z didn't stop. It kept going, heading south on Laurel Canyon. Eddie called it in, straining for a visual on the plates. If only he had an automatic license plate recognition device on the Porsche. No go—the police barely had the budget to install LPR's on black and whites and anti-terrorism units.

A pedestrian had rushed over and was helping the old lady out of her car. So Eddie pulled the bar of lights out from under his seat and slammed them onto his dash. The colored lights flashed as he sped after the Skorpian-Z.

The entrance to the 101 was up ahead. East or west, which way would the suspect go?

Eddie got his answer when the Skorpian-Z lurched right and hit the gas. When the car fishtailed up the ramp to the 101 West, its red tail lights blurred like shooting stars.

By the time Eddie rocketed up the ramp in turn, he'd heard dispatch send an ambulance and a cruiser back to the scene. The whine of an approaching police siren cut the air as he raced after the sports coupe.

It didn't take him long to spot the hit and run asshole up ahead on the freeway. The red tail lights jerked from lane to lane as the car wove erratically through traffic. Eddie figured the driver for another drunk out partying. Like Eddie he must have disabled the car breathalyzer somehow.

The hit and run was bad enough, but the Skorpian-Z ignored Eddie's flashing lights as both cars sped past the Fulton exit. The Z's windows were darkened to an opaque black, preventing any glimpse of the driver, but when Eddie turned on his brights, he was finally able to get a visual on the plates. Eddie called in the number, but stayed on the suspect's tail. It was personal.

He wondered if the Skorpian-Z would take the 405 or keep going West on the 101.

The 101 it was. By the time the intersection with the 405 was behind them, Eddie had heard back on the plates. The car was registered to one Angel Calsado, age twenty-three, with two priors—one for assault, one DUI—and an outstanding warrant for GBH, grand bodily harm. His sheet said Angel was also a low level, but hard case member of the AzteKas, a gang tied to the Juarez drug cartel in the south. The AzteKas were currently involved in a bloody territorial beef with rival gang the Zetas. The war had moved north from Mexico and left headless bodies all over the streets of Ciudad Los Angeles.

By 2:20 A.M. they were just passing the Topanga off ramp. The stars still burned holes in the ink sky. Two cruisers now shadowed the Skorpian-Z and a police chopper circled overhead.

"Angel Calsado," said an amplified voice. "Pull over to the right and exit the freeway." The booming voice came from the chopper overhead, but the sound distortion made it reverberate so that it seemed disembodied...coming from everywhere and nowhere.

One of the black and whites dropped back. In his rear-view mirror Eddie saw the car drive across all four lanes in big S-shaped waves, trying to slow and then stop traffic from behind. Five of the dozen or so civilian cars on the road took the hint and the nearest exit. A few more moved right, slowed and stopped.

As he passed additional cars up ahead, Eddie caught brief glimpses of the open mouths, the wide eyes of drivers pointing fingers as the suspect rocketed past, cruisers on his tail.

And then there was the pair of morons in the gold Corvette with the Co-exist bumper sticker, yucking it up and pointing. Another looky-loo in a black Cadillac Escalade with a Ferrari logo on the back window was also slow to get the message. The Escalade cut his speed as Eddie passed, but didn't stop till one of the two squad cars in the rear herded the driver to the right along with the Corvette.

Eddie and the other black and white kept going.

The chopper kept the spotlight on the speeding Skorpian-Z up ahead. Chatter on the scanner announced the dragonfly launch.

Eddie looked up. The side door of the chopper gaped open. Eddie saw something fall. A shadow, darker than the ink sky. It dropped ten feet then stopped mid-air, hovering as tiny yellow lights flickered on and off, like the blinking eyes of an insect. Then it shot towards the Skorpian-Z.

Eddie sped up. Closer, it looked like more like a toy helicopter than a dragonfly. The black drone sent to surveil the suspect, circled the car, buzzing at the windows. Eddie knew its sensors were scanning. The readings came back over dispatch in seconds: one human heat signature, negative on radiation, two probable firearms in the front seat—a handgun and something bigger.

Eddie heard more chatter over his scanner. The drone trying to nail down specifics on the firearms.

But the Skorpian-Z's illegally blackened windows blocked photos.

The drone shot up and back down, flying backwards as it hovered in front of the speeding Z. It shone a spotlight through the passenger side of the windscreen. But it couldn't get a clear shot inside.

Just past the exit before Las Virgenes the driver of the Skorpian-Z jerked the sport coupe hard right across three lanes. Eddie figured he must have spotted the drone and freaked.

At seventy mph the Z was still racing too fast for them to safely corral him over strips, but Eddie thought he might have glimpsed a fragment of a familiar decal on the rear window: Northstar. He couldn't get close enough to read the tiny registration number. Eddie cut in on the police chatter and relayed the information.

A few seconds later the drone circled clockwise 'round the car and dropped down behind it. It focused the spot-light on the partial decal plastered to the rear window glowed and relayed a picture.

Just past the Parkway Calabasas exit the Skorpian-Z started to slow and lurched to the right. Eddie thought Calsado was going to exit at the next off ramp. Would he take Las Virgenes and try to head to the ocean? There was a sheer drop in the canyon, but it'd still be easier to stop the suspect once he left the freeway.

But the Skorpian-Z passed the Las Virgenes exit.

"Get Northstar," Eddie said. "Shut him down now."

"On it," the voice from dispatch said. "Suspect's blocking the shutdown. Let him go. It's too dangerous."

Eddie swore, but he slowed the Porsche in the far left lane.

Garcia, the P-2 behind the wheel in the other black and white slowed too, staying well back of Eddie, on his right.

That's when Calsado slammed on his brakes, yanked the wheel hard left and made an insane U-turn all the way from the far right slow lane to the fast lane on the left.

Eddie's jaw dropped as he saw the Skorpian-Z's headlights barreling straight at him, the car's aggressive grill grinning as it raced the wrong way in the fast lane of the Freeway.

Eddie moved right.

The Skorpian-Z moved with him. And turned on its blinding brights.

Eddie realized Calsado was going to slam him head on. He *wanted* to hit Eddie. The Skorpian-Z's headlights seared the young detective's eyes. It accelerated.

There wasn't time to do anything but react. At the very last second before impact Eddie shot right. The Skorpian-Z shuddered, but rocketed past. The screeching *paseo* tore off the mirror and stripped a layer of black paint from the skin of Eddie's Porsche. Sparks flew outside his window. Eddie heard screaming brakes, the crash and whine of metal on metal as the Skorpian-Z skidded ahead—and slammed head-on into Garcia's trailing black and white.

The crash sent one of Calsado's twenty-inch chrome rims spinning past Eddie's Porsche on rebound.

Eddie smelled the burnt tire rubber, gas fumes and scorched brakes as he scrambled from his Porsche a few seconds later. Glock out, he made his way towards the mess of metal and plastic smashed together into a nightmare-sculpture. Pellets of windshield glass crunched under Eddie's feet. One look inside the Skorpian-Z told him he wouldn't need his Glock. Calsado had been decapitated.

In the black and white Garcia was pinned like a bug on a board by the steering column which the impact had shoved through him into the seat.

Eddie looked away. He walked back to his Porsche, forcing slow, deep breaths into his lungs to head off the adrenaline shakes. His heart pounded; his blood hummed. He was alive, but Garcia...Jesus.

Eddie felt the cool night air on his skin, and realized with a start he was still bare-chested. He walked back to his Porsche and fished his shirt out of the trunk.

He was still tying his tie with numbed fingers when two additional squad cars and a parade of paramedics and fire trucks arrived a couple minutes later. The fire fighters sprayed the mangled mass that had been squad car and Skorpian-Z with flame retardant to prevent any spilled gas from igniting. The chemical stench of the retardant mingled with the aroma of seared rubber and gasoline.

Eddie's partner Shin pulled up twenty minutes later in a detective sedan. The new police sponsor's slogan, *Firestone protects*, flashed along the running board every time the headlights from southbound traffic crawled by.

"I came as soon as I heard," Shin said. "Traffic's jammed back to Sherman Oaks."

Eddie nodded his thanks.

Traffic updates had gone out to cell phones and navigational systems; amber boards as far south as Orange County flashed alerts, but the morning commute started at four A.M. Closing one side of the freeway inevitably snarled traffic.

"I'm glad you're okay, Eddie," Shin said, patting his partner's shoulder. He circled the wreck. "Poor Garcia."

Eddie nodded again. He wanted to howl. He wanted to hit something. He wanted a drink. Eddie started to pace.

Shin knew his partner's panther-in-a-cage walk, knew what it meant. Shin let him alone.

The homicide team assigned to the case arrived and started separating and interviewing participants in the chase one-by-one. Since he was involved in the fatal incident, Eddie wouldn't be heading up the follow-up investigation.

"Ready for your close-up, *Fast and Furious*?" Shin handed his partner a stick of gum as Eddie watched Detective Greenberger and her partner collect footage from each patrol officer's helmet cam.

"Sure," Eddie said, forcing a grin as he put his hat back on and genially flipped his middle finger at his partner. "Is this my good side?" He folded the gum into his mouth.

The green lights of the helmet cams twinkled. Officer-involved fatalities were closely scrutinized both in the hopes of preventing the next incident *and* heading off any potential publicity disasters or lawsuits that could cost the bankrupt city millions more in pay-outs. Footage from each officer plus the chopper would be played and replayed for the onsite and follow-up investigative teams. Every one of Eddie's actions would be analyzed and questioned. Like they could make him feel worse than he already did.

Shin made another feeble joke. All attempts at kidding stopped when talk turned to Rico Garcia, the P-2 who'd died in the crash. "Garcia was eight months away from his law degree," said one of the guys from his unit. "He's got a wife, two kids and a mountain of debt."

Nobody said anything for seconds that stretched like minutes, but they were all thinking the same thing. *It could have been me.*

After Detective Greenberger had taken his statement, Eddie stood near the bodies in their metal tombs. Calsado's blood had pooled around his seated body, brown-red now, thicker, a blood shadow. Eddie could smell the iron tang of the decomposing liquid by the time the coroner delivered her preliminary assessment to the homicide team.

Shin ambled back to his partner. "Suicide by cop," he said, relaying Greenberger's initial assessment. "Kamikaze-style."

Eddie nodded. He remembered Calsado matching his moves during those last horrific seconds. "Calsado's tox scan?"

"Positive for green ice," Shin replied.

Green ice: The chemically modified dopamine gave a higher high than methamphetamine with a heroin-like chaser. People on ice did crazy stupid things. Still...

"Something doesn't track," Eddie said. He started pacing again.

"An ice addict barrels the wrong way down the 101," Shin said, "and you expect things to track?"

"Prison's just an away game to AzteKas," Eddie replied, fishing a pair of gloves out of his Porsche and tugging on the blue latex as he walked back to the Skorpian-Z. "An outstanding warrant, a DUI? Why off himself over that?"

Eddie stared at the smashed remnants of the Skorpian-Z. The crash had totaled the front end, but the rear was largely untouched. Eddie signaled to Detective Greenberger. The stocky middle-aged brunette cocked her left eyebrow, then nodded.

The release lever was jammed. Eddie put his weight behind it and popped the trunk. Then he walked around to the unscathed back end of the smashed Z, peered inside and sighed.

"Sometimes the night just ends a little darker than it started," he said.

Shin peered over Eddie's shoulder. The muscles of his face went slack and hangdog. He shook his head and gestured to the homicide team. They hurried over, the coroner trailing behind. Eddie stepped back so they could see inside.

Curled in the trunk was the body of a girl in her late teens, wearing a necklace of bruises. She was dressed in skintight pink jeans and a black midriff top. A shovel was tucked next to her.

The coroner slid a temperature scanner over the forehead of the dead girl.

"The drone's sensors only picked up one human heat signature," Eddie said. "She was dead before the chase."

The coroner nodded.

"Looks like Calsado was on his way to dispose of the body when all this went down," Detective Greenberger said, gesturing at the shovel. "He probably figured with his priors he wouldn't beat the rap, so he might as well take one of ours out too."

"*So desu*," Shin said under his breath. He cracked his knuckles. "*Shikata ga nai.*"

Greenberger looked up from the trunk. "What?" she said. "She caught what?"

"*Shikata ga nai*," Shin said, slowly repeating his own words. But he looked at Eddie, not Greenberger.

"It means 'it can't be helped,'" Eddie said with a bitter tinge to his voice.

It was code for the friendly ongoing argument between the partners. Shin was a fatalist who believed karma sorted things out in the end. Eddie thought karma always needed a shove.

Eddie frowned and looked back inside the trunk as the coroner continued to examine the body.

"AzteKas shoot their victims," Eddie said. "And chop off the heads and limbs if they want to send a message. Strangling's personal. Who is she?"

"No barcode," Greenberger said, pointing to the skin on the dead girl's wrist. Where the homeland security barcode should have been tattooed, the skin had been scraped off. "No purse in the trunk, no ID on the body either. We'll match her prints or get facial recognition."

Eddie watched the coroner lift each of the girl's fingers and scan the prints into the system. The dead girl's long nails were painted red with little black and yellow Ferrari logos on each manicured tip.

Shin tapped Eddie's shoulder. "Somebody will call to claim her after the webcasts and news," Shin said, already heading to his sedan. Eddie nodded and started back to his Porsche.

He froze mid-stride. *Ferrari logos on a strangled girl and the way Calsado's car had jerked from lane to lane.* It could mean nothing, or...

Eddie wheeled back around. "Run Calsado's plate with BOSS," he said. "Track where the Skorpian-Z was earlier tonight."

The Back Officer Server System, or BOSS data-sharing network, made Ciudad LA County's one of the most interconnected license plate recognition systems in the country. The LPR devices mounted on the color bars of all squad cars automatically scanned every plate on the road within visual range and stored the electronic data in BOSS. If the Skorpian-Z's license plate had been scanned earlier today, they'd be able to map Calsado's movements before the chase right up to through the crash.

"Why should we care where he was before?" Greenberger said as Eddie peered inside the Skorpian-Z. "What are you looking for?"

"Calsado's phone," Eddie said. "Everybody's got a phone. Where's his? And what's that Northstar number?"

***

Twenty-five miles south, on the edge of the city, Zeta Enrique Morales opened the windows of his black Cadillac Escalade and hurled Angel Calsado's phone off the Vincent Thomas Bridge. The phone spun out over the rail like a Frisbee before dropping into the ocean.

Enrique leaned his head out into the wind. He took a deep breath and howled like a wolf. The sea air was mixed with the smell of oil from the nearby refineries. He took another breath and pulled his head back in, tapping his fingers on the steering wheel. He wanted music and a woman to celebrate. *Soon*, he told himself, *soon.*

Things had gone better than he'd hoped. Two birds with one bullet. Enrique had turned off the log-me-in remote feature on his car's computer right after the crash. He'd told Raul this shit would work, and he'd been right. The remote access his brother rigged allowed him to hack into the Northstar features so he could override Calsado's controls and pilot the Skorpian-Z from afar. The voice-activated steering needed some fine-tuning, but worked pretty well, even the first time out. That computer degree his little brother had talked Enrique into funding had been worth every cent.

Enrique wished he could have seen the expression on Calsado's face when he realized somebody else had taken control of the Skorpian-Z. Calsado had probably tried the Northstar first and then the disabled car phone. After that he must've fumbled around looking for his cell phone. That's when that AzteKa *culo* would have found out it was missing.

It had been easy to lift that cell phone off the wasted loser in the crowded club.

That's what happened when you took a taste of the emerald package. A package that didn't belong to you. Calsado had ripped them off twice, first with Raul's girl and then the green ice.

Without his cell phone, there'd been no way to call for help. Calsado had been truly screwed.

Enrique bet the ass wipe had been scared shitless. He smiled. When you fucked with the Zetas, you paid in blood.

Enrique had watched Calsado exit the club right before two. He'd walked like he was still stoned. Calsado had never even checked the trunk, never dreamed the girl's dead body was right behind him all along.

The crackle of voices from the police scanner app on his own phone told Enrique the cops had just opened the trunk and found the girl's body and the shovel. Enrique touched the cloaked skull of the *Santa Muerte* figurine on the dash of the Escalade, a wordless prayer to the narcos' patron saint. He held his breath.

From the chatter he could tell they didn't suspect anyone but Calsado had laid the body in the trunk of the Skorpian-Z. Enrique exhaled. Then he grinned. Raul owed him big-time now. He was going places man. He'd move up in the organization. About time; he was twenty-four.

Enrique turned off the police scanner app and turned on the radio.

He took one more deep breath and closed the windows of the Escalade.

Enrique saw all kinds of ways to use this tech shit in the organization. Maybe someday he'd even take Raul's spot. Someday.

A chill slithered up Enrique's spine at the memory of how Raul looked when he'd been offered a way out. Stone-faced. Unemotional. Raul had three little tears tattooed near the corner of his left eye. One for each brother lost to the AzteKas. Blood and ink were the only tears those cold black eyes ever cried. Enrique would bet his life on that.

Those black stones Raul had for eyes didn't even flicker while he listened to Enrique detail his plan. Like Raul wasn't involved in the fuck-up in the first place. Like he hadn't caused it, losing control and offing the bitch that way. Raul was chill. You had to give the man that.

Enrique began to sing along with the radio.

He had plenty of time to finish here and get back. It would take a few hours for the cops to identify Mirelle as Raul's girlfriend. Once they knew that, they'd put it together fast. The bitch had cheated on Raul with Calsado. Both the cops and the AzteKas would figure between the sex and the green ice Calsado got a little overheated and offed her by mistake. Calsado couldn't let the Zetas find out if he wanted to see the dawn. But Raul had eyes and ears everywhere between heaven and hell. Calsado had needed to ditch the body to protect himself from Raul's pay-back. But he used. And the ice and the fear made him screw up. And then as far as the cops and the AzteKas knew, everything went south.

The important thing was both the AzteKa thief and that whore had paid. And Raul's hands were clean—thanks to Enrique.

Enrique drove through the dawn and into the morning. He was four blocks from home in East C.L.A. and still singing along with the radio when the steering wheel of his Escalade suddenly wrenched to the right. At first he thought a pothole had grabbed the front tire. Enrique tugged the wheel back to the left, but it didn't respond. Jesus, had the pothole shredded his transmission? This city was really going to the dogs.

Then the SUV pulled to the curb and the engine shut off. Enrique pushed the starter button, but the car didn't respond. He tried the door. It was locked. He pounded, trying to force the door open, but the car wouldn't let him out. Reaching for his Beretta, tucked in the glove compartment, Enrique looked around for something else to break the window. Through the back window he saw the two men exit a black Porsche and walk toward his car, their Glocks out and pointed at Enrique. One was a middle-aged Asian dude. Next to him a young *guero* wearing a steel grey suit and a fucking fedora.

Enrique breathed a sigh of relief. Detectives. At least they weren't AzteKas.

"Don't do it, Enrique," Detective Eddie Piedmont said, keeping his Glock on the Zeta thug. "Put the gun down."

Enrique slowly set the Beretta on the passenger seat and raised his hands over his shaved head. A faint smile played on his lips.

Shin popped the locks on the Escalade.

Eddie hauled Enrique out, and cuffed him. "You're under arrest for the murders of..."

"*Nada*," Enrique said. "I didn't do *nada*."

"*Three* homicides," Eddie said as a sedan with two more detectives pulled up behind the Porsche. "Mirelle Rodriguez, Angel Calsado and Ricardo Garcia. Garcia was a cop. Not *nada*."

Enrique's smile had faded with the first victim's name. "Say what?" he said as Shin proceeded to read Enrique his rights. "You got the wrong *hombre*."

"No." Eddie cocked his head at the Ferrari logo on the back window of the Escalade. The same logo as that painted on the dead girl's nails.

Shin nodded. The rearing black stallion on a yellow shield was a favorite logo of the Zetas and their wannabes. So were certain brands of clothes—like the Ed Hardy tee shirt with the *Santa Muerte* design Enrique wore. His tats of Jesus Malverde, the criminal martyr, and Tweety Bird peeking out from underneath the sleeves were also typical.

"Your fashion sense may be classic Zeta, Enrique," Eddie said. "But your tech advice is dated. The remote-pilot works both ways. Your car left its signature with Northstar the moment you seized control of the Skorpian-Z. We know you caused the crash that killed Calsado and Officer Garcia."

"*Shit.*" Enrique's eyes went dead. He was staring at the black Porsche. The driver's side mirror was missing and there was a long steel scar where the black paint had been ripped off the Porsche's flank. Enrique looked back at Eddie.

Eddie nodded. "Yeah, that was quite a chase you put me through. I pulled your Escalade's identification number off the Northstar computers and ran it with the DMV. Found your plates. Then we mapped your itinerary for the past twenty-four hours."

"You've been on a real scenic tour of the city, Enrique," Shin put in. "Every place but Disneyland."

"That's right, Shin." Eddie gestured to the Zeta. "Enrique here was too busy stuffing the body of the girl he strangled into the trunk of Calsado's Z to visit the happiest place on earth."

"I didn't strangle that bitch!" Enrique said. "No way you can prove I did. It's fucking impossible." When he saw the young *guero* smile, he knew his mistake. His face went pale under the tan.

"I believe you, Enrique," Eddie said. "Strangling's personal. I think her boyfriend killed her. You just helped Raul out by stuffing his girl's body in the trunk of Calsado's car while he was inside the Club Azul. We *can* prove that. You missed a security cam."

Enrique lifted his chin. He plastered a smile on his face and began to hum, softly at first, then louder. He started to sing.

Eddie and Shin both recognized *Hecho in Mexico*, a classic *narcocorrido.* The lyrics recounted a morality tale of the inevitability of the *narco* way of life and the death that awaits its adherents. Enrique howled his fatalistic hymn to the wind as they walked him to Greenberger's sedan.

"See, Eddie," Shin said, wagging his head and grinning. "*Shikata ga nai.*" Shin mouthed the Japanese words as he locked eyes with his partner. "In Spanglish."

"Sure," Eddie said. "Couldn't be helped."

He turned his head to the Zeta. "That's what I'm gonna tell Raul when I let him know it was you who led me to him, Enrique. He'll understand. He's an understanding guy. Just think about that when we stick you in the holding cell tonight. With the AzteKas."

Dance Man

Andrew Jetarski

Dunbar DuWayne lowered himself delicately onto the edge of the brown leather sofa in his study, then almost immediately rose again. He could not sit still, but the wrenching pain in his left knee and lower back made every halting step an agony. He moved like a man twice his thirty-eight years.

The studio's promised "insurance crew" was due any minute. He made his way to the edge of the broad heavy desk by the windows and, agitated, thumbed the morning papers one more time. "Japs Scrap Naval Treaty" and "Strike Threats Sweep Nation" weren't enough to push him off page one. "Hotel Heist" and "Missing Heiress" didn't generate nearly as much copy as "Hollywood Director Blamed." *The Herald* could be counted on to downplay the tragedy, praising his fortuitous survival with only minor bruises and abrasions. But the goddamned *News-Beacon* was still hammering on the drunk-driving angle.

Sam Green was the kind of studio head you did not want to antagonize. Every news rag in town should have fallen into line by now. The fact they hadn't put Dunbar on edge. How unfortunate that he was still ironing out the details of his contract renewal.

At the sound of a car approaching up the drive, he snatched an ornate ebony walking stick from the desktop. No need to have the arrival announced, he thought. Shuffling through the open French doors and along the gravel path, he made his way out the side gate.

Dunbar stepped gingerly into the sunlight dappling the front lawn and scrutinized the car in the sweeping driveway. It was a plain black coupe, boxy and squat, the paint dulled in spots, but clean. A lone man with his back turned slouched near the rear fender.

What were they playing at, sending such a chintzy car for him? The publicity man, Linder, had been adamant about keeping a low profile, but this was really slumming it.

Dunbar spoke loudly to catch the driver's attention. "I'm glad to see at least you're prompt," he said. "I was counting on Linder to get me someone who's on the ball."

He saw a flash of white in the man's hand as he straightened, a scrap of handkerchief disappearing into a jacket pocket. Pride of ownership, Dunbar thought. Polishing his jalopy. The man was tall and lean, his face boney and sunburned beneath small mirthful eyes.

"You the dance man?"

"That would be choreographer," Dunbar said. "And I'm billing as a director now, as you would know if you were in the business." The boney man didn't pick up on the overture. Perhaps star director status did not impress him. Dunbar suppressed a wince as he held out his right hand. "Dunbar DuWayne, Dance Man. Pleased to meet you."

The man burst into a boyish grin, like someone who had forgotten his manners.

"Orville Pine," he said, extending his own calloused hand. "Investigator. Pleasure."

The man's rumpled brown suit looked like he'd been wearing it for days. Dunbar had made a point of dressing for his part: suede brogues on his feet, light cotton twill trousers, burgundy blazer. He had chosen the amber ascot around his neck to offset the large purple bruise on the side of his face.

Pine nodded at Dunbar's heavy cane. "You look to have got yourself kind of banged up."

"The doctors tell me I'll be back to normal within a week. I have no qualms about staying on schedule."

Dunbar leaned on his stick peering at the car. Pine followed his look.

"Dodge coupe. She's not as fancy as you're used to I bet, but she's got a lotta pep."

"You don't have a driver?"

"I'm the driver."

Pine's words seemed to come from the back of his mouth in a lazy flow.

"Well, we both know why you're here," Dunbar said. "Let's get down to the Coast Highway, where it all happened."

Orville Pine's face broke into a smile. "I think that is an excellent idea. Take a look-see."

Pine opened the passenger door and stood to one side. Dunbar saw there was no way he was going to squeeze into the rear, so he sidled onto the cramped front seat. *This is hell*, he thought. *I need a fixer, and they've sent a hayseed errand boy.*

Pine hopped into the driver's seat and cranked the ignition key. The Dodge shivered and came to life.

They coasted down the driveway toward the gates to the street, along a barrier wall of bougainvillea, brilliant with color, which ran the length of the property.

Pine spoke up. "You like more of the chrome, I reckon."

"Excuse me?"

"On your cars, I mean. You must like 'em big and shiny. Eight-cylinder at least."

"Are you a mechanic, Mr. Pine?"

"Did some work around the oil rigs, over in Henryetta. Back where I'm from, Oklahoma."

Oh, swell, thought Dunbar. *An oil monkey, come out to make good in California.* The studio men were drawing from the lower ranks, just to remind him that there were many ranks at Evergreen Studios.

Outside the gate, the street was empty and Dunbar exhaled a long breath. Linder had kept the newshounds at bay. Sunlight broke over the top edge of the bougainvillea, creating a lush riot of magenta cells.

Colors of 1936. That would be the title for his next big picture. By all rights, Evergreen Studios should be the first to come out with a full-color musical extravaganza. Sam Green and his money men might squawk at the added costs, but the audiences would go nuts for it and pour into the theaters in droves.

It felt good to be out in the open air, easing back into the world, watching the light Beverly Hills traffic floating past on the boulevard. *No stray fears, no nagging dread,* he thought. *Push to get back on top.*

Pine was paused at the stop sign at the intersection to the boulevard.

"I don't suppose you actually know where you're going."

"You just tell me the turns and I'll get us there."

"Wilshire to San Vicente then. That takes us to the turn into the canyon down to the ocean."

"You're the fellow who makes them musicals," said Pine. He made "musical" rhyme with "gal." "That must be a lot of fun."

"It's no picnic," said Dunbar. "It's hard work. It demands vision and relentless will to bring it all off. But I do love it. And the truth is, no one can do what I do."

The tall green hedges were giving way to smaller homes and apartment houses.

"I'm sure you've been well-briefed, Mr. Pine. I shouldn't have to tell you why Sam Green wants a full investigation filling out my side of events."

"You're the kind of guy they make sure gets taken care of," said Pine. "One way or another."

"As you know, the incident occurred as I was coming in for a work meeting late on Sunday. We were supposed to begin a major dance number first thing Monday morning and I always check up on my top crew the night before. There were going to be sixty dancers on set."

"How is it you get so many pretty girls in one place?"

Dunbar looked over at Orville Pine, still staring ahead as the world slid past.

"They come to me, Mr. Pine."

"What do you say to 'em? I mean, some of them costumes, whoo!"

"They're not kewpie dolls. The costumes are dazzling, yes, but they have to know how to move in them. They have to show *me* how they can move."

"I mean, you can see right through 'em." Pine gripped the steering wheel and glanced left and right, as if he feared his words might reach delicate ears right here in the middle of the road. He shot Dunbar a meaningful look. "You ever get dates with 'em?"

Dunbar felt a smile ease across his face.

"I get dates. I get plenty of dates. Watch the road, Orville."

They made the turn and began to wind down through Pasture Canyon, a ravine lined with cozy bungalows under towering eucalyptus. A few sported flower boxes in front. This seemed as far removed as you could get from all the battles and glories that had filled Dunbar's life over the past five years. It had always been his favorite escape route to take him down to the ocean in one of his personal fleet of eight sleek automobiles. Make that seven sleek automobiles now.

"I read in the papers you like to drive that Auburn. That's a sweet ride."

"It was a wonderful car. Now it's gone."

"Thing is, you had the bigger machine. That made the difference for you."

Dunbar cleared his throat. He said, "I suppose we should discuss the particulars. Of the accident."

"They're talking murder, right?"

Dunbar turned to stare at Orville Pine's profile, wooden as an Indian's, his eyes glued to the road. Dunbar shifted his stare to his own fist, clutching the knob of the walking stick between his knees.

"There was some crazy talk, from the first cops who got there. They were unhinged. It was a pretty bad wreck."

"But murder, whew," said Pine. "They really got to have it in for you."

As Mirada Drive neared the ocean, it flattened out and broadened, houses giving way to storefronts. Parked cars were angled at the curb in front of the businesses along the roadway: drugstore, hardware store, a restaurant or two.

Why did it have to happen? Headlights suddenly coming, not where they were supposed to be. They should have been off to the left and were suddenly in front of him in a blinding glare. Flying into that light, brighter than any light he'd commanded on a sound stage. Then an empty black nothing, until he found himself stumbling along the roadside in a garish glow. The lone beam of one remaining headlight shone at a crazy angle on a mass of twisted metal and fanning pools of red. He thought he heard a woman's voice, or was it a little girl's, making indistinct moaning sounds.

Dunbar sucked in a breath. "I was in a daze. You'd think they never worked an accident scene before. Once they found out who I am, they tried to hang it all on me. They were calling me drunk. I'm lucky to be alive."

"These automobile accidents can play out like a cyclone," said Pine. "You can't never tell who'll take the hit and who won't, and how the pieces will settle out when they land."

The glittering sea yawned before them as Pine pulled up to the corner where Mirada T'd into the Coast Road.

"About a mile up, you reckon?" asked Pine.

As they moved out into the northbound traffic, the road hugged the base of the cliff before straightening and stretching out beside the wide flat ocean on their left. High clouds danced over the crest of the mountains in the distance.

"This is very pretty," said Pine. "Of course, at night it's going to look different."

"At night it doesn't look like anything at all," said Dunbar.

"Yeah, pretty dark I suppose, pointed this direction. All they would have seen is your headlights coming at 'em."

Dunbar closed his eyes against the bright sunlight. "The father could have been disoriented."

The lighthouse would be coming up on the left, and just beyond that, the fatal stretch of road. He wondered what traces from the crash might still be visible, but didn't want to look.

Pine slowed the car, downshifting to a lower gear.

"Where you think it happened, right along about here?"

The bleached mud on the hillside towered over them on the right. Out over the water a pair of gulls glided through the air. Dunbar looked up as an approaching car suddenly jumped into view and bore down on them. Then the scream of its engine was past and its occupants vanished in a blur.

Pine steered the Dodge onto the narrow paved shoulder

and came to a stop. He reached out and twisted the ignition key. The trembling car went quiet.

"I saw tire marks. You wait here."

Dunbar watched the man amble back along the shoulder. The road curved slightly here, something he'd never really noticed.

The gulls dropped and rose in the invisible currents of the wind and Dunbar followed their movements with a grim intensity.

He turned to look at Pine, sixty or seventy yards back up the road now, stepping and peering down at the asphalt, leaning out like a timid farmboy trying to get a peek at the bearded lady, his head twisting left and right watching out for oncoming cars.

A gull shrieked and he turned back to watch. *I could put this in a dance number*, he told himself. The dips and doodles and carefree calls, Mr. Bird and Miss Gull caught up in love's ballet. He would pitch it to Sol in a couple of days. What the hell, he'd pitch it today, this afternoon, show them he wasn't off his stride from some goddam crash. Three days ago this is where he made his money. He closed his eyes and willed the old magic to return.

The driver's door opened with a metallic snap and Pine spoke through the opening.

"There's some short little skids from the northbound car, like he was just starting to hit the brakes. None from yours though, 'til after point of impact. Big arcs as you spun around. They go down quite a ways. You were moving at a pretty good clip."

Pine hoisted himself back behind the wheel.

"You hit the two northbound cars. Newspapers said you clobbered the Hadens first, the family. Then bounced off to clip the Stott car, with those two other fellas. That how you remember it?"

"All I remember were all those headlights coming at me. And the noise."

"Right there is where everything came to a stop," said Pine. "Just wanted to see it with my own eyes. What say we head on up the road a ways, maybe turn it around, get your angle."

Pine twisted the ignition key and the car growled back to life. He reached up for the gear-shift lever, rested his fingers there and paused.

"They had it you was drunk."

"I had a beer and a sandwich."

"Maybe just another belt or two, knock the cobwebs out before hitting the road?"

Dunbar shifted in his seat and found a rising note of indignation in his voice. "This is nuts. Any other night, any other day and they could nail me on that. Ask anybody in Hollywood. I can hold my own. Three, four, eight. I'll take anybody on and I'll drink you under the table. But Sunday I was focused on the work ahead. I decided to stop for a quick bite. One beer. That was it."

"Where was that?"

"Oh..." Dunbar rubbed his face. "That place on up, on the left. I don't know the name."

Pine craned left to look for traffic behind him as he put the car in gear.

"Well, that shouldn't be too hard to find. Likely they can tell us something."

Dunbar felt pain shoot into his knee as the car lurched and they moved back out onto the highway. He used to listen to this concrete strip humming beneath his tires and imagine it as a willing servant, laying the world before him. Now the road stretched out in front of them like one long tombstone. A knob of rock up on the left loomed like a gate at the Rubicon. Once past it there would be no way home. The air suddenly felt cool on his moistening forehead.

Pine glanced over at him.

"I can tell you from those tire marks I saw back there, looked like you bounced off that boy's car first."

Dunbar shrugged. "He was in front of the other car then. They both got it, what does it matter who was first?"

"Except he wasn't quite in front of the other car."

"Meaning what?"

"Likely that boy, Stott, was coming out from the ocean side of the road, your side, right where the road curves. Making a left turn, trying to skitter out ahead of the car he could see, the Hadens, looking back to see if he could make it. Probably didn't see you at all. And you just weren't expecting him."

"You're saying the crash wasn't really my fault?"

"Like he just popped out there and you looked to try and get around him, holding that shoulder tight. But the road was curving, see, and you just shot across straight into the Hadens. That's all she wrote."

"That makes sense to me now. Surely it must have happened as you say. An entirely plausible explanation."

"Ain't no plausible about it. The tire tracks show it."

"It could have happened to anybody."

"More than likely. Of course now, it doesn't explain your state of mind."

"It's all a blank, I told you."

Two miles down the road a wooden building with a sloped roof appeared on a flat promontory to their left. A sign on a pole at the road's edge read "The Pirate's Roost."

"That the place where you ate?"

Dunbar nodded.

Orville steered the Dodge into the gravel parking lot. The place didn't look too busy, a single car parked at the far edge of the building nearly out of sight. A sign on the window of the double-doored entrance said "Open."

Orville held a hand up toward Dunbar. "How about you stay low on this one? I'll be quick in there. Get the story, or the names of the ones that's got a story."

Dunbar watched Pine disappear through the double doors and felt the throbbing in his knees and lower back begin to ebb. Not such a fool after all, this Mr. Pine. Just a man who knows his job.

Barely two minutes later, Pine emerged again into the glare of the sun. As he slid back behind the wheel, he waved a small notebook. "You look to have some witnesses, Mr. Dunbar."

The Dodge jumped out onto the Coast Highway and they headed back toward town.

Orville glanced over at Dunbar.

"You suppose the Hadens ever saw any of your movies? 'Spose they liked 'em?"

"I'm damned if I know."

"'Course it don't matter now."

"Maybe they smooched in the back of the theater and fell in love because of me. Maybe he got his first feel up her skirt watching one of my dance numbers. Who the hell cares?"

"I guess someone else can buy those tickets now."

Dunbar suppressed a smirk. Pine may have thought he was being subtle, but this was just the sort of move to expect from the studio boys. Catch a man while he's down, offer him salvation with one hand and a leash with the other.

"Are you trying to shame me Orville? You think this is going to push me to back off my contract demands? Do you honestly expect, after all the plays I've had with Sam Green, this will be the one to throw me?"

"Not for me to say."

"You may think I'm some carefree fop, surrounding himself with chorus girls, just in it for the crumpet. Let me tell you, the top-grossers coming out of Evergreen Studios for the past three years, the past three full years, have been Dunbar DuWayne musicals.

"Giving me grief about costs. Yes, it costs money to wow an audience. But do I wow an audience? You're goddam right I do."

They were coming to the knob of rock that jutted between the road and the waves. What had appeared from the other direction as an impenetrable fortress wall, showed now as an arching formation standing sentinel over a small cove beside the highway. Orville slowed and steered onto the strip of shoulder there.

Dunbar leaned forward in his seat. "Go on, why are you stopping? I'm ready to drive through where it happened. I can take it."

From this side were visible the violent marks left years ago by the work crews. The road was notched through what had once been a rocky wall, where they'd had to cut and blast, carving off great jagged boulders that tumbled and splayed to the water's edge. This spot, why were they stopped in this spot? He needed Pine to get moving again.

Orville breathed in the sea air. "Nice here, ain't it?"

The last little section of the wall rose between the road and the ocean, forming a stunted cliff that blocked their view of the water. Fingers of surf spray bounced in the air beyond it.

"That feller back there at the diner, you know, he backed your story about the drinking. Says you walked out of there sober as a judge. It was terrible to have got yourself in that crash just a little ways up the road, but it wasn't because of your drinking."

"It was their fault as much as mine."

"The daddy died instantly. Steering column went right through his chest. He might have done some jerking around at the last, but he was a goner pretty quick."

Dunbar drew in a breath and fixed Orville with a searching look. Pine spoke in a level tone.

"The momma's arms were poking out through the windshield, maybe from the force of the crash, maybe she was reaching out for the baby she'd been holding in her lap. Doesn't really matter. Little thing got fileted like a flounder and spread all over the front of the car. They were still trying to cut through the wreck to get at momma when she died.

"The little girl is a real fighter from what they told me, though her eyes are gone. At least she never had to see what you saw."

This was more than he cared to hear from a studio toady. Dunbar met Orville's eyes without blinking. "Some of us will die better than others, just like some of us live better than others."

"See, I ask myself how someone could come through something like that, see all that, and not be a little bit bothered. You know, how does a man watch a whole family die in front of him, come back down to where it happened, and still be all worked up about costs and contracts?"

Dunbar stared at Pine's sunburned face. "You don't work for Sam Green, do you?"

"You were on your way in to meet with your people about the work next day. People you know, people who will jump through hoops for you. You didn't have to worry about being late, you weren't in no rush. But you were going a good eighty miles an hour when you slammed into those two northbound cars. At about a quarter past ten.

"Fellow back at the diner said you walked out of his place a bit after nine o'clock, just after his favorite show came on the radio. Just now, coming the other way, it took us less than twenty minutes to make it up there, even with our one little stop to look at the tire streaks.

"So a fella could wonder what kept you the extra forty-five minutes along this stretch of road?"

"Just who do you work for, Mr. Pine? Who the hell are you?"

"I was hired by Mr. Charles Penley."

"Penley Petroleum? What the hell business has that got to do with me?"

Pine canted his head with a faint smile. "This is not about the picture business." Dunbar watched as Pine's gimlet eyes followed the rivulet of sweat he could feel sliding down his left cheekbone. Trapped in a tin box on the road outside of town, in this place of all places.

"Were you going to tell about the girl?"

Dunbar felt a surge of rage. "You must be insane."

Pine shrugged. "Nah, not me. But now Mr. Penley, he's a proud man, given to doting on his kin as a proud man will."

A throbbing in Dunbar's temples began to mute the intrusive twang of Pine's voice. The girl.

"His oldest, he knew he couldn't keep her back. She drove all the way out from Henryetta in the car he bought her on her twenty-first birthday, a pretty green two-door ragtop Cadillac Series 60. The one I found parked out here about dawn the other morning."

She had stood out her first day on the set, unable to suppress that extra bit of bravado.

"Her daddy saw to it she called home to her momma at least once a week, so they were all up on her exciting news that she'd gotten herself a job at Evergreen Pictures and what's more she thought maybe she'd caught the eye of this big deal dance director."

Like all the others, covering her eagerness with that phony nonchalance. Edging away whenever he started to move in.

"...over and over about this dance man, her momma warned her, you know all those Hollywood men got just one thing on their mind. 'Oh, don't you worry, Momma,' she said, 'he's a happily married man. Why his father-in-law owns the whole dang studio.'"

What were the chances she happened to be in that diner when he was? She'd glanced at him just once as she walked to the door. There was no mistaking the invitation.

"When she didn't call home Sunday night, Mr. Penley roused me to come check up on her. Filled me in on how much she loved coming out to look at the ocean and some place she called the Pirate's Nest. It didn't take too much to find The Pirate's Roost. The owner ain't so sure he remembers her, but he remembers that bright green Caddie. And he sure remembers you."

He had found her parked by the knob of rock, posing smartly against the front fender, a cigarette smoldering between her upturned fingers.

"I must have driven this stretch of road fifty times in the last three days trying to figure where she would have flown off to. Then I saw how the rock here has got this little place you can't be seen from the road. What a perfect place for lovers."

The breeze fluttering her hair in the dim summer twilight. Her casual confident glance as he approached. All as it should be.

"One thing kept stumping me. If she'd snuck off with you when you left that diner, how come she wasn't one of them got pulled out of that wreck?"

She didn't move or look up until he was almost on her. She feigned surprise as he grabbed her. The stupid bitch actually punched his face as he wrestled her back onto the seat. He was grunting. "You want to be in pictures?" She started to scream as she yanked at his ascot, the white one with the double-D pattern, and somehow, as he yanked back, he got it around her throat. "Shut up," he told her. "You know how it works in this town."

Pine was peering at him. "I got to thinking, those boulders down there must have all kind of hidey-holes in 'em. I went on down to take a look."

The tide should have taken her out before dawn. Three days in the surf. There should be no trace.

"Now, what do you suppose I found?"

Dunbar fingered the amber ascot at his throat. The white monogrammed one, what had become of it?

Pine nodded his chin toward the water's edge. "C'mon out. Let me show you."

Pine popped open his door and stepped out as another car sped by with a gust and a whine on its way in to town. He walked around the front of the car.

Dunbar felt the sweat on the back of his legs and realized he hadn't left this seat since Pine had arrived in his driveway. He'd been promised that the green car was taken care of, returned discretely to her apartment. Linder had seen to it personally.

Dunbar pushed open his door and stepped out onto the rocky ground. Pine stood facing him on the broad sloping shoulder, a thumb idly hooked on the top of his trousers, rumpled coat bunched back.

Dunbar told him, "You don't know how it works in this town, do you?"

"Oh, I learn quick. Showed up at that studio Monday morning, one mention of your name and I got the bum's rush. So it took me that extra day or two to go asking around at the diner, poke around these rocks. And find this."

Pine pulled the white ascot from his coat pocket and held it fluttering in the breeze.

"Her name was Annabeth, in case you were wondering."

Dunbar felt short breaths catch in his chest, his mind racing. *Got to buy him off, convince him. Stop him one way or another.*

Pine smiled and shook his head. "I suppose if you hadn't panicked, maybe tried to bring her into town with you, she would have been just one more body pulled out of the wreck. You could have got away with it."

Pine's sad smile faded. "Now, be a sport and show me where you put her in the water."

Pine turned and moved toward the base of the rock wall, shoving the ascot back in his pants pocket with one hand, while he reached up to scratch his armpit with the other.

Dunbar began follow him, feeling the heft of the heavy walking stick in his hand. A few more steps and they'd be out of sight of the cars passing above them. Make it quick and sudden, no room for error. Just one more dumb dead Okie by the side of the road.

He shifted the stick into his waiting fist, ignoring the stab of pain shooting up through his hip. He took one good measured stride to close the distance and with both hands raised it as a club over his head.

Pine whirled. The glint of the gun barrel in his hand brought Dunbar up short. He hadn't noticed the shoulder-holster. Pine squared his stance, calmly gripping a .45 automatic.

"I needed you to make that play just to be sure I got me a murderer," said Pine.

Dunbar felt his arm waver. He shifted half a step and groaned.

Pine wagged the barrel. "You want to settle that crutch back down? If I have to put a slug into your knee, it's going to be a job getting you to climb back in that car. And you won't be showing anybody any dance moves for a considerable long time."

Dead Man's Curve

Paul D. Marks

The wind screamed through my hair, all the windows down, as I raced down the canyon toward Sunset Boulevard in my friend Joe's '67 GTO. A *real* car, that drove like a *real* car and looked like a *real* car, not one of those modern *jellybean-looking* things. Fifty years old and the smell of the leather seats singed my nostrils as if the car had just driven off the showroom floor.

Little GTO by Ronnie and the Daytonas blasted out of the GTO's bitchin sound system on the surf and rod playlist that streamed out from Joe's iPod, which I had a hell of a time figuring out. I know, I know, the original GTO didn't have no iPod input... Joe had done some updating, especially to the sound system.

409, then *Drag City*.

Damn if I didn't feel like somebody again. A winner.

Shut Down. Little Deuce Coupe.

Newer stuff like *Sober Driver* by Dengue Fever.

Hell, I hadn't felt this good in years; just sitting in that black leather seat took ten, no twenty, years off my life. I almost felt like a teenager again, cruising the Strip and Pacific Coast Highway, listening to the Beach Boys. Looking for girls.

Sure, things had changed in all these years—decades. But LA still had the sun and surf and cars.

And driving Joe's muscle car—even if I was just doing an errand for him—gave me a sense of purpose for the first time in ages. I needed that. Needed it more than anything.

Whipping onto Sunset, heading toward Beverly Hills, I thought of Susie Evans, a girl I'd dated a long time ago. Long, straight blonde hair. Eyes as blue as the ocean—does that sound corny? And, man, did she look good in a bikini. Real

California girl, the kind the Beach Boys' *Surfer Girl* or *California Girls* was written about. I met her on the beach when her Frisbee went astray. We'd dated for three years.

I skipped ahead on the iPod to *Surfer Girl*. That was Sue. My old girlfriend. Joe's on again-off again girlfriend. Seemed that she was on the bench these days, second string, to a bunch of younger hotties. I'd read it in the tabloids.

I slowed down slightly—but only slightly—as I tore through Beverly Hills.

"What the f—"

Some damn black Beamer was about to kiss my tail. I was flying, so when I saw the Beamer growing large in my rearview mirror I was surprised. My first instinct was to jam on the brakes—like I used to—play games with him. But I just kept her steady. The guy came right up on my tail, maybe a foot between us.

"Cool it, man. Get off my ass you son-of-a-bitch." My hand shot in the air, giving him the three-fingered salute. He screeched into the curb lane, blowing by me on the right.

"Fuck you, asshole!" I flipped him off again. The chase was on.

He shot out, slicing in front of me with inches to spare. Smelly acrid burning rubber overpowering the sweet leather smell of the GTO. But hell if I was going to slam on my brakes. The big GTO barreled up on him. He didn't like it—jammed on his brakes, red lights flashing in my eyes.

He cuts me off, then wants to play.

I'm game.

I gunned the engine. Slid alongside him. Flipped him the bird. He zipped ahead. I hit the pedal harder. I knew I shouldn't be doing this. I was doing an errand for Joe in his car. I was a mature man—well, not if you asked my sister.

I hammered pedal to metal. Shot out in front of that anemic Beamer.

Hell, it might as well have been 1967 again.

The GTO tore down Sunset, nearly airborne.

Hit the brakes. I had to slow for a car crawling along in the fast lane—the Beamer passed me on the right again. It went back and forth like that for a couple minutes. I hoped there weren't any cops hiding out.

By some twist of fate or destiny—whatever you want to call it—*Dead Man's Curve* came blaring out of the speakers just as we careened into that famous hairpin turn. The same Dead Man's Curve that Jan and Dean had sung about in 1964. The same Dead Man's Curve that Jan and his Vette had spun out on in real life in '65, an accident that had brain-damaged him for life. And even though they'd straightened out the hairpin turn somewhat since then, it was still a hell of a twister.

I shot around the slow jerk, came up on the Beamer's tail, cut out—jumped past him. Was about to leave him choking on my 1967 polluted exhaust when I came up fast on a plumber's truck in my lane. I smashed down on the brakes. Tires spinning. Black rubbery smoke rising. Trying not to fishtail. I yanked the wheel hard, turned out onto a side street, crunching up and over the curb. If I'd stopped on Sunset I would have been rear-ended by the car behind me. Guess I was lucky.

The Beamer sped past, laying rubber, flipping me off through the sun roof.

The GTO came to a stop, half on the sidewalk, half in the street. My head whiplashed—no headrest to stop it. The trunk—which Joe hadn't even given me the keys to—popped open.

I sat there a moment, head reeling—seeing my life passing before me. A series of band gigs and dead end jobs that I once thought were glamorous. Girls and groupies—there is a difference. I waited till I got my equilibrium back. Slightly dazed, I got out of the car. Surveyed it. Seemed to be in pretty good shape, lucky for me. Headed toward the rear to close the trunk.

"Asshole probably thinks he won."

I came 'round the back of the car.

"Shit!"

My head was swimming—I had to get the hell out of there.

I couldn't believe my eyes. No wonder Joe hadn't given me the keys to the trunk. He might as well have given me the finger like the guy in the Beamer. In fact, he gave it to me in spades.

What was I gonna do now? Go to the cops? Run? You know what they say, you can run but you can't hide. I knew I wouldn't be able to hide.

I stared down at the dead body in the trunk. Flung it closed.

What the hell was I gonna do now?

I wanted a do-over, but there aren't many do-overs in real life. At least not for me. I should've learned that lesson a long time ago. Still, I wished it was a week ago. All I wanted then was to be somebody—again. Now I got more than I bargained for and I could be somebody heading for jail.

A week ago, I was the aimless slacker that I'd been for the last couple decades, wandering around in a haze of dope and delusion, still thinking it was the 1960s or '70s. Not a drifter exactly, since I had a small pad, shabby as it was—*shabby chic*. No, the real thing. Real shab.

That long week ago, my bare feet burned in the Huntington Beach sand, as I walked toward the shore, long board under my arm.

"Dewey Weber died twenty years ago," I said to no one in particular. More like thinking out loud. "That should count for something."

"Who the hell is Dewey Weber?" a man walking parallel to me said.

"Made the best damn surfboards in the world. Some might argue. But they didn't know Dewey. And what the hell are you doing at Huntington Beach if you don't know the name Dewey Weber? It's only fucking Surf City, U-S-A. And you don't know Dewey Weber."

The man looked like he could either fight or flight—he walked off. Probably thought I was some crazy beach dude, talking to myself and all.

I walked alongside the pier, heading for the water. It was a warm spring day, a weekday. Most people should have been at work or school, but the beach was fairly crowded. Sometimes I wondered if anyone in SoCal ever really worked.

A guy with a paunch and a receding salt and pepper hairline came up to me. Trouble on the horizon?

"Hey, don't I know you?" he said.

I squinted, checking him out. Didn't think I knew him.

"Sure, didn't you used to be Ray Hood?"

"Still am." I was flattered to be recognized.

"My mom took me to see you and The Zumas when I was fourteen. She loved you guys—I did too." He grinned. "I wish I had something for you to autograph."

Shit, he looked old. What did that make me?

"I knew it was you," he said. "But you sure don't look the same."

In my head I didn't think I'd changed that much. Neither one of us had paper or pen. He walked off. I was just as glad; there was nothing more to say. And I didn't need to be reminded that my once-blonde hair was now at least half gray—and that I was probably lying to myself when I said only half was gray.

"The California girls aren't the same either," I mumbled, looking around. The whole place had changed. Not for the better, not for the worse. Just changed. Still, sometimes I felt like I was in a foreign country. A stranger in my own strange land. But I would never leave. The beach was my home.

That damn long board got heavier every time I took it out. I hauled it past a thousand different people blasting a thousand different sounds from a thousand different boom boxes—hadn't they heard of iPods and earbuds?

I stabbed the board in the sand at the water's edge, needed to catch my breath before going in. An angular kid—maybe twelve or so—glared at the board, then at me.

"Get outta my way, old man. This is my beach."

"It used to be mine. I used to be somebody."

"Well, you're not anymore." He laughed. Jumped off with his buds.

"Old man," his words echoed in my head.

"Hell, I used to be somebody," I said out loud, as I hauled my board up the threadbare stairs to my crummy apartment. "At least half a somebody."

I leaned the board against the wall, locked the door behind me. Stood in the entryway, bent over, sucking in air. Getting harder and harder to lug that monster up those stairs. When I regained my breath I grabbed my old, beat up Gibson J-50 acoustic—still sounded fab, scratches, buckle rash and all—walked through the open slider to the balcony, where, if I craned my neck, I could see a straight-edge of ocean three blocks west. Couldn't really hear it, but I could pretend the sound of the cars whooshing by was the crashing of the waves.

I strummed a few random chords, eventually segueing into *Surfer Girl.* That turned into *Distant Shores.* And that turned into silence, as I sat there staring out over the rooftops, not really seeing them. I saw an echo, a memory of the past. Good times, bad times, I had my share of both. These days it was bad—had been for a long time. But nothing is permanent. Luck can change.

I flashed on the pictures on my walls. The Beach Boys on tour—and who was that guitarist stage right? Me, a baby, still in my teens—what a trip. Jan and Dean. I played lead for them for a while after Jan recuperated somewhat. And who was that sleek blonde kid riding the nose on a Dewey Weber stick? Who had a curvy blonde California girl on each arm?

And who had lost it all? To dope, to booze and to sheer exhaustion.

Nope, nothing is permanent.

It took a while, but I finally realized this.

"How the hell did I end up in this dump?" But I knew—and I knew it was no one's fault but my own. I had let it go to my head. I thought my guaranteed fifteen minutes of fame would turn into a lifetime's worth. And the emotional ricochets of my busted dreams kept bouncing off the walls. I ducked them as best I could, but you couldn't dodge every one of them.

I glared at the phone, willing it to ring. I'd called a couple of old buddies. Left messages with their secretaries or assistants or whatever they're called these days. "Tell them it's Ray, Ray Hood. I'm back. Limber. Sober. And playing just as good as ever."

Willing—waiting for—the phone to ring, but it never did.

I made myself a peanut butter and blackberry jelly sandwich. I lived on those and Franco American Spaghetti, though it seems they were taken over by Campbell's, so I guess I ate Campbell's spaghetti these days. Nope, nothing is forever.

Damn if the phone didn't ring.

"Hey, Sis." My sister, Rhonda. I liked hearing from her, but I won't say I wasn't disappointed that it wasn't Joe Moria or Tommy Di Falco.

She wanted to stop by.

Five minutes later, she was at the door, with two large bags of groceries.

"Thanks for the food, Sis, but you know I do shop on occasion."

She opened the fridge to see my stash of peanut butter, jelly, bread and beer. "I can see that. Well, at least this should give you some variety for the next week or so. I even bought those little sandwich cookies that you like so much."

I didn't like her mothering me. On the other hand, I did like those cookies. Gave her a hug.

"Why don't you come home? Visit the family, see your nieces and nephews. There's nothing for you here anymore. I know you don't like the burbs, but we don't live all that far away."

"Bor-ring."

"You can't relive the past, Ray." She walked around the apartment, scoffing at the pix on the walls from my *glory* days.

"Something's gonna break. I put calls in to Joe Moria and Tommy Di Falco. They're still two of the biggest record producers in town."

"And how long ago was that? Hmm?"

"A week, I guess."

"They don't want anything to do with you. You burned your bridges with them a long time ago when you became a tweaker."

"I can still play."

"I don't mean to be cruel, but you're yesterday's papers, Ray."

"But you are cruel, Rhonda."

"Only because I want to shock you into reality."

"I live fucking reality every fucking day. This is my fucking reality." I swept my hand across the *vast* expanse of my dinky, crappy, cluttered pad.

"You're nothing but a dreamer, Ray. Nothing but a goddamn dreamer."

"Yeah, well, I used to be a doer."

"But you're not anymore."

"I will be again. I can still play." I picked up my blonde 1968 Fender Telecaster, turned on the Twin Reverb amp. Snaked through some riffs. "I'm not that old and decrepit. I can still play—"

"You're good, I'll give you that. But they want younger guys. Guys who didn't burn bridges."

"And I can still surf." I didn't tell her that every time I hit the beach in the last year or two I never made it to the water. But I knew I could do it—I knew it. "Hell, the only Beach Boy that really surfed was Dennis. At least I can surf...and play guitar." I tried to go for bravado, but I even sounded pathetic to myself.

She walked over to the sink. I cringed inside, hoping it wouldn't show on the outside. She picked up my box of Clairol Shimmer Lights Beach Blonde hair color.

"And what's this? You're not twenty-two anymore. Oh, Ray, stop living in the past, grow up and get a real job."

Rhonda didn't stay long. And she wasn't gone five minutes when I dropped some bath salts, got tweaked. My hands shook. I couldn't play the runs I'd played for her just a few minutes before, but I felt mighty fine.

The phone rang. I thought it might be Rhonda calling to say she was sorry for rushing out so quickly.

"Ray." It was a man's voice. "Joe Moria, long time, buddy."

Now my hands really began to shake.

We met at Joe's house in the hills above Sunset. When you're one of the hottest record producers with a string of hits as long as your arm—hell longer—you can afford prime real estate and more. He and another guy were waiting for me at the back of the driveway, in front of a garage that looked as big as an airplane hangar.

The other guy's brush cut said former military. And I knew if he lifted the shirt covering his flat stomach it would reveal one solid six pack. Joe introduced him as Stash. That's all—Stash. His real name? Nickname? I had no idea.

Behind them, on an apron of cement you could have landed a jet on, sat part of Joe's classic car collection, including the '67 orange GTO, with the three-speed Turbo-Hydramatic automatic transmission, and black vinyl top, that I'd always drooled over. I could feel my eyes widen at the sight of it. So damn pretty. So damn hot. And so damn fast. Behind it was a sampling of Joe's other classic cars, '68 Dodge Charger, '63 Stingray, and a bunch of other sixties muscle cars, Mustang, Camaro, Barracuda, Road Runner. Some guy in greasy white coveralls was washing them by hand. Another guy was waxing them. It must be nice to have money.

I wasn't sure how to greet Joe after all this time, but he came up to me, threw his arms around me.

"Good to see you, Ray. Sight for sore eyes."

It was like all the years, all the bad vibes had just washed away. I felt good—like a human being—for the first time in ages.

We sat on Joe's patio, overlooking the city, talking about old times. Stash didn't say much, but I felt like he was appraising me every second, his eyes boring under my skin, trying to see what made me tick. I didn't know if I should broach the subject of possibly doing some studio work or even touring with one of Joe's bands. But he saved me from having to humble myself.

"I wanted to talk to you about a job, Ray."

"I may have had some rough times, but I can still play. I practice every day. Still a good session man."

He didn't respond right away. Finally, he said, "Uh, it's not about a gig—at least not a music gig."

He must have seen the disappointment on my face, though I tried to hide it.

"But if it works out then maybe we can talk about a gig afterwards. And I'll pay you well."

"What is it?"

"You just need to drive a car from my house here up to my ranch in Napa."

"I thought—"

"I know we've had our differences, but I think I know you pretty well. And I know I can trust you. It's a simple job—just deliver a package from here to there."

"Illegal?"

"Do I look like I need to do anything illegal?" His eyes scanned his huge house, vast property and collection of classic cars. He looked toward my old, beat up motorcycle that I'd ridden over on. My guitar and small rucksack were bungeed to the rack. "You got a valid driver's license?"

I nodded.

"I saw you looking at the GTO out back. You always had a hard-on for that car. Tell you what, you do the job and you can use that car and when it's over it's yours, on top of the cash."

"And then we'll talk about a gig—a real gig? Doing some session work or touring?"

"You got it."

We had a lunch of kale, black cod and something called quinoa, prepared by Joe's personal chef, and wine from his own private label on the patio overlooking the city. Reminisced about old times. I wanted to ask him about Susie Evans, but there was bad blood between Joe and I about her. Though it was a long time ago, blood under the bridge, so to speak. In the past—hopefully in the past.

I agreed to do it. I guess my desire to work—to be somebody again—outweighed my better judgment. I wanted to go home, clean up, change my clothes. But Joe said the job had to be done right away, so I'd have to get going soon. He also excused himself for a meeting, but not before giving me the key to the GTO and instructions on where I had to take it.

"Why me?"

"When you left your message a couple weeks ago sounded like you needed a break."

He handed me a stuffed envelope. "Here's three hundred for expenses. You'll get the full cash end of the deal on delivery at the other end."

"Seems too good to be true and you know what they say about that—"

"Well, not in this case. This is just one friend helping another."

I walked off to admire the GTO.

Joe didn't give me a trunk key. I figured the package I was supposed to deliver was in there, but I didn't want to ask too many questions, make waves. They say desperate men do desperate things. And I was that desperate. And stupid men do stupid things—and I was that stupid.

And now here I was, just off Sunset Boulevard, with a dead body in the trunk—and I knew why Joe hadn't given me the trunk key. I kept staring at it until I forced myself to look away. What was I gonna do now?

I closed the trunk as best I could. Felt my way back to the driver's door. Got in. Floored it into reverse. Music still spilled from the car's speakers—Chuck Berry's *No Particular Place to Go.*

Instead of going directly back to Sunset, I drove up farther into the hills, just in case the cops were roaming around down there after my run-in with the Beamer.

"Fucking Dead Man's Curve—of all places," I said, as I turned onto Mulholland. The city spread out to the south of me, the valley to the north. I could turn right. I could turn left. But like the song said, I had no particular place to go.

"Fucking Joe."

Should I call the cops?

Call Rhonda?

Should I try to complete my mission for Joe? Yeah, my mission. A dead body—a fucking dead body.

Was I a patsy? The more I drove the more I thought so.

I hit the San Diego Freeway, drove south to Huntington Beach instead of north to Napa. I didn't know where else to go.

I walked under the pier, sat in lapping water, trying to figure out what to do. The salt stung my skin as I watched the flaming sun sink into the ocean.

Joe Moria lit one Gauloises cigarette off the one he had going. Three lines of coke straddled a small mirror on his desk. He leaned toward the white powder but forced himself to pull back. He loved coke, but he also knew what it did to him. That's how Sandy Baker got dead.

Sure, Sandy needed killing. He was fucking up Joe's business. But there was probably a more *elegant* way than just shooting him here, in his home studio. But all buzzed on coke, well, it just happened.

Joe waited for the goddamn phone to ring. Hell, he could get just about anything he wanted with a simple order. But he couldn't get the goddamn phone to ring.

Stash should have called by now. He was Joe's Go-To man these last few years. He was overpaid, but he could be counted on to keep his mouth shut. *Maybe*, Joe thought, *you couldn't really overpay someone who would do that.*

It had been Joe's own idea to have Ray drive the GTO up to the ranch. That way if he got stopped by the cops Joe could deny any culpability, say Ray stole the car, a car he'd always coveted, and put the murder on him. That pathetic schmuck Ray had called at just the right time. Ray had known Sandy. And there was bad blood between them. Ray's calling was like manna from heaven.

The world could live without Ray. A loser who had nothing to offer. Was just stealing air and food from people who deserved it. The perfect patsy.

All he had to do was take the body from Joe's house in the Hollywood Hills up to his ranch. From there Stash would get rid of it one dark night. But where the fuck was Ray? According to the GPS Stash had put on the car, Ray was heading south when he should have been heading north.

And where the hell was Stash's call?

Of course, Joe could have called Stash too, but—

The damn phone finally rang.

"What the hell's happening?" Joe shouted into the receiver.

"Your boy rabbited."

"Looks like he's down in Huntington Beach."

"Maybe he went home to change and clean up, like he wanted." Stash laughed.

"Okay, so it wasn't such a good idea using him. We gotta pull the plug. Get on it."

"An orange GTO won't be hard to find, especially one with a GPS locator on the undercarriage."

I was starving. Maybe dead bodies made me hungry. I didn't know—I'd never seen one before, unless you count my grandfather's open casket that I had to endure when I was eight. I headed topside, walked along the pier. Bought a hot dog on a stick.

Two men were headed in my direction with definite purpose in their step. Definitely not dressed in beach casual. As they got closer one of them looked familiar. Stash, Joe's bodyguard or whatever he was. The strong, silent—and I assumed—deadly type.

I didn't have much time to think, but in the split second my survival instincts kicked in I realized that I probably knew the pier—the whole area—and they didn't. I took off running on my old legs as fast I could pump them. Maybe lugging that long board down to the beach every day did me some good after all.

I ditched them and, huffing and puffing, ran to the GTO. I looked around. They hadn't left anyone by the car. Just the two of them, somewhere still on the pier. I threw the door open, jammed the key in the ignition and took off.

I drove up PCH, trying to keep as close to the speed limit as I could, knowing the cops wouldn't appreciate finding a dead body if they stopped me. On the other hand, maybe that was my best way out. Nope. Cops are almost never the best way out—at least not for someone like me.

I rounded the corner—and there they were, three cars behind me. I could tell Stash's brush cut anywhere.

"I lost them. How the hell do they keep finding me?" I pummeled the gas pedal. "If I have to keep driving this fast the cops are bound to bust me."

I seemed to have ditched them again. I gave the wheel a hard right, then a hard left. *Diddy maoed* down to a little spot I knew about, one of the leftover oil fields. A bunch of obsolete derricks, some of them still tick-tocking in the late afternoon sun. I drove in through a break in the fence. Nobody was around. I jumped out of the car, surveyed the site: time-worn, dilapidated buildings with roughhewn wooden sides. Derricks that looked like praying mantises, reaching for the sky. Pools of tarry oil here and there—I knew this site was waiting for environmental cleanup. The trunk wouldn't open. I found a long flat piece of metal, something like a crowbar. Shoved it into the trunk, gave it a push. It flew open. Working up a sweat, I managed to pull the body out, drag it across the dirt. I dumped it in one of the oily, black pools, closed the trunk, ready to get the hell out of there. A glint of something shiny under the bumper hit me in the eye. I reached for it. It was stuck to the chassis. Looked like an iPod or one of those iPads. What did I know? I couldn't afford that fancy electronic stuff. I examined it a moment—it was a GPS system and it had been attached to the undercarriage of the GTO. No wonder those mothers could find me even when I'd left them in the dust.

I couldn't leave it here—it would bring them and maybe the cops right to the body. I figured out how to turn the thing off, put it on the seat next to me and now I got the hell out of there.

I felt like I was in Dante's Ninth Circle of Hell—treachery. Adrenalin slugged through my veins like it hadn't done in years. I'd never been so freaked out or exhilarated. I felt alive and scared of dying all at the same time.

Just as I turned onto PCH I was lit up by a CHP car. I pulled to the shoulder. I might have been driving fast. Or maybe Joe had put out an alert; I was sure he had connections with the cops. Either way, I was screwed.

Two officers approached on either side of the GTO, their hands hovering over their holsters. My hands were in plain sight at the two and ten positions on the steering wheel.

"License and registration, please," the younger chippie said, officiously polite.

"What'd I do, officer?"

"Sir, license and registration."

I rooted in the glove box for the registration, explaining the car was on loan from a friend. Came up with the insurance card and the registration. They ran it through their computer and since there was no stolen car report and I had no wants or warrants they couldn't bust me on that.

"Mind if we search the car?" the older cop said.

What could I say? If I said no they'd make me wait around for a warrant. Or they'd make my life a living hell. If I was lucky there was no coke under the seats and no traces of the body in the trunk that would be visible to the naked eye. It had been wrapped up pretty good. And I hadn't noticed anything left behind after I'd dumped it at the rigs.

"Go ahead. But can you tell me what you stopped me for?"

"Broken taillight."

For a broken taillight, they made me stand off to the side under the watchful eyes of the older officer while the younger one searched the passenger compartment. He didn't seem to find anything. Went around to the trunk.

"Trunk key."

"I lost it and the ignition key only works the ignition. But it doesn't close all the way anyway. You can just pop it." Trying to be helpful—I hoped I wasn't helping myself into a six by eight cell.

He asked me to open the trunk. After my little session with the metal bar at the rigs it popped easily.

"Step back."

He looked through the trunk as if expecting to find something. Seemed disappointed not to. He traded positions with the other officer so maybe a fresh pair of eyes would find something he couldn't. No such luck.

He came back to me. "Cool car, sir. What year is it?"

"Sixty-seven. 389 under the hood. They don't make 'em like this anymore."

"You can say that again. Wish our cruisers were more like this baby," the older cop grinned. "Get that taillight fixed."

Reluctantly, they let me go. "You have a good day, sir."

I put on my blinker and eased out into traffic. A rock or something must have kicked up in the oil field, breaking the taillight. Just my luck.

I figured Joe would have let me take the blame if I was caught with the body in the car. That was the plan. But even if I'd made it up to Napa, what would he and Stash have done with me? I doubted they'd just let me drive off in my new GTO. No, they'd want to clean things up and up there, on his ranch, who would know—and who would miss a loser like me? Fuck that Joe. He was really trying to burn me.

They say revenge is a dish best served cold. I wanted revenge. And I would serve it hot—hot as lead. I would fuck him—fuck him good. Or die trying.

I drove the GTO up to the Point. By now the sun was almost completely hidden behind the horizon and there were few people out.

I walked across the cool sand, straight into the breakers, the salty sting of the air slapping me sober—even though the only thing I was stoned on was fear and exhaustion. I walked out into the ocean as far as I could. Then I began to swim until my arms got tired and my muscles burned. I thought about continuing out, so far out that I wouldn't be able to make it back to shore, ending it all right there. But I wouldn't let them beat me. I ducked under a wave. When I came up I felt like a different person. Somehow cleansed, almost like a baptism—a baptism by fire.

I swam back to shore. Showered off in the public shower. Hit a thrift store on PCH and bought what was once an expensive suit that still looked nearly new and fit perfectly. I bought shoes and a shirt and tie to go with it. All for less than fifty bucks. I spent another twenty on a haircut at Supercuts. The first time in decades my hair was shorter than John Lennon's on the cover of *Abbey Road*. And slicked back. I looked like an aging movie star if I say so myself.

I gassed up the GTO, headed north on PCH.

Heading toward Joe's.

Not sure what I'd do when I got there.

But at least I felt like I had a purpose—revenge.

I turned onto Sunset, zigging and zagging up the winding curves. Past the Self-Realization center, the fancy houses in Brentwood and Bel Air, UCLA.

I wanted to know who the dead guy was. I thought he looked familiar. But he had been bloated and it was hard to tell.

About a mile from Joe's house I turned on the GPS, hoping he'd still be looking for a signal from it. I started cruising around his neighborhood. Just circling. Waiting. Hoping to lure him like bait on a fish hook.

Headlights loomed in my rearview. I sped up a little. Figured that was the wrong move. Slowed down to a full stop. The car passed me. Not Joe. I was relieved and disappointed at the same time.

I heard it before I saw it. The roar of the Barracuda's four barrel carb and dual exhaust. It echoed through the canyon, bouncing off the walls. The headlights came on me quickly. So quickly I barely had time to think. I peeled out. The chase was on.

I led him down the canyon onto Sunset. We zigzagged back and forth. I prayed no cops would be waiting around the next curve.

We cut in and out of the sparse late night traffic.

I had a plan. I didn't think it would work. But if it did, the irony would be perfect.

Dead Man's Curve was coming up in less than a mile. I jammed on the pedal. The GTO whipped up Sunset. The Barracuda stuck to my tail. Did he know Dead Man's Curve was less than a hundred yards ahead?

Now only a hundred feet to go.

I turned into Dead Man's Curve, cut my wheel and my speed. Joe went zooming past me on the left. Couldn't make the turn. The Barracuda spun out—flipped over three times, before crashing into someone's perfectly coiffed lawn and bursting into flames.

The early morning news the next day said that famous record producer Joe Moria had died an excruciating death in the flames of his burning classic car. I didn't feel a thing, good or bad. I was just glad it was over.

Well, not completely over. I hoped with Joe dead Stash would want to get out of the state and just forget about me. One can always hope....

I drove to Susie Evans' house. I knew she still saw Joe. Of course, she was too old for him to have a steady relationship with now. But I guess he still had some feeling for her 'cause in between the twenty-somethings Susie was always there.

"You," was all she said when she opened the front door.

I pushed past her, waited in the living room.

There were no tears in her eyes. She just stood opposite me. Didn't invite me to sit or have a drink. Why would she?

"You look different," she smiled a tiny smile. "Good."

"What'd you expect, an unshaved has-been bum?"

"I heard it on the news," she said. "He was chasing you, wasn't he?"

I didn't answer. But I wondered what would make her go there.

"You know the whole story, don't you?" I said.

It took a minute, but she nodded.

"Why me?"

"You're a loser, Ray."

"The perfect fall guy, huh."

She nodded.

"And maybe, just maybe he was still a little jealous of you and me. We had something he could never have 'cause he could never give anything of himself—not really."

Now there was a tear in her eye. For Joe? For her and my lost relationship? Didn't matter. It was all in the past—but maybe the past informed the present.

"Who was it?"

She knew I meant the dead guy.

"Sandy Baker. He and Joe had a falling out. Not everything with Joe was on the up and up. Sandy threatened to turn him in."

"So he kills two birds with one stone, so to speak." Not that I particularly liked that expression here.

I split from Susie's. The GTO purred and *Surfer Girl* and those other oldies played in my head. For a split second I wondered if Susie and I could ever be an item again. But the thought vanished in a puff of exhaust smoke. What would be the point?

Do you realize how hard it is to find a payphone these days? Almost impossible. But I managed to find one in a drugstore parking lot. And the Huntington Beach police received an anonymous phone call telling them where they could find Sandy Baker's body. I didn't know him well, but I knew he must have a family, someone who cared about him and wanted to give him a proper burial.

Then I drove the GTO up the coast, past Zuma Beach. And I played *California Girls* and *Surfer Girl* on the iPod and thought about Susie and knew she was the past and that you can't go home again. I drove all the way up to Mavericks, a wild break near Half Moon Bay, where the Big Wave riders go. I parked, ran my hand over the GTO's smooth orange paint. I loved that car. I loved it even as I put a large cinder block on the gas pedal, put the car in gear and watched it fly off the cliff into the ocean. Fuck Joe and his GTO. I'd buy my own GTO one of these days with my own money.

I hitched back down PCH to my apartment. The light on the answering machine was blinking.

"Hey, Ray. Tommy Di Falco. Long time no hear. Listen, if your chops are still good, maybe I can get you a gig. Call me."

My luck was changing. Or was it going to be another Joe Moria experience? What the hell? I dialed Tommy's number.

Identity Crisis

Lynn Allyson

Every morning I wake up with the same regret: If I hadn't gotten into that stupid car, I wouldn't be stuck in this wheelchair.

"Don't say stuck," my physical therapist, Ronnie, says. "It's a self-fulfilling prophecy."

"Stuck. Stuck. Stuck. Stuck."

"Dude, you can still drive a car. Twenty years ago they didn't have that kind of technology—not at an affordable price, anyway."

He thinks I'm lucky. I'm only a paraplegic. I can still move my body above the waist. But what does he know? He can still take a piss standing up.

"We're moving out of the grieving phase into the doing phase," Ronnie says.

But I'm still in the I-hate-your-guts-leave-me-alone phase.

I pretend I'm a surfer just to fuck with Ronnie's head. "How am I going to get back on my board?"

"We'll find a way, dude. We'll find a way."

He's an idiot.

Now a detective named Milo is trailing my ass. He usually shows up right before dinner, upsetting my mother.

"Hi, Kevin. I'd like to ask you a few questions, if you don't mind."

"Do I have a choice?"

"Son, I'm just trying to understand what happened."

"Isn't it obvious? My brother's dead and I'm a cripple for life."

Detective Milo doesn't flinch. He's probably seen worse—triple homicides, crack babies, bodies dumped in the ocean.

This was just a car accident with a bad ending. There wasn't even a celebrity involved.

"I'd like to know the details. Maybe prevent this from happening to someone else."

My mother looks at me with pleading eyes. She's already been through so much. I don't want to cause her any more pain.

"Whatever." I wheel myself into the living room and stare out at the blazing pink sunset, compliments of LA's dense smog particulates.

"What do you remember from that day?"

"Not much," I say.

I don't tell him we wanted to meet our friends at the beach, especially LuAnn Willis. She was the shortest girl in class until last summer when she grew a foot and got boobs. Not the normal kind, but the big, crazy kind that look fake. You knew they were real because even in LA a fifteen-year-old can't get a boob job. My brother said if we were lucky she might go skinny dipping in the ocean.

I pull a folded-up newspaper clipping out of my pocket. The front page picture shows a mangled Mustang at the bottom of a ravine. "Danny loved that car."

Detective Milo looks away. He's probably thinking about his kids, wondering what kind of car they'll want when they turn sixteen. He sure as hell won't let them have a convertible.

My mother hovers between the kitchen and living room. "The doctor says Kevin's memory will improve over time. Lost events will come back in bits and pieces as the brain heals itself."

A bell on the stove rings. My father pulls up in the driveway.

Detective Milo hesitates, then takes the hint. "I'll come back later. I don't want to interrupt your dinner."

The spinal clinic is packed. Spring must be a dangerous time. Ronnie rolls me onto my back and bicycles my legs. "Dude, they just had a monkey move a robotic arm with his thoughts. You picked a good time to get crunched."

"That's me, perfect timing."

"If it were the middle ages you'd be dead."

"When exactly were the middle ages, Ronnie?"

"That's not the point, dude."

Apparently, almost anyone can become a physical therapist assistant at a spinal cord recovery center, even in a tight economy.

"How did you get into this field anyway?" I ask him.

"It was my destiny."

"Right."

Everyone in the clinic believes in some destiny bullshit. They think that Jesus has a purpose for them. I don't know why Jesus couldn't just tell you what he wants before he ruins your life.

My two new best friends are quadriplegics, a life form one step up from a vegetable. Jeremy dove into a pool that was too shallow and Fernando crashed his motorcycle into a tree after drinking a keg of beer. Way to go. Now we live in our dreams. Jeremy runs on the sand, Fernando sprints past the fifty yard line and I frantically search through the trees looking for my brother.

"See." Ronnie points across the room to Fernando who's trying to move his toe. "That kid has a good attitude."

"Yeah, he's a real role model."

Detective Milo is at my house again. He thinks there was something unusual about the accident, something strange about how our bodies landed in the brush. I wouldn't know. I missed the physics class on projectiles flying out of a moving car. Maybe if I had paid more attention I would have landed on my side instead of my back.

"Have you remembered any other details?" Detective Milo asks. "Can you remember where you were sitting?" He hands me a stick of gum. Spearmint.

"In the passenger seat, where the passenger sits."

"And your brother was driving."

"Of course he was driving, it was his car." This investigation is starting to get on my nerves. "Does it really matter now?"

"I just want to get the facts straight."

We both know if I was driving I could be charged with vehicular manslaughter.

My mother wipes her hands on a towel. "Kevin, just answer the questions. I'm sure Detective Milo would like to go home."

I look at my watch. "I'm sorry. I don't have to worry about being late for track practice anymore."

Detective Milo stares at me straight on. No pity. I like that. He thinks he's tough, but tough is facing that chair every morning, 24/7, with no time off for good behavior.

I shouldn't have even considered going to the beach on Saturday, but my brother talked me into it. "Don't be a pussy," he said.

"If I don't finish my report, I'm going to flunk history."

"Come on. You've got all Sunday." He dangled the car keys in the air. "What's the point of having a convertible if you don't drive it?"

"Bro, I don't want to end up in summer school."

"How much have you written?"

"I haven't started."

"Are you serious?"

"Sorry, I'm not organized like you."

"Shit. I'll write the paper."

"Really?"

"Consider it my graduation present."

We stopped at a 7-Eleven and I picked up a six-pack of Coors and a cheap bottle of vodka with my fake driver's license. Then I locked our wallets in the glove compartment so we wouldn't lose them in the sand.

"You know there's going to be a full moon tonight," I said. "Which means you have a seventy percent chance of getting laid."

"Why is that?"

"Chicks dig full moons. It does something to their hormones."

"Did Danny ever let you drive?" Detective Milo won't let it rest.

"Are you kidding? He worked three years at KFC to buy that old piece of junk. He wouldn't let anyone touch it. He said it was a classic."

"Something seems funny."

"Yeah, the whole thing is hilarious."

"Danny's blood alcohol was off the charts, not to mention all the prescription drugs in his system. I can't imagine him getting the key in the ignition, far less driving up the canyon. Didn't he seem out of it to you?

"I don't really remember, going into a coma and all."

"You two were identical?"

"A matching pair."

"Was there any way to tell you apart?"

"Danny had a mole on his arm."

I pointed to the jagged red scar on my forearm, where the ER team had stitched my shredded flesh back together. "I heard my brother looked worse."

"Car accidents are never pretty."

We had cut across the valley on Topanga with the music cranked up and the top down. Past the 101, past Mulholland Drive. We snaked through the canyon until the Pacific stretched out in front of us with its endless blue waves. Then we headed south on PCH, past the Santa Monica pier, past Marina del Rey, through the wetlands to Dockweiler Beach. Suddenly, it hit me. In four months my brother was going off to Stanford while I tried to improve my grades at a local junior college. He was leaving me behind.

All of his studying had paid off. He was the new hero in my family, the first person to do anything worth talking about. My mom couldn't shut up about it. Even though we still looked alike, we were no longer equal.

"Are you going to remember me after you move out?" I asked.

"Not if I can help it."

"Asshole."

"Dickhead."

My brother drummed his hand on the door. "I expect to see your ugly face every six weeks."

"If I can't find anything else to do."

We grinned at each other, mirror copies.

"Who's the designated driver?" I asked.

"You are, bro. Tonight I'm going to party."

Our entire senior class was at the beach. Everyone had their own combination of liquor and organic fruit juice from Whole Foods. LuAnn was leaning against me in the sand, her breasts bulging out of her yellow tank top. Someone poured more vodka into my drink.

My brother was fighting with Gena, an old girlfriend he couldn't get rid of. At some point, after the sun went down, their argument escalated. She slapped him across the face. It was a loud dramatic hit, the kind you see in the movies. My brother stood up next to the fire pit and raised a bottle of wine in the air.

"This calls for a toast," he said. "After all these years, I'm finally getting rid of this bitch."

Our friends cheered and Gena stomped away.

Thirty minutes later she was back, sucking up to my brother with a fresh batch of margaritas. Classic doormat.

"It's a shame you boys weren't wearing your seat belts."

"No shit."

"Is there anything else you remember?"

"Not really."

Around midnight the party started to break up. I was wasted. My brother wanted to take one last swim in the ocean. He stripped off his clothes and slipped the leather cord of his necklace over my head.

"Don't lose that," he said, touching the baby abalone shell encased in silver. "It's good luck."

I don't remember getting into the car that night or driving up the canyon. I don't remember the blinding lights of a car coming toward us, or the sound of metal collapsing followed by the long empty silence.

It was my mother's voice that brought me back. She was holding my hand, tears rolling down her face. "Kevin, can you hear me? There was an accident, Sweetheart, a horrible accident."

I didn't even need to ask. I knew my brother was dead.

The guilt of killing my twin was almost more than I could bear. How could I have been so irresponsible?

"But you're still here, Kevin. Thank God, you're still here." My mother's voice was raw.

I couldn't tell her the truth. I couldn't tell her the twin she had hung all of her hopes on had died. It would have been too cruel. Kevin had to live. He had to live for both of us. I squeezed my mother's hand.

"I'm here," I said.

But Gena knew. She kept stalking me, watching my every move.

"You're not Kevin," she said, after I got home from the hospital.

"Gena, stop it. I can't take any more drama. Everything is hard enough."

"Is the tattoo on my ass a heart or butterfly?"

"I don't know. It took me two weeks to remember my birthday."

"You picked it out." She sat down on Kevin's bed and rubbed her hand across the pillow. "Have we ever had sex?'

"No."

"Have you ever felt me up?"

"Don't you have someplace to go?"

"I warned him not to leave me, but he wouldn't listen." She pulled a loose thread on the comforter and watched it unravel. "Big mistake."

"What are you talking about?"

"I gave him the triple crown. Prozac, Valium and Ambien. Didn't the police tell you? Your brother's system was a toxic waste dump. He probably stopped breathing while you were driving."

I felt woozy. "What are you saying?"

"I had to do it. He was going to leave me."

"That's what people do after high school. They go away to college."

"I wasn't going to let anyone else have him."

"Why are you telling me this?"

"So you won't feel so bad about the accident."

"What if I call the police?"

"You'll never tell. You'd have to go back to being Danny, the loser twin."

"Get out of my room," I screamed. "Stay away from me."

She walked to the door and pulled down her shorts. The tattoo was a butterfly.

August twenty-fourth my mom made me a birthday cake. It used to be the best day of my life. Now it was the worst. Detective Milo showed up on our doorstep.

"Come in," my mother said. "We're having a little celebration."

The cake stuck in my throat like glue. I didn't deserve a party. I didn't deserve to be alive.

Gena was on the couch, stuffing her face as usual. She wouldn't leave me alone. She wanted me to marry her, threatened me with the truth.

"If you say one word, you'll end up in jail for murder," I whispered.

She smiled and mouthed the word "Danny."

I wanted to strangle her with my bare hands.

Detective Milo finished his cake. "I know this is a hard day for you, Kevin, but I wanted to take you for a little walk."

Gena jumped up and slipped on her sandals.

The detective raised his hand. "I want to talk with Kevin alone, if you don't mind."

Gena gave him a dirty look.

I wheeled myself to the end of the cul-de-sac. Then Detective Milo took over pushing me down a road that curved into a little park. We stopped in front of a man-made lake and Milo sat down on a bench.

I hoped he knew. I couldn't take it anymore. My nerves were shot. I hated myself. I hated my life.

"I've finished the investigation," Milo said. "Did you know that Danny was taking all kinds of drugs?"

"No."

"Did he seem unhappy to you?"

"No."

He turned the chair around so we were eye-to-eye. "If you live long enough, you'll understand bad things happen to everyone. But I want you to promise me something, Kevin. If you ever feel that life's too hard or that you can't handle it anymore, reach out for help." He handed me his card. "You can call me any time, day or night."

For the first time since the accident I started to cry. I was tired of pretending. I wanted to tell Milo the truth. I wanted to tell him who I was.

"You have an incredible future ahead of you, Kevin. Don't let anything stop you."

A mother with her young son strolled to the edge of the lake and threw a handful of breadcrumbs to the ducks. They both looked so happy. I wished I could start my life over again.

"Can I ask you something?" I said.

"Shoot."

"Who was at the funeral?"

"The whole damn town. They had to have the service on the football field to accommodate everyone."

"My brother would have liked that."

I'm not sure if stealing someone's identity is a crime, but I'll be going to Stanford in September. Of course, I'll be going part time until I feel stronger. And Gena is out of my life forever. She had an unfortunate overdose of acid and ended up in a mental hospital, locked up tight. I found my emergency supply of recreational drugs when I was cleaning out my dresser. I'll miss Ronnie. Before I left town, I stopped by the clinic to show off my new modified car. He was totally impressed that I was driving. I can still see his hopeful face as he waved goodbye.

"Make us proud, dude," he yelled.

"You got it, Ronnie," I said, waving back.

But in my heart I knew it was too late for that.

The Last of the Recycled Cycads

Bonnie J. Cardone

If I had known my husband and his girlfriend would be on *The Tonight Show*, I wouldn't have turned on the TV.

I'd stayed late at the studio to catch up on paperwork. Once home, I walked into the living room and paused to admire the view. Below me, the bright lights of LA sparkled in a crisp, remarkably clear evening.

I pressed the power button on the remote and the TV blinked on. Jay Leno finished his monologue and the audience erupted in applause. When the commercials began I went into the kitchen and opened the ancient fridge. A pathetic selection of edibles greeted me. Managing Quiero's Photography leaves little time for grocery shopping. I chose a not-so-fresh apple and a Diet Coke, leaving an even less appetizing looking apple and a small carton of orange juice for breakfast.

I returned to the living room as Leno was saying, "Please welcome celebrity photographer Ted Quiero and super model Willow."

WHAT!

Ted strolled out from behind the curtains with a beautiful young woman clinging to his arm. He'd left the studio early, telling me he had an interview. He hadn't mentioned *The Tonight Show* and he hadn't said Willow was going with him.

I was well acquainted with Willow. She was a rising star in the modeling world and Ted had photographed her several times, most recently for a magazine article they were probably promoting now. I hadn't liked the way she looked at him then and I didn't like the way she was looking at him now.

I had to admit, however, they made a striking couple. Ted is tall and slender, with curly, close-cropped dark hair—I'd made the appointment to have it cut yesterday. Willow is tall and reed thin, with long blond hair and flawless skin.

Ted wore his usual outfit, jeans, boots and an untucked long-sleeved dress shirt. Willow was almost wearing a skimpy, wispy nude-colored gown.

I collapsed on the sofa and took a bite of the apple. The crunch echoed throughout the large, sparsely furnished room.

The next few minutes were pure misery. I didn't hear what was said; I was watching Willow cast adoring glances at my husband while batting her obviously false eyelashes. Twice she brought one of his hands to her lips and kissed it. That made me nauseous. The next time she did that I ran into the bathroom and threw up. When I returned, she and Ted were walking off the set holding hands.

I turned off the TV and I walked over to the floor-to-ceiling windows. In a corner of the patio on the other side of them, I saw those weird plants Weasel had left. There were at least a dozen of them, all different sizes. If a pineapple plant and palm tree mated, this is what their progeny might look like.

Weasel and Ted are best friends and have known each other for decades. Weasel is a nickname, coined by Ted when they were in junior high, and it fits his buddy perfectly. Weasel is always involved in some questionable enterprise, usually one doomed to failure. For reasons I am loathe to admit, Ted and I love hearing about them.

Thinking of Ted caused big, sloppy tears to drip down my cheeks. I'd ignored his infidelities in the past—all geniuses are flawed, aren't they? This time, however, he'd gone too far. Now the entire world knew he cheated on me.

As I turned from the windows my eyes fell on our wedding photo, perched on the fireplace mantle. That little redheaded girl—me!—had learned a lot in eight years of marriage, most of it the hard way.

Maybe it was time for a change. I'd put my own photography career on hold to further Ted's and this was my reward: he'd humiliated me by appearing on national TV with his girlfriend. Well, there was a man who loved me unconditionally and would welcome me with open arms. My dad still lived in Cliffview, the little town in which I'd grown up, about eighty miles north of LA on the California coast. I'd go home. It wouldn't be the first time I'd shown up on his doorstep unannounced. There, with the only person who thought I was perfect, my broken heart and severely bruised ego would mend.

It took several minutes to find a suitcase because I couldn't remember in which of the nearly empty closets I'd put it. I didn't have much to pack. Ted and I own very little. We rent a big house in the Hollywood Hills above the Sunset Strip to impress Ted's celebrity clients, though we'd never dream of inviting them inside. The rent is low because the house is a fixer-upper. In my opinion, "tear-down" would be a more accurate.

Our few furnishings were purchased at thrift stores. While Ted has had some really lucrative assignments recently it will be a while before his business makes a profit. Until it does, we are in debt up to our eyeballs.

I tossed toiletries, lingerie, jeans and T-shirts into the suitcase. I knew *The Tonight Show* was taped hours before it aired and Ted would be home soon. I didn't want to be around when he got here.

It had been a while since I'd last done laundry. I dumped the dirty clothes hamper on the floor and picked my things out of the pile, stuffing them into a plastic garbage bag. I would wash them at Dad's.

My van was parked in the garage, accessed via the kitchen. I stepped into it and pushed a button on the wall. The garage door slid up as Ted was getting out of his red sports car, which he'd parked behind my van.

"Cinnamon, sweetie. Where are you going?" he asked.

"I saw you on *The Tonight Show*."

"I'm sorry, baby. I wanted to tell you about it but I was afraid you'd misunderstand. It was all an act, honey. Willow means nothing to me, absolutely nothing. We were just trying to get a buzz going, attract some attention. It's good for her and it's good for us."

Ted stood in front of me, his face wearing his most sincere look. For once, I was not buying it.

"You made a fool of me on national TV. How is that good for *me*?"

Ted sighed. "It was a publicity stunt, sweetie, everyone will understand that." He put his hands on my shoulders. "Come into the house. We can work this out. We'll have a little wine, talk it over."

When Ted turns on the charm he's nearly irresistible. Trouble is, I recognized the loving look on his face. It had been trained on Willow not long ago.

Ted stroked my cheek, just like he'd stroked Willow's on *The Tonight Show*. That made me mad, hopping mad.

I pushed his hand away. "I'm out of here, Ted. Move your car."

"Please don't go, I need you. I'm nothing without my little redheaded girl."

Now Ted's face wore the "poor, poor pitiful me" expression. Why had I ever thought that was genuine?

Since Ted's car was blocking mine, I walked over to it, opened the door and threw my suitcase, purse and the garbage bag inside. Ted had neglected to take the keys out of the ignition as usual. I got in and started his car.

Ted's face appeared in the window next to me.

"I'm begging you, darling. Don't go. Please. You know how much I need you."

A cynical thought occurred to me. Was it Cinnamon the wife he'd miss or Cinnamon the trusty photo studio manager and all-purpose lackey?

I put the car in reverse and began to back down the long, steep driveway with Ted following on foot. I glanced in the rearview mirror as I drove off. Ted stood on the sidewalk, his cell phone to his ear. He was probably calling Willow. I had already been replaced.

I didn't get far. When I stopped for a red light at the bottom of the hill on Sunset Boulevard, the car sputtered and died. Ted had gotten home on fumes. No doubt that was my fault; I'd forgotten to remind him to buy gas. Now I saw the folly of not renewing my Automobile Association membership and spending the money on something for Ted instead. I couldn't just call and have gas delivered to me; I'd have to go get it myself.

If I'd been driving my ten-year-old van, I wouldn't have attracted much, if any, attention. But I was in a sleek, expensive, apple red sports car. Within minutes, two boys on bicycles appeared. They asked if I needed help and when I admitted I did, they pushed the car to the curb in the only space available on Sunset, which of course was a no parking zone.

Casting admiring glances—at the car—one of the boys asked, "Are you a movie star?"

"No," I said, "but my husband and I photograph them. Just last week we shot Johnny Depp for the cover of *Rolling Stone.*"

While that was a lie, it was an effective one. One of the boys offered to get gas at a nearby station. However, when he realized his friend would be left with the beautiful car and a woman who knew movie stars, he rescinded his offer. The boys began to bicker. My suggestion they both go was ignored. In the end, I borrowed a bike from one of them and peddled off to the nearest station, leaving them sitting in the car. I was hoping that would be enough to prevent the car from being ticketed or hauled away.

Getting gas was easy enough, although the attendant insisted on keeping my credit card until I returned the can. That upset me. How did I know he wouldn't use the card to buy a bunch of stuff while I was gone? We argued about this for several minutes. I lost. As I biked back on Sunset, I realized that taking Ted's car had been a big mistake. Besides being a gas-guzzler, it was leased and required a sizable monthly payment, unlike my van, which was free and clear of financial obligations. True, the van objected to going more than fifty, but who needs speed?

The boys and the car were still there when I got back, along with a big fat parking ticket. The novelty of car sitting gone stale, the boys hopped on their bikes and vanished. I poured the gas into the tank and drove back to the station to return the can. After retrieving my credit card I headed up the hill for home, where I intended to exchange Ted's car for mine and set off for Cliffview.

I wanted to make the switch without Ted's knowledge and it looked as if that was possible. My van was where I had left it. I was surprised, however, that the garage door was still open. Couldn't Ted do anything without my prompting?

I moved my suitcase, purse and the garbage bag into my van and got in. As I started it all hell broke loose.

The door from the kitchen to the garage burst open and Ted and Weasel ran out, screaming "Help, help!" at the top of their lungs. Right behind them were two men, one of whom was gigantic.

Ted yanked open my door and jumped into the van, shoving me into the passenger seat. He stomped on the gas pedal and the van lurched backward.

Weasel was halfway into the back seat of the van on my side. Unfortunately, the sudden, jerky movement shook him off and the incredibly ugly giant pounced on him.

We'd gone only a few feet when the second man wrenched the driver's door open and dragged Ted out. Ted uttered an ear-piercing scream as he hit the ground.

The van went over a bump and gathered speed as it rolled down the driveway. I kicked the suitcase and the garbage bag out of the way, got into the driver's seat and set the emergency brake.

That slowed the van a little. I finally found the brake pedal and that slowed it even more, but by then I was near the bottom of driveway. The van continued on across the street and ran into a streetlight. Though it was a low speed impact, I was momentarily stunned.

When I regained my wits, I fumbled around in my purse, found my cell phone and called 911. Then I put the van in gear and drove back up the hill, avoiding a body just outside the garage that turned out to be Ted.

He looked awful and was barely conscious. As I knelt next to him, I heard sirens. The two strangers jogged by, headed for the street. The garage door slid down and all the house lights went out. I heard a truck start up and speed off.

Minutes later, two LAPD patrol cars arrived, followed by a fire truck and an ambulance. Emergency medical personnel pushed me out of the way and began to work on Ted. Not long afterward he and I were in an ambulance, headed to the hospital.

Ted was in the ER for a couple of hours. While I waited for news of his condition, Weasel called. I have to admit, I had forgotten all about him.

"Ted okay?" he asked.

"I don't know but I should know soon."

"Keep me posted," he said.

"Okay."

"And look, Cinnamon, if anyone asks, I wasn't at the house tonight."

He hung up before I could demand details.

Not long afterward, I finally was able to see Ted, though the visit was brief. His face was a mass of bruises. The doctor told me he had a concussion and a broken nose, along with various internal injuries, none of them life threatening.

As I left the ICU, two LAPD officers stopped me. They introduced themselves as Mike Mitchell and Carl Grady. I knew they had not been allowed to speak to Ted. I let them drive me home.

Back at the house on the hill, all was quiet. I inspected my van. There was a dent in the rear where it had struck the streetlight. That didn't look as if it would impact driving it as much as it would my budget.

We went into the house. The cops admired the view from the big windows. And I noticed, but didn't process the fact that there were no longer any funny-looking plants on the patio.

"Tell us what happened here, Mrs. Quiero," Officer Mitchell said.

"I am married to Ted Quiero but I use my maiden name, Cinnamon Greene," I said, before relating an edited version of the night's events that didn't mention Weasel.

When I had finished, Mitchell said, "A neighbor heard you and your husband arguing earlier this evening. What was that about?"

"I'd rather not say," I huffed. I didn't want to tell them about that humiliating *Tonight Show* episode. They'd find out soon enough on their own.

"You had a fight with your husband. You drove off in his car, then came back and ran over him with your van." Officer Grady suggested.

"That's not exactly what happened. I took his car to get gas. When I returned, I parked his car and got into my van. That's when he ran out of the house with two strange men right behind him. He got into the van with me, but one of them dragged him out and began beating him up. He fell under the van and it ran over him as I was trying to get into the driver's seat to stop it. It was an accident. You can ask Ted when he's feeling better."

But Grady wouldn't give up. He made me go over the story again. Then it was Mitchell's turn. Both officers tried to get me to talk about the argument but I refused, saying it involved a highly personal matter I didn't wish to discuss.

Officer Grady asked, "Mind if I look around?"

That set off alarm bells. I watch enough police shows to know that letting cops wander around in your house is a bad idea. Besides, while hardly luxurious, the living room is the best part of our home. I was grateful an overgrown hedge blocked the view of the pool and its empty, crumbling interior.

It was very late and I suddenly realized I was very tired. "You want to look around, get a search warrant," I said. "And before I answer any more questions, I'll want my lawyer present."

After the men left, I took a hot shower and went to bed. Although I was exhausted, I couldn't sleep. The night's events kept flashing through my mind. After a couple of hours I got up and wandered into the kitchen, looking for breakfast. The good fairy had not restocked the fridge. I grabbed the orange juice and the ancient apple, then brewed a pot of coffee and took a cup of it out on the patio. I intended to sit on the edge of the pool and dangle my feet in the nonexistent water as the sun rose over the city.

That was not to be. The pool cover was on, which was very puzzling. I lifted up one edge of the ratty, sun-bleached tarp and peered in. The deep end was no longer empty; it was full of those funny looking pineapple/palm tree plants.

I'm not much of a gardener. Did those plants need to be kept in the dark like some of the bulbs my mom used to grow? I sat on the edge of the pool and drank my coffee. The plants had been moved from the patio to the pool after Ted and I had our confrontation on the driveway. Four people were in the house after that. I doubted the two strangers would move the plants so it must have been Ted or Weasel. I settled on Weasel. There had to be a reason he didn't want the cops to know where he was last night.

By then I was hungry. A woman cannot live on ancient apples, orange juice, coffee and Diet Coke alone. I needed something more substantial.

The nearest supermarket offers one stop shopping twenty-four hours a day. It has a bakery, coffee shop, deli, dry cleaner, movie rentals, a pharmacy and a florist, along with a branch bank, an ATM, a photo department and a copying machine. At the bakery I bought two still-warm crullers—one butterscotch, one chocolate—and gobbled them down as I perused the aisles. I was about to push my cart past the florist's area when I saw a young man restocking the plants and cut flowers. Inspiration struck.

"I'm intrigued by some plants I saw," I told him. "They look like a cross between a pineapple and a palm tree. I'd love to buy one but I don't know what they are."

"Probably a member of the cycad family," he said. "Maybe a king sago palm. Those are quite popular. They don't need a lot of water and will even grow in sand. Small ones are reasonably priced but mature ones can be worth several thousand dollars. There's been a rash of sago palm burglaries recently, both from nurseries and private homes. If you buy one, don't plant it in your front yard."

Bingo.

I bought two coffees and drove to Weasel's small, nearby apartment. I banged on his door till he got out of bed and opened it. He had a black eye and bruises on his face. I handed him the grande latte I'd bought him.

"I want the truth about what happened last night, Weasel. I found the palms."

"Oh," he said.

"Speak."

Misery flooded Weasel's face. It wasn't something I'd seen very often; Weasel is almost always cheerful and upbeat no matter what mess he's created.

"I got a really good deal on the plants," he began. "I knew I'd be able to sell them for a lot more than I paid for them. Only it was a scam."

"Imagine that," I said. "Didn't you wonder why they were so cheap?"

Weasel took the lid off his coffee. "The guys I bought the plants from were into recycling. They'd sell the plants to someone, then steal them back. They knew nobody would report the thefts because the plants were hot to begin with."

"Was Ted in on this?"

"No, no, no. I didn't have room for the palms here and asked if I could store them on your patio. I told him they were for a gardening job I'd gotten."

"So what happened last night?"

"Ted phoned me as you drove off. His parents and brother had seen *The Tonight Show* and had given him an earful, and now you'd left him. He was very upset. I went over to keep him company.

"I'd only been there a few minutes when the two guys who sold me the cycads barged in. They must have followed me from here. They wanted the plants back. One of them is this big bruiser. Really, really big. Ugly, too. Ted and I ran. You saw what happened next. When they heard the sirens, the bad guys took off.

"I knew we'd be in big shit trouble if the cops found those plants. I locked all the doors and turned out the lights. I put the plants in the deep end of the pool and covered it. When I finished, I snuck out of house and walked down to Sunset, where I caught a taxi."

"The cops drove me home from the hospital and came into the house," I said. "They wanted to look around. Good thing I didn't let them."

"We need to clean out the van in case they come back," Weasel said. "There might be a cycad leaf or two in it."

"Palm fronds in my van?"

Weasel sipped his coffee and avoided looking at me. "I used the van to pick up the palms a couple of days ago. Ted didn't think you'd mind."

"You used my vehicle to move stolen goods?" I said. "That's great, just great. The cops already think I ran over Ted. If they find those plants in the pool, I'm dead meat. We've got to get rid of them right away."

"I know," Weasel admitted. "But they won't all fit in your van. It took me two trips to move them to your house. Besides, what would we do with them?"

There was silence as we contemplated those questions and the possible answers. Or rather, as I did. Weasel toasted a bagel and ate it, then showered, shaved and got dressed while humming Beatles tunes.

When he finished he said, "Let's call the hospital." So we did. The nurse told me Ted was resting comfortably and would probably be discharged in a couple of days.

"Do you still have the trailer that came with the horse?" I asked.

Several years ago Weasel had bought a racehorse that turned out to be lame and had to be put down, dashing his hopes for a Derby win. The horse came with a trailer.

"I haven't found a buyer for that yet," Weasel admitted.

"We can use it to move the plants," I said.

"All right!" Weasel said enthusiastically. Then he added, "Move them where?"

"We'll give them back to the guys who sold them to you," I said. "That should get them off your back."

"Jeeze, Cinnamon. Those are really bad dudes. I don't want to go anywhere near them."

"If we do it right they won't even see us," I said. "Do you know where they live?'

"I have the address somewhere."

It was locating the trailer that took some time. Weasel had left it with friends in the San Fernando Valley who had passed it on to a rancher in Ojai. The rancher was using it to move stuff around on his property. While it looked decrepit, it was still in working order. It did not, however, have a license plate.

"There's no VIN, either," the rancher told us. "Someone got rid of that a long time ago."

"Stolen?" I asked.

"That would be my guess."

The rancher helped us hook my van to the trailer and I drove back to LA cautiously. I didn't want to attract the attention of any law enforcement types.

It was late when we got to Hollywood. We loaded the cycads into the trailer. That took care because the leaves of the plants have very sharp edges. I was glad I was wearing a long sleeved sweatshirt, jeans and an old pair of leather gloves I found in the garage.

It was early the next morning when we finished. Traffic was nearly nonexistent as I drove to South Central LA. With Weasel acting as navigator, we easily found the thief's house and, even better, an empty lot across the street. We parked there and started taking the plants out of the trailer as quietly as possible. Even so, our activities were noticed; the big bruiser came out of his house before we were finished.

Standing on his front porch he roared, "What the hell do you think you're doing?"

"Oh oh. We've got to get out of here," Weasel said. We did the only one thing we could do in those circumstances. We unhooked the trailer, jumped into the van and drove off as if the devil was behind us.

That someone would leave something instead of stealing something in that neighborhood was such a novelty that the big bruiser stopped to consider it. While he stood gaping at the horse trailer and the three cycads we'd managed to unload, we made good our escape.

Leaving the mysterious trailer in South Central had consequences we never imagined. Worried it might contain an explosive device, a neighbor called the police. Since they were unable to determine exactly what was inside, the LAPD Bomb Squad evacuated the neighborhood and used a specially designed robot to examine and, ultimately, blow up the trailer. The spectacle was broadcast live, nationwide, and kept millions of Angelenos glued to their TV sets right through what would have been rush hour if they'd gone into work.

There was no gridlock in the city that morning—except in the area surrounding Weasel's cycad-filled horse trailer. There, chaos reigned. News helicopters jockeyed for space in the sky while LAPD vehicles with flashing lights, ambulances, fire trucks, news vans and food trucks clogged the streets on the ground. Fisticuffs nearly erupted several times among the hordes of reporters competing for definitive sound bites.

The next day, the front page of the *LA Times* carried a spectacular full color photo of the explosion, showing shredded cycad leaves and mangled trailer parts raining down from the heavens.

An anonymous tip received during the bomb scare resulted in a search of the big bruiser's yard and then his house, where police found more king sago palms. Smaller photos in the newspaper showed the thieves in handcuffs. The *LA Times* headline read: "Stolen Palms Blown Sky High, Thieves Caught."

That was the last I heard of the recycled cycads.

Not My Day

Stephen Buehler

Damn it, stuck again. I hate the 405. Since my CD player burned out, I blast the radio. I can't find a station with any good stuck-in-traffic music. I try what's always my last choice, the news: *"We repeat, the police say soon they'll have an update concerning the Freeway Killer. Two more people with multiple head wounds were found along the freeways, bringing the total to nine over the last two months."*

I shut off the radio. That doesn't take my mind off of my problem. It's two-thirty in the stinking hot afternoon and I have a job interview in fifteen minutes. Fifteen minutes! For a mindless medical billing job. There's no way I'll get to the Wilshire exit by then. I need this job. Shit, I've already rescheduled once. I can't believe the dying grandmother excuse still works.

It's bumper-to-bumper, we move maybe five feet every two minutes. Of course the cars to the right are going faster than my snail paced lane. I see an opening and take it. I gradually edge my car in even though the guy behind me isn't liking it. I'm guessing that because his arm is sticking out the window and his middle finger is pointing up to the cloudless sky.

Now he's pounding the steering wheel and even from here I can see his face turn red. *Hey, I'm in the same boat, buddy*, I want to shout. He's driving a Benz and I'm in a Civic. I'm the one that should be pounding the steering wheel. And what's his problem anyway? He's only one car back. One car! What's that mean, he'll get to where he's going ten seconds slower since I'm in front of him?

"Out of the way, douche bag," he yells.

There goes his horn. Like I could move any faster. He won't stop honking that fucking horn. I can't take any more of this. I stick my head out the window and yell, "Suck it." That doesn't seem to help.

With the horn still blaring, I notice mist or smoke blocking my view. It takes me ten seconds before I realize it's me, well not me, but my piece-of-shit car. This can't be happening. My engine knocks several times. Stops knocking, now it's dead. There goes that stupid job interview, my day is officially screwed.

I try the ignition. The radio comes on but the engine does nothing. I'm stuck. I keep trying the starter and pressing the accelerator but it's deader than squashed roadkill. Not a sound except for that asshole behind me.

I'm two lanes from the side of the freeway. The afternoon traffic is so tight I feel like we're all cholesterol moving through clogged arteries and my broken down car just gave the freeway a heart attack.

It's all connected. If I got the job then I'd be able to afford road-side assistance. But since I don't, it's all up to me. I have to move the car over to the side by myself. I take a deep breath and reluctantly get out. Every driver gives me that, "you've got to be kidding me," look. I don't glance at the car behind me, even if the horn has stopped. I open the hood and motherfu...burn my hand. I try to wrap it in my last good shirt, the "interview" shirt. Smoke billows out. I'm hoping to find a loose wire or bolt.

A figure pops out from my right. It's the asshole who is behind me. He's big. Linebacker big. "What's the problem?" he asks in a concerned tone. He doesn't look pissed. This is scary.

"I haven't a clue." I wait for him to choke me out.

"Let's push it off to the side." I'm taken aback but agree. "I know something about these things," he adds. It takes us fifteen minutes with me mainly holding up my arm to stop the cars and him doing all the pushing. I offer to help but he refuses which is okay with me, I'd probably get hurt anyway. I wait by my car as he goes back for his. This time it's much easier as drivers realize that the sooner they let him through, the faster traffic can crawl again.

I refer to the side of the freeway as the "loser lane" because every day I see broken down losers kicking their tires and waiting for a tow truck. Now I'm one of them. I switch the radio back on but it's still the news. At least I'll hear I'm not the only one having a lousy day.

I go to the front of my car. I see water coming out on the right side of the engine. I look closer. The linebacker returns. I point, "Take a look at..."

"Hey, asswipe," is all I hear. I see an arm. With a wrench. About six inches from my head, coming down, fast...

"It's three o'clock in the afternoon, time for local news. We are the first news station to bring you this bulletin. Predawn the police captured the Freeway Killer. We repeat, the Freeway Killer was apprehended early this morning. Details are slowly trickling in. We'll keep reporting them as we get them. Okay, let's get back to today's topic; the many forms of road rage. You know, sometimes it's suppressed until..."

To Kate— Enjoy the ride! Miko

By Anonymous

Miko Johnston

In Los Angeles, your vehicle defines who you are. Girls who lick around the edges drive Civics, tree huggers buy hybrids and rebels go for big old gas-guzzlers unless they're rich, then they drive Porsches. Instead of 'baby on board' decals, the joke now is that Volvos come standard with an NPR bumper sticker. And show me a guy with a grey beard and his last three hairs knotted in a ponytail sitting behind the wheel of a Corvette and I'll show you a boomer going through male menopause. My partner Pacer and I have been studying this phenomenon since high school. We're now halfway through our masterpiece: a twenty-first Century triptych created out of auto and human detritus—unbeknownst to Moira.

Moira Goldberg, who used to be Moira Olsen, perches with the least ass-to-cushion ratio she can manage on the worn chair in my auto body shop. She blabbers and all I can think is she isn't going anywhere in those five inch heels. She probably regrets wearing that tight cream suit. Every time she shifts, the skirt rides up her still shapely legs in those tiger print stilettos and her face turns redder than the rubies studding her trio of gold bracelets. I halfheartedly listen as she explains her problem with the expectation I'll solve it for her.

"The insurance adjuster keeps telling me she can't total the car unless the damage exceeds eighty percent of the resale value..."

It took months of Googling and reconnaissance to track her, but thanks to texting while driving, she needed an auto mechanic and picked me. I wonder if that thought will cross her mind before I'm done.

"...but my husband negotiated such a good price that it's worth more now than what we paid for it."

She doesn't remember me. Granted, I've aged thirty years, but still. You spend three years with someone in high school and figure they'd look at you with a glimmer of recognition and even if they didn't make the connection they would acknowledge some familiarity, ask with a curious smile, "*Where do I know you from?*"

But she looks at me like I'm a billboard, there but not significant. She only pays attention to me because she thinks I'm going to help her. But I'm not. She's going to help me.

"No matter what you do to it, the resale value will be half. Half!"

The car she's referring to is a new Cadillac Escalade, black, with cocoa interiors and a bashed-in front end. It's not how I remember her. Cadillac girls went to private school. They brought cloth napkins with their lunches and held contests to see who could go the longest without wearing the same earrings twice. But this is who Moira has become.

She used to be a cheerleader at Northridge High, cute and sassy, with long chestnut hair and a slender, almost boyish figure. The hair's now shorter, streaked with blonde. She's gotten thick in the waist and has a small but noticeable pot belly. I almost feel sorry for her, but Pacer doesn't. Moira was the one who provoked the bully who hurt us while the teacher looked on.

Now she's demanding, "Can you guarantee the car will be totaled?"

I'm rethinking my artistic vision for her. The centerpiece of the triptych must be an inspired blend of Moira then and now, the Cheerleader and the Cadillac Wife.

What a shame you missed the first part, ERIC, which went on display almost a year ago in the Northridge High parking lot. It's been taken down, but the police have plenty of pictures in their open case files and undoubtedly some parts tucked away in evidence bags. The words they used to describe it prove that cops don't understand art, but we were proud of it.

Moira is still talking to me when she interrupts herself to take a call from her husband. She raises her voice because to her I'm just a mechanic with grease-stained hands. I don't count.

"No," she growls to him. "That's not good enough. Tell them to find me another Cadillac. If they can't, I'll take the Mercedes...I don't care if your mother doesn't like German cars, I'm not driving around town in a Camry." Her free hand shakes as she argues; her ruby bracelets clink together like tinny wind chimes, loud and equally annoying. "Then rent the Camry for yourself and I'll drive your Escalade!"

Little flecks of spittle fly from her mouth. I can tell she's used to yelling at her minions. Moira lives in a diva mansion within a gated and guarded community in West Hills, an overpriced abscess that borders on rugged chaparral to the west. A few miles east are the industrial parks of Chatsworth, where auto shops coexist with small factories that make everything from foam rubber to porn flicks. Here the gates are chain link topped with barb wire; the guards have four legs and the coyotes, two.

Moira's still snarling at her husband. I'm getting some wonderful ideas for the project, but I haven't finalized which car to use. It has to be something cheeky, leaning towards vintage. A Beetle won't do, it's too earthy for Moira now. I've kept a red Mini Cooper on stand-by. Pacer thinks it's a bit obvious, but if I can envision something spectacular for MOIRA, it'll work.

This piece will be more challenging than ERIC. Eric was the bully who picked on me. He would call me names in the hallways and flip me the bird. When I caught him trashing my car in the school parking lot, it got me angry enough to finally confront him. He punched me so hard my mouth bled. Then Moira goaded him on until he threw me on the hood, denting it.

Dave, our home room teacher, saw the whole thing from his bike. He did nothing but smirk, the iconoclastic bastard. I'd planned to begin the triptych with him, but Pacer and I want to use a Saab and they're hard to find, so DAVE had to be put on ice.

With ERIC, car and concept were easy. He drove an F-250 pick-up tricked out with oversized wheels, chrome trim and obscene mud flaps, exactly what we'd have chosen for him. So I cut off his head and his hands and mounted them on the hood. It took some doing to get his middle fingers to point upward, but the expression on his face was nearly perfect. Who knew terror could resemble anger?

Moira has ended her call and is staring into space. I'm enjoying her discomfort. Her expression has changed to something more familiar; not anger or hurt, but one I can remember seeing in the halls of Northridge High. Dark eyes fixed on her victim, her head down and forward, lips parted and curled back, exposing her teeth. A look of ferocity, like a wild animal.

Thank you, Moira, you've inspired me. Pacer will agree to the Mini Cooper now.

Her cell rings again.

"I'm about to leave the shop...no, I don't know how long I'll need the rental. It depends on whether my car is totaled."

As she talks, Moira turns her back to me. Her chestnut hair spills forward, revealing a tiny mole at the base of her neck. She ends the call and shoves her phone into its special pocket inside her purse before asking, "Is there some place nearby where I can get a light lunch?"

"They make a decent sandwich at the Ralph's on Devonshire."

She looks at me like I'm bird droppings on her windshield.

I try again. "I hear the Radisson Hotel on Topanga has a nice restaurant. I can drive you, if you like."

"In your truck?" She winces.

"I have a car. The hotel can order a cab for you. Just give me a minute to lock up."

Moira follows me into the shop and waits until I roll down the bay doors.

"Are we taking that red Mini?" Her voice is sweet. She likes the car we've picked for her.

"There's no motor in it." I fight back a smile as I direct her to the rear door, which leads to the little garage where I keep my art equipment. She waits until I open it and stops dead when she spots my car, a bulbous, earth-toned anachronism on wheels.

"What the hell is that?"

She doesn't recognize it. "A '74 AMC Pacer, very rare."

"Fortunately. And you drive that on purpose?" The searing tone in her voice transports Pacer and me back to that day in the parking lot. I had to clean up the mess, fix the damage. For thirty years I've gotten paid to clean other drivers' messes and fix their damage, until we got broadsided by a speeding pick-up last year. Pacer was seriously hurt, but the driver never stopped, just flipped me off. As I pounded out the damage, an idea was born and a vow made.

This time, I wouldn't be the one who bled.

Moira's taunting no longer stings, so I encourage her to continue by asking, "Don't you think my car is unique?"

"No. It's ugly and stupid looking." There's condescension in her tone now, but her fitful pacing tells me she's uncomfortable.

"I've been searching for another car," I tell her. "Something a bit more iconoclastic. Ideally a Saab, but they're really hard to find."

For the first time since she stepped into my shop, Moira looks directly at me. I can see a flicker in her eyes, as though she realizes something in my face. I almost hope she does. But she marches to the passenger door and stands there, arms folded in impatience, waiting for me. And then she shakes her head and says, "You're wrong. Nothing's more iconoclastic than a Citroen."

I gasp at her brilliance. It had never occurred to me, but she's right. We're deeply indebted to Moira now, so we'll have to make this special. And we know how.

"I'll be ready in a minute. Help yourself to a bottle of water, if you'd like," I tell her, pointing to the chest freezer in the corner.

I wrap my hand around the handle of the screwdriver in my tool belt and savor every moment as she reaches for the freezer latch. The timing has to be precise to make this flawless.

Standing behind her as she opens the door, I wait for the inevitable reaction. It takes a few seconds to register what she's seeing, but Dave's severed head is quite distinctive even through plastic wrap. As soon as the scream passes her lips, I plunge the screwdriver down into the mole on her neck, careful not to break the skin in the front of her throat. She jerks like a marionette with tangled strings before crumpling to the ground. I roll her over to see her face. Wonderful. I've caught her in mid-scream, eyes wide open, ears pinned back, mouth agape, teeth bared. Just like a wild animal.

I shut the freezer to preserve Dave's parts for another day and focus my attention on MOIRA. It's half past noon. By one a.m. we'll have her cleaned, gutted and mounted on the hood of the Mini like a tiger rug, body splayed, wearing nothing but those stilettos, her head reared up with wires attached to her scalp and pulled back toward the windshield.

Another hour to put on the finishing touches, then haul the artwork into my truck, drive it to Northridge High's parking lot for display and finally home to study the reviews. We can hardly wait to see the flood of coverage on TV. I'm breathless just thinking about it.

Once everything calms down though, Pacer and I will have to get back to the real world. Fixing cars. Ordering parts. And finding a Citroen.

DAVE's waiting.

Road to Revenge

Nena Jover Kelty

Something's up! Lately, Charlie's not been his usual man about town, dating a different bimbo every night. He's down to one girl—Terry, a blonde with straight shoulder-length hair. Lately, things have not gone well between them. "Commitment" crops up in almost every argument. Terry may not want to believe this, but I'm Charlie's number one love interest. He even paid ninety-four dollars for the Vanity Plates I'm wearing. It says "IMNO.1" What more proof do you need? He treats me well. My gas tank is always full, he washes and polishes me regularly and keeps me snug at night in his garage. I'm his treasure.

Well, talk of the devil, here he comes. He gets in and pushes my button—He really knows how to do that! I purr as we glide out of the driveway. We're off for our usual Saturday ritual—the car wash. When we arrive, I hear that wonderful word, "Detail." Oh, heaven, Charlie's getting me the works. If I were human, I'd be covered in goose bumps. He's even emptying my trunk and the glove compartment!

After we get home, I take a nap to get rested up for the big date that must be coming up. Imagine my shock when at nine o'clock he closes the garage door and goes to bed! I am flabbergasted. It bothers me so much I have trouble falling asleep. Finally, nature takes over and I just nod off, but one nightmare follows another. They seem so real. I am convinced someone is creeping around the garage opening and closing my doors. At midnight, I wake with a start, thinking that was the lid of my trunk! I doze off again telling myself it is just a dream.

Morning finally arrives and I'm exhausted and feeling groggy. My rear end is sagging, feels weighted down.

Charlie's up early for a change. It's a beautiful day. Maybe we're going for a drive in the country. We go slowly through Beverly Hills, until suddenly we turn into a business establishment. "Used Cars" the sign says. I almost throw a rod. What are we doing here? Is Charlie selling me? Is he tired of me? Does he want a younger flashier car?

He turns my engine off and a man immediately appears at the window. "Good morning, sir. Murphy's the name."

"Hi! I'm Charlie."

"Great car! Interested in selling it, sir? I just happen to have a client looking for this exact Mercedes model. He even said red would be perfect."

I fear Charlie's answer.

"Yes, I have a great job offer in New York—lead in a play, then maybe a movie. I heard you're better off not owning a car there."

My tires almost go flat. Charlie's going to New York! What about me? I try to hear more as Charlie points out all my extras, wonderful condition and low mileage, giving my left front tire a casual kick for good measure.

Ouch! Charlie! Don't add insult to injury! I feel further violated when two other salesmen come over and begin inspecting me as if I were a piece of meat. I am so angry I could pop all my lug nuts.

"Would you mind opening the trunk, sir?" Murphy asks Charlie.

"Sure!"

And that is when all hell breaks loose. There is a blood curdling scream "No!" from Charlie and a "My God!" And several swear words from the other men. I am beside myself. What on earth...? I can't see into the trunk and am frantic with concern. I can hear Charlie sobbing, "Terry! Oh, Terry! "

"You know her?" Murphy asks.

Charlie's voice is unrecognizable as he says, "Yes. It's Terry. She's my, was my fiancée. What's she doing in the trunk of my car? What happened to her?"

All the men start talking at once and I don't know who is saying what, but I do hear, "Somebody call the police!

Nobody leave! Look at that knife! And the blood! Don't touch anything! Poor girl! She looks so young. Who would do that to her?"

They must have all looked at Charlie because he gets very upset and starts shouting, "Don't look at me! I didn't do it! If I did do it, do you think I'd be stupid enough to put her in the trunk of my car then come here?"

The others mumble something and I can hear feet shuffling. I am stunned, sorry for Charlie as I know he would never hurt anyone. And poor Terry! I must admit I never liked her but would never wish her murdered because that's what it sounds like happened. I think of the creepy nightmares of last night. If only I could talk! The wailing siren of a police car interrupts my thoughts. It pulls up next to me and a cop gets out.

With notebook in hand and pencil poised, he walks over to the open trunk of the car and says, "Everybody stand right where you are. I'll need all your names and identifications." After getting the basic information, he says, "Does anyone here recognize the victim?"

"I do," says Charlie. "Her name is Terry Barnhill. She was my girlfriend."

"Whose car is this?"

"Mine."

"Your car looks exceptionally clean, sir. When did you have it washed?"

"Yesterday morning. I was getting it ready to sell. I'm leaving next week for a new job in New York."

"I'm sorry, sir, but you will not be leaving for New York any time soon. And your car will be impounded as detectives go over it for evidence. Stay there while I call the coroner."

The next thing I see is the coroner's arrival. A black van marked "LAPD" pulls up behind him. The coroner walks over to my trunk, glances in, turns to the policeman and says, "I'm going back to the lab. Send me all the information you have as soon as possible. My assistant will put her in a body bag," and with that he left.

The police officer turns to Charlie, "Do you know her next of kin?" Charlie says he doesn't know any of Terry's family, but she did have a roommate who was a good friend.

"I'll need her name, address and telephone number.

"Of course. How long will I be without a car?"

"That's the least of your troubles, sir. I'd like you to come back with me to the station now. There are some questions I need to ask you."

And with that Charlie is gone. I watch the tail lights of the police car disappear around the corner. When will I see him again? Even though I was furious about being sold off, I feel lost without him.

What's this? A tow truck just lumbered onto the lot. The driver exchanges a few words with the policeman and then walks over to me. His hands are on my front bumper! What is he doing? Suddenly, he lifts up my front end and before there is time to recover I'm moving forward, absolutely terrified. Where is he taking me?

Now, I'm in a sort of hangar. It reeks of chemicals. The odor overwhelms my car freshener. The driver of the tow truck unhooks me. It feels good to have my front end on the ground again. He leaves and two men approach wearing protective gear and tiny ID tags. I can barely read: Mike and Fred. This is a nightmare! What are they going to do with me?

"Are we going to strip her, Mike?" Fred asks.

Strip me? What kind of a place is this? I can't believe what I'm hearing.

"No. This isn't a narcotics case—it's murder. For now it's just fingerprints and blood."

The men go quietly about their work, turning on some bright lights and getting out the paraphernalia they needed. Oh! Oh! They're tickling me! I can't stand it!

"This car is so clean, we probably won't find many prints," says Mike, as he uses his tickling brush on my rear fender. Oh, I wish he'd stop that!

"The trunk's going to be the most interesting," says Fred. "Apparently, the victim had a knife stuck in her stomach. It hadn't gone in far, so there wasn't much blood. There was something odd about the scene. The coroner told me to look for anything unusual."

"Is he trying to tell us how to do our job?"

"Okay," says Mike, "let's tackle the trunk."

I am so glad to hear them talk. At least I'm not entirely in the dark.

"Get the camera so we can get a picture of that scrawl on the side there. It looks like some kind of writing."

"No it isn't a word—more like a circle that isn't quite finished. And it looks like it was done with a woman's hand as the fingerprint at the end is small."

A circle that isn't quite finished! That could be a C! C for Charlie! Oh, no! That would be just like Terry. Blaming Charlie for everything!

"Well, that about wraps it up," says Mike. "Let's go type up our report."

The door slams and I am suddenly alone. Now what? How long will they leave me here? I feel utterly abandoned.

It isn't long before my driver's door suddenly opens and a strange man gets in. He pushes my button, but it is not like Charlie's touch. We drive out of the building and onto the streets of Los Angeles, finally pulling in to what looks like a junk yard. I am surrounded by the dregs of carmanity. Every car is covered in dust. Some have sustained huge damage and others sport bullet holes. I am devastated. Surely I deserve better treatment than this! I know I'm vain, but puhleeze!

I lose all sense of time. A few cars leave and some new ones arrive, until one day who should be standing next to me but Charlie.

"God, Rosie, you look a mess!" He only calls me Rosie when he is upset about something.

The lot manager walks over with a release form for Charlie to sign. "I guess you're free to go now, sir. I bet you're glad it's over."

"That's for sure! I was the main suspect until the detective found out the truth."

"Well, who did it?"

"She did it herself. It was suicide, but she did her best to make it look like I had done it."

"No kidding! Well, good luck, sir. You deserve some."

They shake hands and with a "We're off to the car wash!" we leave. He has no trouble starting me up. I am anxious to get out of there. He runs my windshield wipers long enough to make a little hole to see through. I can barely keep my mind on driving as I go over the conversation Charlie had just had with that man. How vindictive Terry was!

We've only gone a few yards when Charlie's cell phone rings. It is hands free, so I can hear both sides of the conversation.

"Hello, Charlie!"

"Oh, hi, Bev! I was going to call you!"

It's Beverly, Terry's roommate!

"I wanted to thank you for what you told the detectives. You saved my life!"

"You don't have to thank me. I only told the truth."

"Well, as Terry's friend, I thought you might want to protect her reputation and bend the truth a little. If you hadn't told the detective about her prescription for Xanax..."

"Don't even think about it. She just wanted to frame you. She could be vindictive, but I never thought she'd go that far. What do you suppose drove her to do it?"

"It was when I broke our engagement. I really thought she was the one for me. I caught her cheating on me and called her every rotten name in the book. She took it hard and begged me to take her back, but I'd had it. Did you know the other guy?"

"I met him once and I didn't like what she was doing to you. I'm so sorry for everything you had to go through, Charlie. I wish you the best. It was nice knowing you. Take care!"

"Bye, Bev. Thanks for calling. " And with that, he hangs up.

We go through the car wash and I feel a thousand times better. It's a little drafty in my trunk without carpeting, but I'm sure Charlie will replace it soon.

I'm snug back once again in Charlie's garage, but don't feel secure about my future. What are Charlie's plans? I still don't know how Terry managed to point the finger at Charlie, how she got in my trunk and why the detective concluded that Charlie had nothing to do with her murder. It's so frustrating not knowing!

The next morning, my heart sinks; we are back at the used car dealer. Murphy immediately runs out of his office.

"I saw you drive in," he says, as he tries to catch his breath. "I knew you were innocent from the beginning. The look on your face when we opened the trunk said it all. You can't fake that much shock and horror."

"Thanks for believing in me," says Charlie. "For a while, I was really in trouble."

"How exactly did that girl try to frame you?"

And then I finally hear the rest of the story. Charlie says, "I got all the info from Terry's roommate, Bev. Terry was so angry with me that she told Bev, 'Charlie is going to pay for calling me all those horrible names. I'm going to have it out with him. Just because I've had a couple of dates with George is no reason to break up with me.'"

Can you believe such thinking?

"She then flounced out of the room saying she had to make a phone call. Shortly after, the doorbell rang and it was George Taylor, the man she had been dating behind my back. She invited him in and they went into her room where they started a very loud argument that Beverly couldn't help but overhear. 'I don't love you! I never said I did. I love Charlie. I'm going to see him tonight. We'll make up or I'll die in the attempt. I'm that determined.'

"'You're nothing but a two-timer! Charlie's welcome to you!'"

Amen, George. If Terry were a car, she'd have been turned in as a lemon long ago.

"The next thing Beverly heard was George slamming the front door as he left. Terry came out of her room carrying her purse. Beverly noticed the bottle of Xanax she dropped in before closing it. 'Charlie said for me to come to his house. We're going to discuss our situation over a glass of wine.'

"'That's a good idea. Good luck!'"

I don't think it's a good idea at all, but who's asking for my opinion?

Murphy interrupts Charlie at this point, "But we found her in the trunk of your car with a knife in her stomach. How did she manage that?"

"Even though she was under the influence of a lot of Xanax, she was able to concoct a devilish plan. I hadn't invited her over, but she drove to my house, lifted up the garage door—I never did get around to installing an automatic opener. She opened the driver's door of my car and pushed the button that opens the trunk. She climbed in, pulled down the door, then stuck the knife she was carrying into her stomach. As if that wasn't enough, in a final gesture of revenge, she put her finger in the blood then started to write my name on the inside of my car."

That explains the sleepless night I had. Who says dreams don't mean anything?

"Why did the coroner conclude she had killed herself?"

"Well, the knife had barely pierced her skin—the wound wasn't severe enough to kill her, so he examined the contents of her stomach. She had taken a lethal dose of Xanax. And alcohol was also involved."

"What are your plans now, Charlie? Did you lose that job in New York? Are you going to keep the car?"

I hold my breath, fearful of his answer.

"The company really wants me for the part, so they delayed the play's opening. I'm selling the car. Do you think your client is still interested?"

"I'd have to call him. You might have to lower the price. He may not be interested knowing it was used for a suicide."

"I understand."

Murphy steps away to make his call. After a short conversation, he comes back all smiles. "Mr. Brad Tennyson is still interested. He knows all about the suicide and is not bothered. He works close by and is coming over right now. Perhaps you can make a deal today."

"That would be great!"

What's great about it? Maybe it's great for you, Charlie, but what about me? How can you get rid of me so casually? I'm so depressed and for the first time, feel my age. Lost in thought, I hardly notice the dark blue Buick turn into the lot, but come to full attention when out steps the driver—a six-foot tall gorgeous hunk with wavy black hair. As he is introduced to Charlie, he sticks out his hand and flashes a smile that would melt the heart of a stone. He catches sight of me and walks over, eyeing me from one end to the other, caressing my fenders as he peeks through my windows. And his eyes! They dwell with such longing on my soft leather seats! I'm totally smitten and instantly fall madly in love.

The deal goes through. Brad says he'll bring the check the next day and Charlie says he'll have the pink slip. I have mixed feelings; furious with Charlie, but thrilled at the thought of a future with Brad. Charlie is beside himself with joy. He gets on the freeway and drives fast, pounding my steering wheel and shouting, "I did it! I did it! Damn! I'm good!"

Why are you so happy to be rid of me? I think, thoroughly crushed.

Then Charlie reaches into his pocket and pulls out what looks like Terry's engagement ring. He holds it up to the light and shouts, "See, Terry! Did you enjoy the wine? Good combination huh? Wine and Xanax! That's what you get for cheating on me! Was it worth it?"

When I hear that, I think my radiator will explode. There is no word in the English language to adequately express my outrage at the discovery of Charlie's true character. I feel thoroughly betrayed.

I'm not sure if it is something I did or if it is sheer coincidence, but at that very moment, my left front tire suddenly blows out and we crash into the cement divider of the 110 Freeway.

Unfortunately, Charlie had not fastened his seat belt and so he hurtles through the windshield, landing on my hood, his beautiful face shredded and all of him quite dead. I wonder as I contemplate his remains if Charlie would think his recent actions were worth the results and if Oscars were ever awarded posthumously.

I sustained critical injuries, but am spared the dreaded designation of "totaled." Damages repaired, Brad, who still loves me despite all my scars, brings me home where we will grow old together.

Traffic Control

Eric Stone

"You gotta admit, Paul, traffic's never been better on the Westside."

"So you're saying the guy's some sort of traffic control genius?"

"It's working, isn't it?"

"Sure, but shooting someone at every damned entrance and exit on the 405 and the 10 is a little extreme, don't you think?"

"All I'm sayin'..."

"Yeah, right, just another disgruntled commuter with a .38."

"Don't forget the .22 and the .44 and the .45 and the nine. The guy is really mixing it up."

"We so sure it's a guy? I've seen my share of really pissed off females, too."

"Traffic in this town's a bitch, enough to piss anybody off. Hell, I've had some moments."

"Who hasn't, but still..."

"Must've made your commute a lot easier lately. I don't know why the hell you ever bought that place in Venice anyhow. It's an expensive dump in a traffic hellhole."

"You kidding me? It's worse. No one dares get on the freeway on the Westside. Surface streets are fucking parking lots. You think people used to go postal on the freeway during rush hour, you oughta see Washington these days, Jefferson, Adams, it's looney-tunes out there. I've got that crack whore informant. I'm thinking of renting her place from her. It's a shithole but it's right by the station. I wouldn't have to drive across town."

"Yeah, the wife'd really love that."

"Long as I keep turning over the paycheck she doesn't... Hell, my crack whore's cheaper."

"Least it isn't easy for her to get to Rodeo Drive to go shopping anymore."

"It's not like Santa Monica doesn't have too many overpriced shops these days. We'd better nail this fuckwit soon or everybody in town's gonna start shooting."

"On your side of town, at least."

"Don't get smug with me, asshole. Just 'cause you got that bank repo palace in Echo Park."

"You're just jealous. I've got seven freeways within twelve minutes of my place. What've you got in Venice? Two? No, wait, I forgot the Nixon, two and a quarter."

"Yeah, yeah, rub it in. Wanna get some lunch? I don't know what we're doing here on the Overland off-ramp now anyhow. Our killer only shoots people at rush hour."

"Yep, and only in fancy cars. Maybe if we'd require anyone with a car costing over sixty grand to spring for bullet proofing—problem solved. What's there to eat around here anyhow? Tofu burgers, some vegan shit?"

"There's actually a pretty good Indonesian place not far."

"Ethnic? On the Westside? This I gotta see."

Sam watches the cops start up their prowl car and drive away. Must be lunch time. Probably off to fill up on donuts. There's bugs in the bushes between the rec center and the road. And it's commuters who are the problem, not just any poor soul getting off the freeway in the middle of the day. Lunch sounds right.

The Indonesian place is good. And they don't hold back on the spice either. The Vespa takes about two minutes to get there.

But what the hell are the cops doing here? They don't eat Indonesian food. Well, maybe Indonesian cops do. These guys aren't that. Couple of white boys, a fat one and, well, the other one is pretty good looking. Maybe in another world, some other life.

Sam flashes him a smile when she sits down.

Brooks flashes her one back. She's hot, he thinks, really hot with that short bob of jet black hair coming to a fringe above bright blue eyes. Gotta be contacts, but it's working for him. Great teeth with that small gap between the two front ones and a bit of an overbite. Even before he bothers running his eyes down below her long, slender neck his brain is fumbling for any right words it can think of to say to her. Maybe she's got a thing for cops. He hopes so.

Sam sees him seeing her. It's hard to miss. And it's just as hard to miss that he likes what he sees. And so does she. But no, oh no, this is a really bad mistake waiting to happen.

Brooks wishes he knew what the woman is thinking and he gets up to talk to her. "Hi, uh, I don't mean to be too forward, but can I buy you a drink or something?"

She laughs at that and it's a tinkle that tickles Brooks out to his spine. "Well, officer, this isn't a bar, you know."

Sam swallows hard, hopes he didn't notice how she said that. She can't possibly have just said that and leaned forward a little and maybe even lowered her eyelids a little and flashed him another big smile. Not a cop. Not now, not when every cop in the city is looking for her and not in a good way. Is there ever a good way for the cops to be looking for you?

He blushes, just slightly but enough. She didn't even know that cops *could* blush and something inside her melts a bit seeing it. And oh shit, oh shit, oh shit. Her head knows she's got to blow him off, but her body isn't cooperating. It's telling her she might need to make some new mistakes to help get over the last batch.

Brooks sees the woman blushing now, too, and that gives him confidence. He gestures to the other chair at her table and sits down before she can say yes or no. "Maybe that's the kind of drink I'll mean next time. If there is a next time. Right now I meant one of those drinks with the beads in it that you have to suck up through a big straw, or maybe an iced coffee."

Oh hell, Sam's trying to figure what's she going to do now? That was cute and she likes his voice, too. It's deep but with nice soft edges and expressive. "So, what are you going to do if I say you can't buy me a drink and you shouldn't be sitting here? Arrest me?"

"It's a thought."

Damn him, why's he got to have that smile, that nose, those deep deep heavy-lidded brown eyes and lips fuller than they ought to be?

A movement just past his left ear catches Sam's attention. It's his partner, waving. Sam's relieved. Maybe that's her out.

"I think your partner wants you."

Brooks looks around and shakes him off. When he turns back, he catches a small hint of fear in her look, in the set of her mouth, in the crinkles around her eyes.

"Hey, look, I'm sorry. I don't usually do things like this, really I don't. My name is Brooks and, well there's just something going on here. I think you feel it, too. I'll give you my number and I hope you call me. I'm not such a scary guy. Just that, I don't know, something struck me."

He pulls a pen out of his pocket and writes his number on the edge of the paper placemat. He tears it off and hands it to her, aching a little when the tips of his fingers touch hers briefly.

"Can I ask your name?"

Sam wants to tell him, wants to take his hand, wants to give in to the snap, pop and crackle in the air between them. She closes her eyes and squeezes them for a moment to take control.

"Maybe I'll call you, Brooks." She didn't mean to say his name. Something about it sounds like a promise that she knows better than to keep. It would be suicide.

It sounds like a promise to Brooks, too. He leaves her with a big grin.

It's not long before everybody's back in place. Brooks and Paul are in their unmarked car on the Overland off-ramp. Could anything be more obvious—a Crown Vic? Does anyone other than cops ever drive one of those?

They'd got their food to go. Whatever the hell that fish paste stuff they use in Indonesian cooking is stinking up the car. But it tastes good.

"Cute girl, Brooks. You get her number?"

"Gave her mine."

"She'll never call."

"She will."

"How can you be so sure?"

"Just a feeling."

"Got any feelings about our Commuter Killer?"

"You read the *Times* this morning?"

"Just the sports. Fucking Dodgers. Why'd they let Kemp bat in that homerun derby bullshit? I hate that shit."

"Some joker wrote an op-ed. Said we ought to get the shooter to agree to just wound someone every so often, help solve the traffic problem."

"Yeah, right. Asshole."

"Maybe the asshole's got a point."

Paul throws him a look. They've only been partners a little over a year. Maybe he doesn't know Brooks all that well.

Sam's hunkered into the crook of some branches of an acacia next to the Manning / National entrance to the 10 East. Her scooter's parked out of sight but near enough for a quick getaway. The prowl car sitting on that on-ramp is around the bend, closer to the actual freeway.

Her fingers keep going to the outside of her right front jeans pocket, feeling the crinkle of the torn piece of placemat with the cop's phone number. She'd folded it and put it there. Finally, she takes it out to have a look.

He's got strong, clear writing, block letters, no frills. If he was issuing a ticket there'd be no appealing it on grounds that it was illegible. She'd got out of one once that way. Maybe she would call him. Wouldn't that be a gas—the most wanted woman in LA dating a cop?

She's not sure how much longer she can keep this up anyhow. She's already made her point and it's getting a lot harder to find targets. People aren't stupid, at least most of them. Even the regular people, the working people in their Chevys and Fords and Toyotas, the ones who are safe from her, are keeping away from the freeways. Luckily some of the pricks driving Mercedes, Hummers, Beemers, Escalades are still arrogant and unimaginative enough to think she won't get them.

There was that guy yesterday in the Bentley. He had his window down, arm on the sill, like he was taunting her. It was a good shot, one of her longest. It was kind of a shame that he veered off the north-405 ramp at Wilshire and crashed into all those tombstones in the veterans' cemetery. Sorry about the graves and the car. That had been a beautiful vehicle.

Things could have been different. She'd been happy teaching high school English in Hawthorne. Maybe she was even making a difference in some of those kids' lives. And then they had to fire her ass for being late all the time. It wasn't her fault. It was the 405, the fucking traffic.

And the very day they sacked her she got home and found her supposed boyfriend in bed with her best friend. Payback, he said. He was sure she was having an affair with the auto shop teacher because she was getting home late most days. Traffic again, fucking traffic.

And the day after that, parked near the unemployment office, her piece of shit but long-owned and well-loved Corolla got sideswiped, hit and run, totaled by a fucktard in a gold-flecked Mercedes SUV.

It was the perfect shit storm. Her dad had been a gun nut, a lifelong NRA guy who'd only ever bought from the black market—no serial numbers, no registered ballistics . She went to the storage locker where she'd put all his stuff after he died and emptied the gun cabinet.

"I hoped you'd call, but I thought it might be a few days."

Sam and Brooks are sitting across from each other in a dive bar in Koreatown.

It had been a long wait for someone dumb enough to drive past Sam on the on-ramp. By the time they did, a little after six in a fire-engine red Ferrari, she was too slow to get off a shot. She cursed herself for that. She would have liked to have wasted that guy, just like he was wasting that magnificent car. Poor thing probably never got out of second gear in the city.

But she was tired and distracted. What was it about that cop? She'd never had a thing about uniforms and he wasn't in uniform anyway, just cuffs and a gun and the other guy with him who definitely looked like a cop and that ridiculous Crown Vic. She couldn't get him off her mind.

So she climbed down from the tree and called him. She wasn't so far gone that she didn't remember to block her number from caller ID, but she had told him her name when he answered.

"Hi, it's Sam. I'm..."

"I recognize your voice."

He had just got off duty. So had she, is the way she thought of it. An hour later and here they are.

"I don't like to play games."

"And you like single malt scotch. I'm learning at least a few things about you."

"I'm not all that girly." Sam nods her head toward his Cosmo and makes a face. "Bet you don't order those when you're drinking with your cop buddies."

Brooks laughs, obviously at himself which gives her something else to like about him.

"You got me there. But you're girly in the ways that matter."

"What ways are those?"

"Thought you didn't like to play games."

Two whiskies, one-and-a-half Cosmos, a fifteen-minute drive and they're at his place in the hills overlooking downtown.

"Great view."

Sam doesn't have much time to appreciate it before they're kissing, then falling onto the sofa together, then untangling themselves from the tangle made by the unzipping, unbuttoning and unhooking of clothes, then in the bedroom, then on the bed.

She wakes up before he does, a skewer of sunlight stabbing through a crack in the blinds and into her eye. He's snoring softly. There's something comforting about it. Last night was great, too great. Holy shit, what has she done?

Coffee's going to be awkward, she's sure of it. So she slips out of bed hoping not to wake him, but she does.

He makes good coffee. He's got fairly fresh corn tortillas, good cheddar and a bottle of her favorite hot sauce and they come together well on a hot pan on his stove. It's a whole lot easier, more comfortable than she thought it would be, than it ought to be. He even gets the paper and reads it, not just the sports section either.

What the hell has she done?

"You need to get to work. Just drop me off at a bus stop, I can get home okay."

"No one takes the bus in LA I'll give you a ride. Where do you live?"

She'd gone home after calling him, left her scooter there then walked to the bar. It was only a few blocks. She didn't want him to know where she lived. This was crazy, but she wasn't stupid.

"No, really, you've got a killer to catch." Did she wince when she said that? She hoped not. "I'm used to it. I always take the bus. It's good people watching."

"Yeah, I do need to get to another fun-filled day sitting with my partner twiddling our thumbs on a freeway on- or off-ramp."

Maybe she can get some information out of him, if she's careful.

"Who's going to be catching all the other bad guys around town if all of you are sitting in your cars on the freeways? There's a lot of ramps."

One hundred fifty-four, to be exact, in the area that she thinks of as the Westside, her territory.

"Why? You hoping to rob a bank?"

She laughs. "Could be my best chance."

Brooks figures there can't be any harm in talking to Sam. They've just spent the night, a fantastic night, together and they've already got plans to see each other again tomorrow night. Plus, a girl like her, who's she even going to know who might know a psycho killer and say something? That's pretty far-fetched.

"We don't cover them all, only about a third of them at any one time. We keep switching it around. Luckily tomorrow I'm back to my normal running down and catching perps, at least for a few days. With any luck we'll have caught the guy by the time I'm supposed to hang out on a freeway again."

With any luck they won't. That would be a sorry end to the start of what could be a good relationship. Sam hears the thought clear enough in her head that for a moment she's almost afraid she's said it out loud. She shivers.

"You cold? Someone walk over your grave?"

She laughs, punches him on the shoulder.

"Better be getting me to the bus stop, copper."

That afternoon, with tomorrow night's date to look forward to Sam is more careful than usual. For the first time she uses her dad's beloved H&K PSG-1 sniper rifle and wears a disguise: a long blonde wig and baggy clothes stuffed with padding. She sneaks up to the roof of the Courtyard Los Angeles Marina del Rey hotel. It overlooks on- and off-ramps on the 90, what was going to be called the Richard M. Nixon Freeway until it got cut short because of lack of funds and then Watergate happened. She hasn't targeted anyone there yet, but it's still within her range.

It's going to be a tough shot, at a distance, through a car window, probably a moving car. But her father used to take her shooting a lot and this was his favorite rifle. She's had practice. She's also got a really good scope.

But she can't hang out here forever. Even up on the roof she's more exposed than she'd like to be. Normally this time of day she'd be spoiled for choice, lots of high-end cars going to and from the boat slips and multi-million dollar condos of the Marina. There's not much traffic now though. And the few cars that do brave the freeway do it fast, swerving back and forth thinking they can dodge bullets.

Finally a fool volunteers himself. He's driving a bright yellow Hummer that's practically vibrating with the deep bass of stereo speakers that Sam can hear all the way up in her perch. The windows are dark, even the front ones tinted beyond what the law allows. She guesses he figures that will keep him safe. He figures wrong.

Cruising slowly along the slight curve north and east entering the freeway from the south on Lincoln Boulevard, the Hummer invites Sam to pierce its un-tinted front windshield and the driver behind it. She does, slowly squeezing the trigger the way her father taught her to, not letting herself be rushed. In the split second after the bullet leaves the barrel the target moves forward a split second too, straight into the steel-jacketed high-powered projectile. With her eye still to the scope Sam sees the neat hole open in the glass, the suddenly red hole open in the driver's forehead.

She's packing up and moving before she can watch the man slump forward onto the wheel, watch the monster vehicle skew off to the right and into one of the skinny palm trees lining the parking lot next to the freeway entrance. She can hear a car horn, but she's not sure it's his, doesn't pause to find out.

Sam's down the back staircase, out the back door and driving away on her scooter before the horn even stops.

Brooks and Paul get the call on the radio. They've been babysitting the entrance to the eastbound 10 at Bundy and that's not too far away from the shooting. A flock of helicopters—police, news, maybe medical—chudder overhead on their way to the Marina.

Paul's driving, slow and careful like always.

"Step on it."

He gives Brooks a look.

"What's the hurry? From what they said on the radio it doesn't sound like the victim's going anywhere."

He's right. It'll be at least twelve minutes before they get there. The scene will be crawling with black and whites, paramedics who won't have anything to do, maybe some detectives will have already got there, the coroner. There'll be a bunch of looky-loos. In the past there would have been reporters, too, but now they seem to stay at their desks and work the phones or the internet instead. In some ways that's good, they were a nuisance. In others not so much, the coverage is even dumber than it used to be.

"So, why are we going there?"

"Beats me. We got the call. That's the job."

"How many does this make? It's been what, a month?"

"Three weeks. Five, six... this is the eighth DOA, plus two wounded."

"I just had a funny thought."

"Funny? About this? You've really lost it."

"No, really, three weeks? I wonder how many DOAs we get from freeway crashes in a normal three weeks and how many we've had while this was going on."

"You are sick in the head, you know that?"

"We should look it up. I'll bet the city's coming out ahead on this."

"Man, you need to see the department shrink. You like this guy, don't you?"

"Huh? Fuck no, of course not. But you gotta give him some respect."

"I don't gotta give him anything."

Sam's in Brooks' bathrobe across the table from him. They're leafing through the Sunday *Times*. She's on her third cup of coffee. He makes really good coffee. He'd asked, again, when he was ever going to see her place. She changes the subject.

"You guys still looking for the Commuter Killer?"

"Why, something in the paper? Sure."

"Yeah, but it's been a month since he shot that guy in the Marina. Nothing since."

"Thirty-six days but there's no statute of limitations on murder. Even if there was it'd be a lot longer than this."

"Traffic's getting bad again."

"People have short memories."

"If it gets back to the way it was, think he'll come back? There's another op-ed saying it might not be a bad thing."

"Killing people's always a bad thing."

"This guy's saying maybe he should come back once a month and just wound somebody. Remind us all he's still out there."

"Yeah, right, he volunteering to be one of the ones who gets wounded? Fuckwit."

"Remember that jerkwad columnist in the *Times* a month ago? The one who thought the Commuter Killer ought to come back and wound someone every so often?"

"Yeah, last time you called him a 'fuckwit' I seem to recall."

"Well, maybe he's got a point."

He'd had to drop off his prowl car and partner at the Westside station. It'd taken him an hour and a half to get to her place in Koreatown, thirty minutes alone spent driving the five blocks from Butler Street to the freeway entrance.

"You're in a mood. You need a drink? All I've got is scotch."

Sam had finally let Brooks come over a couple of weeks ago. His place is a lot nicer, so they spend most of their time there. This time of day though, it's another half-hour at least to get the somewhat-less-than four more miles to Echo Park. Once she'd put the guns back in her dad's locker there wasn't much point in keeping him away.

"Figures. I've got a better stocked bar at my place. Maybe you ought to give up this dump and move in."

"Are you asking me to move in with you because you've got a better bar?"

Brooks laughs, that nice charming laugh that's as much at himself as anything else, the one that melted her when they first met.

"I guess that's one good reason."

"Any others?"

"You know why."

She does. They've been spending every night together for the past six weeks. The 'L' word even put in its first hesitant appearance about a week ago.

"The traffic? In this city everything's about the traffic. Anything we can do to cut down driving times..."

"Yeah, right, the traffic, too. My place is closer to your new job."

She'd finally found work teaching English as a second language at a community adult school on the north side of downtown. It was only ten minutes from Brooks' house, even during rush hour.

"Hmmm, that's even a better reason than the bar."

"You know why."

Sam's getting really tired of this. She dropped one of her evening classes so that she could be home when Brooks gets home, cook dinner for him some nights, have it just about on the table with one of his girly drinks ready when he walks in the door. But since he got transferred to the Westside station a very long six weeks ago, things have taken a bad turn.

It's the promotion from hell. An hour to work in the morning, hour-and-a-half, sometimes two home at night. And when he gets home he's in a foul mood and who can blame him? It's wrecking everything and probably his liver, too. The girly drinks are mostly vodka at this point.

It's been two months since Brooks got promoted and asked her to marry him. "Yes," she told him, "yes." But, she told him, she wanted to use the rings she'd got from her father and mother. They fought about it briefly, he wanted to buy the rings, isn't that what the man is supposed to do? But he gave in. It was a nice idea after all.

That was the last time she'd gone to her dad's storage locker. She got out two of the bullets for the sniper rifle and took them to a jeweler. It wasn't hammering guns into plowshares, exactly, but they made beautiful rings. She'd picked them up two weeks ago but every night when he got home he'd been in too terrible a state of mind for her to bring them out.

Sam's got to save this relationship. She loves him, the jerk. Something's got to be done about traffic in this town.

She makes another trip to the storage locker.

The Lowriders

Avril Adams

Salvador Bernstein stepped in front of the bathroom mirror. It would be his final check of his appearance before taking the long concrete staircase that wound down to La Palma Avenue from his home on the hilltop overlooking Chavez Ravine. His dark brown hair, long on top, clipped above the ears, gleamed from the oil he'd raked through it. Tonight he wanted to impress the other fellows and especially the girls with his white tie and lavender shirt and the black calf-length coat that squared and widened his shoulders so he could pass for a man of twenty-five years and not a child approaching seventeen.

Leo Bernstein, Salvador's father, stooped over a large piece of white cloth spread out upon a broad tailor's cutting table, his bald scalp yellow under the hanging bulb, yards of blue seersucker rolled up beside him. "Where do you think you're going dressed like that," he said without looking up from his work. Salvador stood in the doorway of the cramped living room, his new-found macho self-assurance diminishing by the second under the withering scrutiny. His father was not supposed to be home from his shop, yet there he stood like an old *chucho* barring the gate to the outside world. Salvador concluded with a sinking heart that his first night as a boulevardier on La Palma would end before it had begun.

"I'm goin' out with my boys, Dad, to a fiesta," he finally said.

"Fiesta?" said Bernstein as if his hearing had failed him. "There's a war on. What's there to have a party about?"

Salvador cringed at his father's harsh tone and rough German accent which had not smoothed out in the two decades he had lived in Los Angeles and the seventeen since he had moved to the barrio with his Mexican wife, Amalia. Salvador was mortified at the way Leo spoke such primitive Spanish, his crude manners, casual atheism and rigid social conformity. "Yes, Dad, there's a fiesta tonight, we're going to have fun for no reason at all," he said.

"Well, you look like a pimp. Look at those clown pants. Look at that silly hat, with that feather in it." Leo wagged his head disapprovingly. Reluctantly, apprehensively, Salvador stole a glance at his wide pleated trousers and the object in his hands, a dramatically broad brimmed hat of the finest felt, a single feather in the band, the salesman said had come from a Mexican eagle. His fingers curled tightly around the brim. Leo ended his reproach with a story about another barrio boy beaten by a gang of sailors in a downtown movie theater for sporting the same ridiculous costume. Salvador had heard similar stories, but the guys who got thumped by the sailors couldn't defend themselves as he could. They were just *putos*, weren't they? He shrugged.

"You look like a *schwartze* in that Zoot suit, showing off like that, Sal. Do you want to look like a Negro? No, wait a minute," he scowled. "You're dressed up like one of those greaser lowlifes ... one of those hoodlums ..." The angrier his father became, the thicker grew his accented English. He declaimed his indignation in his native tongue, then in Spanish. In his business, tailoring movie stars and crooks he had learned all the bad, insulting invective of every language because it suited him to use it. And yet, to Salvador's dismay, he couldn't order a bowl of *caldo* in a barrio restaurant without pointing at the picture on the menu.

"The word you want to call me is *pachuco*, Dad, lowrider. We're not pimps or Negroes, Dad. We're Mexicans and proud of it even if we make you ashamed."

Leo flung out the long end of the white fabric like a fisherman's net, pulling it down flat on the table. He began to scissor along the lines already chalked in the clear shape of a tuxedo coat. "*Vaya*, then, *vaya*; break your dead mother's heart. Get out of my sight, I have things to do."

Salvador closed the door behind him. There would be trouble with his father later. But already, outside he had a heady feeling of exhilaration gazing out into the semi-darkness of the poorly lit streets. He was sixteen and free for the moment, not to be called to fight in Europe or Asia for nearly a year. He descended the crooked stairway through the hills, walking almost a mile before he saw the first vehicles, signs of the weekly *procession de los Pachucos* making their leisurely drag down La Palma. Inching along, the last car in line was a chopped, chromed-out Chevy coupe, the rear bumper dropped to within inches of the asphalt, its deep maroon, "kandy" paint job radiant under the street lights. It was Benny Cisneros' car. Salvador would know it anywhere because he had helped to sand the metal and re-chrome the convex hubcaps the boys called spinners. Benny was doing thirty days in The Can for boosting spinners.

He stepped up his pace to catch sight of the driver. It was Junior Salcido, back from El Paso, behind the wheel of Benny's car, his bulky arm around the shoulder of his girlfriend, Alma. Salvador gave his friends the high sign and walked on, proceeding at roughly twice the speed of the flashy, creeping cars. All the pretty girls were there in their short vaquero skirts and bolero tops. He gave some of the unattached young ladies the appreciative eye as he strolled by. Some girls looked him over, too, just as much. How, he wondered, could his father not understand what all of this meant to him? He was sure the explanation was that his father was from a cold, forbidding country full of evil, mean spirited men, some of whom ate *borchst* and *kreplach*. And how boring it must be to cut cloth for a living, losing your eyesight! How could he understand the flaming Mexican spirit of Aztlan *pachucos,* their hot food, hot blood, hot times? Despite his green eyes and light skin, Salvador considered himself a Mexican through and through, a true Aztlan like his boys.

A few cars ahead drove Hector, his cousin. Hector's side of the family had been in the ravine so long their arrival there was part of the misty past. It was so much more legend than fact that Hector only laughed when the subject was raised. He often said, "We owned the whole place before that *pendejo*, General Santa Ana, got his *culo* kicked. Now look at us, we're squatters." Hector drove a two-tone green '42 Fleetline Chevy. It had cost him all his savings working at a rubber fabricating plant. He'd chopped down the factory sheet metal and support posts between the roof and the body making the windows appear tough and short sighted. He put his face close to the glass, peered out of the custom windshield, signaling to Salvador.

Salvador stepped onto the running board and climbed into the passenger seat. He threw a quick glance into the back seat and felt a twinge of disappointment that there were no pretty girls chattering away behind them. It was no surprise though. Hector was a loner. He toyed with the ladies but didn't take them to heart. Salvador thought it was because he was ashamed of his messed-up leg from coming down with polio when he was fourteen. Hector was the only older guy Salvador knew without a wife or steady girlfriend.

"You got the bumper really, really low," whistled Salvador in admiration. The bumper was just a hair above the asphalt paving. Hector smiled, showing large white teeth and fearsome canines. "It's the sand, man. It's all in the sand, *mi amigo.*" Salvador nodded thinking of all the sand bags he had loaded into Benny Cisneros' trunk to achieve the same effect.

After a few moments bouncing along with the rest of the caravan, ogled by the usual cohort of car fanatics, most of whom Hector knew by name, Hector said, "Later tonight a few of us are gonna peel off for a drive to Hollywood. Wanna come along?"

"I don't know, man. I don't know. I've heard about some rough stuff, like sailors off the U.S.S. Trident banging heads down there and my dad wouldn't let me ..."

"It's just a few miles," interrupted Hector. "Take Vermont to Franklin west and you're almost there. Then cruise down the boulevard to the Chinese Theater. You know—Buster Keaton, Jimmy Stewart and them are playing. They got some hot cars up there. We can show them what we got, too. But if you're scared you can stay here, *muchacha.*"

Salvador considered the cars he'd seen when he drove through the wealthy white neighborhoods with his father delivering tailored suits and tuxes. There were plenty of new auto models in that part of town, mostly foreign, a few Cadillacs and Buicks, plenty of custom, coachbuilt jobs and tricked out Deuces. He liked the Deuces. It would be fun to see them if the drive didn't take too long.

Hector seemed to read Salvador's mind. "It won't take long," he said. "We'll be back before that *pinche* Nazi you live with knows you're gone. If it weren't for all that fabric you can get from him ..." This was Hector's usual rant against Leo, the disagreeable outsider in the family.

Salvador responded as he always did to that particular foolishness: "Dad's a Jew, Hector. He's a German Jew. He hates Nazis. He hates Hitler."

Hector rolled his eyes and laughed. "Yeah, so what? Anyway, so what does that make you, a half-*joto*?"

Salvador thought sometimes the boys just didn't get it. "Okay, Hector, let's go. Two hours. No more. Got it?"

Hector grinned, the glow of triumph in his face.

At the end of La Palma Avenue, a remarkably short street of ten blocks at most, the lowriders and their girlfriends debarked and gathered for beers and impromptu music. At some unknown signal, four or five dropped down Chevys reconnoitered, as Hector had promised, to dispatch to the virgin territory of Hollywood-land. Breaking out of the customary phalanx of the barrio, the cars cruised singly through quiet downtown streets, keeping to speed limits and avoiding attention. They changed the planned route taking side streets north until they could turn west on to Hollywood Boulevard. There they re-formed into a casual convoy keeping just within sight of each other. Alfonso Perez in his bright red Ford coupe reached the Chinese Theater first. He and his lady hopped out on to the sidewalk to press their hands and feet in the impressions left in the concrete by famous film stars. A cop on the beat, when he saw their *pachuco* drag, tapped his Billy and gave them a threatening stare. They clambered back into the car, laughing.

Hector's car was the last in the convoy. He seemed fascinated by the lights and glamour of the city. He looked at the women wrapped in expensive furs and clucked his tongue.

"Why they got all this and we got nothin'?" He spat his disgust.

"Watch what you're doin'" said Salvador. He noticed with irritation that Hector had taken his eyes off the road and missed the turn-off that the others had taken. They were now on an unknown side street and would have to double back to the boulevard. Salvador glanced at his watch and groaned. "Two hours, man. That's what this was supposed to be. How're we gonna to make that now?"

"It's not so bad, I know where we are," said Hector.

"I don't think so," said Salvador.

A car pulled up beside them at a light. It was a black '28 Model "A" hot rod jacked way up in the back and down low in front, giving the impression of a tabby pouncing on a mouse. Dramatic licks of painted orange and red flame flared along the side and doors. The two blond men inside made a point of staring them down.

"Look what we got here, Salvador" said Hector, "a whatchacallit—an adversary; a *pinche* challenger." He laughed, staring back too long at the other men, gunning the V6 engine to a muffled roar.

"I know what you're thinking, Hector," said Salvador, "but not here and not now." Panic rose in his chest.

Hector ignored him, interested only in the hot rod revving beside him itching for a fight. "You know why we drop our bombas low, Sal?" he asked casually. "Because these *gringo cabrones* jack theirs up." He laughed.

"You can't take him, Hector," Salvador protested. "Not with this Fleetline body dropped so low. Give it up."

"Shut up. I've got plenty of bounce in this bomba. And that rod's an A-bone with a four. I'll burn him up."

Salvador was thrown back against the seat as the traffic light changed and the cars screamed off, burning rubber. The lightweight Model A took the lead pulling ahead by a couple of lengths until the more powerful Fleetline caught up, crowded it in a turn and forced its larger body in front. Hector hit a bump and the Fleetline, not as nimble as the rod, spun out. The A-Bone exploited the advantage darting around it, taking the lead again and giving Hector and Salvador a blast of exhaust as it pulled away. But the rod was going too fast. It took a curve on the rims of the tires and side-swiped a four-door Buick. It hit a skid and spun around, facing the wrong direction. It slammed to a stop at an angle, blocking the street. The A-Bone's doors flew open and its occupants jumped out. Hector hit the Fleetline's brakes, not willing to risk a scuff or a ding to the hand-rubbed finish. With the guys in the rod piling out Hector expected a face-off. He reached for the tire iron secreted under his seat. He opened his door, dropped his bad leg on to the ground, pushing the rest of his body out of the car with strong, workingman's arms. Salvador climbed out, too, but hung back, not willing to play the game for keeps, not ready for the childish duel to turn deadly.

Hector saw a .38 in the rod driver's hand. "Thought so," he shouted at the men. "You *cabrones* can't drive. I bet you fight like *chicas.*" Salvador held his breath. He knew things weren't going to end well. Hector's blood was boiling. The fearless Aztlan warrior was ready for the noble charge.

"Take off that suit, greaser. You know wool is being rationed by Uncle Sam, you punk. You unpatriotic wet-back, I should get a large bolt of the Stars and Stripes and shove it up your a...."

"Why don't you put down that gun and take it off me, Mama's Boy?"

The guy with the gun flipped-open a walleted gold badge and held it aloft. "LAPD. greaseball, off-duty, but not too off duty for you. If you know what's good for you, take off that suit." The muzzle of the gun briefly shifted to point at Salvador. "You too, scumball," someone shouted.

Salvador, trembling, removed his coat and tie placing them carefully on the Fleetline's hood. Slowly, painstakingly, he unbuckled the belt, afraid of even thinking about the bleakness of his situation. He realized his cousin hadn't moved. Hector clutched the tire iron at his side.

"Drop the iron, greaser," said cop number one.

The A-Bone's driver raised the revolver to his hip in an I-mean-business gesture. After agonizing seconds Hector sent the tire iron clattering to the pavement but his fists remained clenched.

"Do what he say," whispered Salvador to his cousin.

"You do it, half-*pinche*. You were never one of us to begin with, *patron*."

Salvador wanted to make Hector see reason. With Hector's bad leg he knew fighting was not an option and if these rodders were off-duty cops he and his cousin had the chance of a snowball in, well... But Hector was proud, abundantly so, not about to back down. He stood his ground, feet spread in a belligerent stance, compensating for his weak leg.

The second man, the passenger, moved closer, pulling a baseball bat behind him. "You fellas are in luck, tonight. We were looking for a ball for a game and you're gonna be it." He patted his palm with the bat as had the foot patrolman with the Billy on Hollywood Boulevard. He arched the bat high over his shoulder and rotated it like Lou Gehrig at home plate waiting for a home run pitch. "The officer's peacemaker says take it off, greaser," said the second cop. "Take off that Zoot Suit—and come to think of it—everything else. Give us a look at the *cajones* you greasers are so proud of."

Hector limped forward in answer, letting them know what he thought they could do with their *bate de beisbol.* The cop swung the top of the bat toward Hector's head a few times and each time, Hector leaned back like a boxer gracefully eluding a wild jab. The cop popped the bat a fourth time and Hector tried to grab it but missed. The cop swiftly drew it back and swung it hard, landing the business end of the bat on Hector's collar bone. It nearly crumpled him. If the shoulder wasn't broken, thought Salvador, it was badly bruised. As if intending to act in concert with his partner, the cop with the gun fired a bullet into each pane of the Fleetline's windshield, shattering the glass.

Hector was defenseless now and both men seemed to know it; the Mexican aware that now the bat could do its work mechanically and efficiently, the rod driver sure of the same. The next blow came with plenty of warning, landing on Hector's left hand. Salvador heard the sickening thwack as the tiny, complicated bones imploded. It was Hector's turn to groan. The cop pivoted and with the full force of his considerable weight, slammed the Babe Ruth slugger into

Hector's right shoulder. Hector dropped like a sack of rocks. The cop rolled Hector over and yanked at his striped calf-length coat, rolled him back again and ripped off the shiny black shoes and oversized pants. The pocket watch with the long chain found its way into his pocket. Not finished yet, after stripping all the clothing, the cop roughly removed Hector's underwear. He held his nose at the under pants, laughing as he tossed all the confiscated clothing, all the Aztlan warrior's plumage in a pile and set it ablaze with lighter fluid and a cigarette lighter. As the fire burned, the cop returned to the prostrate body on the ground. Salvador vomited as the man used the bat to deliver a home run hit to Hector's temple. The first cop came over to take a look.

"I would definitely call that resisting arrest, wouldn't you?" he said to his partner, while delivering a gratuitous kick to Hector's ribs that lifted him slightly off the pavement but otherwise made no impression. "Too bad about your suit, greaser," he said to the body.

One of the cops remembered Salvador. He squeezed a pair of steel handcuffs on his wrists. "We're taking you both in," he said; "reckless driving, suspicion of car theft and assault on a police officer."

At the police station Salvador sat shackled on a hard wooden bench near the booking station. His near nakedness seemed to juice up the onlookers. All the men, police and prisoners alike, made smooching sounds as they passed him or invited him to have a look at what they were saving specially for him inside their pants. Salvador shivered, not only because he wore only his underpants on a chilly winter night, but because whatever pride he had in himself and his people was cooling on a slab in the coroner's office. Finally, the cops allowed the nearly naked boy to make his single phone call. He swallowed his trepidation and phoned the only man who could rescue him now and make things right.

The call was quick. Salvador explained that he was in police custody, that Hector was dead, killed by a vicious cop's blow to the head. They had stripped him of his Zoot Suit leaving him nearly naked. Salvador's father was quiet for what seemed a long time. Salvador thought he heard the sound of tears but dismissed the idea. His father wouldn't shed them, would he?

"I'm coming now, son," said Leo Bernstein in his thick coarse accent. "I won't let them have my only son. I'll bring you something you can wear."

Leo hung up the phone. In Salvador's closet he found a calf length coat, a pair of oversized pants wide and pleated at the waist, fitted at the cuffs. He took a black shirt and white tie from the dresser. He searched for a hat, one with a wide brim but didn't find one. In time he would remedy that situation. What he had found would have to do. But his only son would walk out of the police station with his head held high as an Aztlan warrior.

Driving Dead Daisy

Laura Brennan

As I stared down at the dead body, I unexpectedly thought of my favorite grandmother. Not the French grand-mere who hated me, but my unflappable Nanny Joyce. "Theresa, my darling," she would have said to me, "this one's a puzzler."

Not that there was any mystery whose body it was. Even if I hadn't been chauffeuring her around town for the past three months, I would have known that signature sunshine-yellow couture anywhere. Daisy Mac, born Deborah Anne McCullough, had shot up the pop charts almost as fast as she'd taken over the covers of tabloids everywhere. Gorgeous, talented, dysfunctional as hell. The world was waiting for her to crash and burn. Now she had.

Right in the back seat of my limo.

But she'd had help shuffling off her mortal coil. The bruising on her neck was a dead giveaway, if you'll pardon the pun. I was appalled at myself as one irreverent thought after another popped into my head, until I realized my legs were giving out. I found myself sitting down suddenly and hard on the manicured lawn. It was as close as I'd ever come to fainting and I refuse to be a woman who faints.

I scrambled to my feet and took a quick look around. Robbie Voth's estate, like most in the Hollywood Hills, was really an oversized lot with an ugly modern house and ridiculously high walls to keep out the paparazzi. A couple of security cameras monitored the front gate and the yard, but I knew for a fact they had been disconnected at the time of the murder because I was the one who had shorted out the system. So while there was no visual record of me nearly fainting, there was also no footage of the guy who had killed her.

Definitely a puzzler. I ran through my options. Calling the cops was out. They would want to know why, after helping Daisy's current beau into his house—where he promptly threw up and passed out—I hadn't returned right away to my equally-drunk client. It would take very little digging to discover that I'd been mucking with the security system for the last couple of months, ever since Daisy's social calendar had given me access to Robbie and his garage. After weeks of carefully-crafted gremlins and false alarms, Robbie hadn't even bothered to set his system tonight. It was the moment I'd been waiting for. My team was ready and waiting for my call to relieve Robbie of his 2010 Ferrari 458 Italia. By morning, it would have disappeared onto a cargo ship, in a crate marked, truthfully, if you think about it, "used car parts." With it would be six other high-end vehicles destined for private buyers in Hong Kong. All I'd had to do was short out the security cameras one last time...

Oh, yeah. That would go over big with the cops.

When I'd made the career move to grand theft auto, I'd known it would come with risks. I'd done my best to minimize those and maximize profits. It had taken me two years to slowly develop contacts in Africa, South America and Asia. Over the last six months, we'd tested the waters with several small batches of specialized parts, untraceable to a specific chopped car. It had been lucrative, sure, but it was chump change compared to tomorrow's shipment. Now, finally, my patience would pay off. Robbie's Ferrari was going to tip us over the million-dollar mark and make us the go-to source for our overseas clients. Steady seven-figure paydays were worth a few hazards.

Already, Daisy's death was slipping away from tragedy and into the realm of hideously bad timing. I shook it off. I had a responsibility to my team and I'd delayed long enough. I pulled out my phone and dialed a number I knew by heart. Frankie answered, over-eager as always. I had found him eight months ago, trying to smash-and-grab a Mercedes. He was so green he didn't even know the car's windows don't shatter. I shook my head at the memory as his voice squeaked over the phone.

"Are we a go?" Frankie wanted to know. "I got everything ready at the garage."

I told him to shut up—not too unkindly, he's a good kid—and to put Grey on. Grey Smith was my right-hand man and sometime lover.

"Grey left an hour ago," Frankie said. "The team's already in place." That bespoke confidence. Or nerves. Usually the crew didn't leave until after I gave the go-ahead. "Are we a go?" Frankie asked again, insistent.

I took a deep breath. "Code Yellow," I replied. Then I hung up and dialed Grey's cell. I had two hours while Frankie and the rest of them dismantled our entire operation and covered our tracks before vanishing into the night. It was a hell of a call to make right before we got the biggest paycheck of our lives, but money loses some of its luster when you're doing fifteen-to-twenty. Grey picked up on the first ring. He always did that, impatient for the conversation to be over before you even said "hello." I filled him in and told him we'd gone to Yellow. There was an uncharacteristic pause.

"Sounds like a Red to me," he said finally. Code Red, the panic button. Everyone grabs their personal stuff and gets the hell out of Dodge, never to be contacted again. I wasn't ready for that.

"Not yet," I answered. "There are only two guys I can think of who wanted Daisy dead. If I can figure out which one killed her, I may be able to keep the cops from looking into us."

"You said Voth is passed out drunk?" Grey asked. "Maybe he did it."

"No, she was alive when I took him into the house."

"Are you sure?" he asked.

"Of course I'm sure. She helped me get him on his feet..." Then I realized what Grey was saying. Let's dump this on the rich drunk and be done with it. I paused a second to wonder why I hadn't thought of that myself. The answer was instant: I might be a car thief, but in my heart I wasn't a killer. Setting up a lost soul like Robbie, who was even gentle as a drunk, felt like drowning a puppy. I couldn't do it, no matter how much I wanted to get my hands on his car.

"Take Russell and Linc back to the warehouse and help Frankie clear it out," I said. "I'll check in soon." I hung up without waiting for an answer. I had a body cooling in the back seat; this was no time for democracy.

It was also no time to be squeamish. I reached under Daisy and felt around for her purse, a hideous neon sunflower confection some up-and-coming designer had created for her. My initial instinct when I'd met Daisy Mac had been utter revulsion. Her clothes, her makeup, her lifestyle had all screamed "look at me!" It had nearly been more than I could handle. I'm sure my team thought I'd become a limo driver in order to steal cars, but in fact it was the uniform that had drawn me in. People see a uniform and rarely look deeper. In livery, I became invisible. As my white driving gloves rummaged through the yellow clutch, I wondered if Daisy's unique sense of style had served the same purpose. The flamboyant armor had kept all eyes on her but made them unable to see deeper than her outer trappings. The inner woman had been private. Safe. Well, until tonight.

I found her phone. To me, social media was a modern circle of hell. Besides, what would I tweet? *Just lifted vintage Jag. RT if you loved #gonein60seconds.* Not my thing. But it was Daisy's. She tweeted, posted and pinned her every move. So did everyone else in her circle, including her quick-tempered ex. Malcolm Dread was a British punk rocker and my best hope. I was heartened to discover he was in town, at a club not fifteen minutes away. Twitter might lie but Foursquare didn't.

I buckled Daisy in and started the limo.

Not having a celebrity to unload, I parked on a side street a couple of blocks from the club. I wiggled out of the livery and slid into my back-up uniform: a Spandex mini clubwear dress that fit in the glove compartment and guaranteed no one seeing me would look at my face. Fingerprints trumped fashion; the driving gloves stayed on. I ditched the cap and let my hair down. I glanced in the mirror. An oversexed club bunny stared back at me. One of a million in Hollywood. Perfect.

I hated to leave Daisy in the car, but a dead body is not a trendy accessory. I slid her sunglasses on her face, which made her look pretentious and hung-over, but alive. A close peer through the tinted windows might reveal her silhouette, but there was no way even the nosiest neighbor would see the damage done to her neck. I patted her shoulder because I couldn't think what else to do, then I left for the club.

It was after midnight and the dance floor was packed. As I navigated the drunken, gyrating bodies, I once again thought of my grandmothers. Nanny Joyce would have clicked her tongue. All these young souls, she would have said, so desperate to connect. But her foot would have tapped to the pulsating beat. Grand-mere would've been too busy scouting for unattended purses to notice the music.

I paused halfway up the stairs that led to the VIP lounge and surveyed the bar. No sign of Dread. I was resigned to sweet-talking my way into the lounge when I heard raised voices above me. Two burly clichés were giving a green-haired drunk the bum's rush right past me and down the stairs. I recognized Dread at once, though less from the hair than from the inventive curses pouring forth with a South London flair. A woman was hurling anything she could find at the back of his green head. She had run out of ammo and was slipping off a silver sandal when I stopped her.

"Better not," I said. "He's not worth ruining a Jimmy Choo."

She turned bloodshot eyes towards me and struggled hard to focus. "No," she managed. "He's not." She tottered a little. I steadied her as she got the sandal back on. "Men!" she added.

I nodded in sisterly commiseration. "Although he must've set a world record," I added, "for getting thrown out of this place." She looked puzzled, so I continued. "I thought I saw his green 'do slide in the doors ten minutes ago."

"Nah," she said. "Couldn't have been Mal. We've been here forever. He kept promising Daisy Mac would show, then Rihanna... Shit, all we got was a glimpse of the vampire guy. Not even Edward, the other one." She glared at me, the unfairness of this fueling her rage. I made sympathetic noises, but forged on.

"Are you sure he didn't run out for a bit, say, half an hour ago?" I pressed. "I was so sure. I almost asked for his autograph... " I let my voice trail off as she snorted.

"Half an hour ago, he was in the men's room screaming my name," she said. "Be nice if he could remember it now. But hey, honey, you want a rocker on your scorecard, you can have him. Good luck." She stalked away. I let her go. Much as I wanted Daisy's killer to be Malcolm Dread, it looked like he had an airtight, if pissed-off, alibi.

That left one possibility. Alexander Sorovsky.

Sorovsky was a celebrity photographer, but he was paparazzi like I was a chauffeur. Snapping pics for trashy mags got him access to the stars and the illusion that he was part of their lives. His—let's call it "intensity"—had bordered on stalking for several young starlets. With Daisy it had progressed into the realm of scary. The stream of calls and texts had been followed by Photoshopped pics of the two of them together. When he broke into her house to "borrow" some lingerie, she was finally able to get a restraining order.

He was fighting it under the guise that it prevented him from doing his job. Since his job was to take pictures of Daisy without her permission or even her knowledge, I thought this was a ballsy defense, but it was winding its way through the courts. In the meantime, Sorovsky stayed just far enough away from us to stay out of jail. A dead Daisy would make his life a lot easier, but was he crazy enough to kill his fantasy girl?

Only one way to find out. Sorovsky would be harder to track down than a flamboyant punk rocker and the clock was ticking. I did the only thing I could think of: I texted him. From Daisy's phone.

Where R U? I waited a couple of minutes. No reply. So I sent, *My neck hurts. What happened 2nite??* If he'd killed her that should suitably freak him out. Sure enough, I got an answer this time: *Is this a trick? I'm not supposed to contact you.* I texted back: *Stupid judge. We can talk it out. Where R U?*

I held my breath. If he were smart, he'd turn off his phone and call his lawyer. But he wasn't smart. He was obsessed. The lure of meeting Daisy one-on-one proved irresistible. He texted back an address.

Sorovsky lived in a ground floor apartment off Franklin. I double-parked in the shared driveway, blocking a BMW that had seen better decades and a funky VW bug complete with flowers on the dashboard. Now I needed something to prove my bona fides...

I needed Daisy's underwear.

When I was a child, I had spent a blissful month every summer with Nanny Joyce, but when my parents died, it had been my grand-mere who had taken me in. From the first, I'd wondered why. Certainly it hadn't been from any joy in having me around, or even a sense of obligation, since she had cared for nothing after my father's death. Finally, I'd settled on the idea that I was a mulligan, a do-over, a chance for her to shape a child into a mini-me of her own paranoid self. Trust no one, love no one, leave no trace of yourself wherever you go. What had really stuck was her favorite phrase. "Theresa," she liked to say, "you're not very smart. But you're smart enough to let people think you're dumber than you are."

I don't know if sex made men dumb or if looking like I wanted to sleep with them made men assume I was brainless. But I knew dangling lacy lemon-yellow undies in front of Sorovsky's peephole would guarantee me entrée. I rang the bell. I heard footsteps, then a pause. The door flew open.

It took Sorovsky a few seconds to realize I wasn't the object of his desire. It was long enough for me to cross the threshold.

"What the hell's going on?" he asked. I could smell the alcohol on his breath. A loaded stalker with a quick temper? Better and better. "Where's Daisy?" he demanded.

"In the car." He turned to glare at the limo and took a step towards the door. I swung it closed and leaned against it, holding out the underwear. "She doesn't feel well," I continued. "She sent me with a peace offering."

Sorovsky waivered a moment, then snatched the underwear and turned away. “What does she want?” he asked. He wandered deeper into the apartment. I followed. The rooms were dark and the walls were covered with photos. Shots of dozens of celebrities, mostly women, mostly young. Mostly Daisy.

“Something happened tonight,” I said.

He snorted and threw himself into an armchair, reaching for a bottle of Old Crow.

“Tell me what happened,” I pressed.

“Why don’t you ask her boyfriend?” He snarled the words. I was surprised. He had always come across as creepy and delusional, but never vicious.

“Robbie Voth is dead to the world,” I answered. I circled him so I could watch his face as I said “dead,” but there was no reaction. Possibly he was too numb from the whisky to react at all.

“Not him,” Sorovsky growled. “The other one.”

“Who do you mean?” I asked. Daisy had been a mess, but a serially monogamous mess. I couldn’t picture anyone who would fit the bill, unless—

“The one making out with her in the limo.”

I felt a surge of energy. This was it, it had to be. “You followed her tonight?”

“What if I did?” He was instantly on the defensive. “I have a job to do. You’re not a celebrity unless someone celebrates you. Without my pictures, she is nothing.”

“Of course,” I soothed. “Daisy knows that. She understands.” He fingered the underwear and allowed himself to be mollified. “You always make her look so lovely in your pictures. The other photographers aren’t as kind.”

“That’s because they don’t care,” he said. “No one cares like I care.”

“Daisy knows,” I repeated. “She can see it in your photos.” He glanced over towards a desk and I saw a professional-grade digital camera with an immense zoom lens attached. “I bet she’d love the pictures you took tonight.”

His eyes narrowed. I’d pressed too quickly. I shrugged and moved away. “But then we both know you couldn’t have taken any photos tonight. It would violate the judge's order." But the subtle threat was the wrong tack as well. He simply looked mulish. I sighed.

"Daisy's dropping the lawsuit," I told him. "After tomorrow, you won't have to worry about it ever again."

"You're lying," he said, but it came out automatically.

"I'm not," I told him. "But there's a price." At that, he looked up. "I need to see the pictures you took tonight. I don't need to take them with me and I won't tell anyone you took them, but I need to see them. Daisy trusts me,"—that was true, although the tense was wrong—"and she needs me to look at those photos. Alexander... " I leaned over him and breathed his name. I was no Daisy Mac, but my cleavage was ample enough to distract a drunk. "I promise you, Daisy will be forever grateful. Grateful that you were there."

He was wavering. "I've already downloaded them," he warned. "It won't do you any good to hit delete."

"I won't try." I kept my gaze steady. I didn't want to spook him. If I had to, I could pepper spray, snatch and dash. But I didn't want to, which made no sense at all. There was no time, my Code Yellow was running out, I had to see those photos, yet I felt bound by my own spell.

I held my breath, and I held out my hand.

"For Daisy," I said. Whatever I felt, he seemed to feel, too. Without a word, he picked up the camera and handed it to me. I turned it on.

It occurred to me why Sorovsky didn't do well as a celebrity photog: he hoarded the best pictures for his own walls. Certainly the shots I was scrolling through wouldn't make him much. There was a close-up of Daisy and Robbie in the limo. I had opened the door, but luckily I remained out of frame. There was another of Daisy helping a stumbling Robbie to his feet, then close-ups of her as I, unseen, walked Robbie to his door.

Then I clicked on the money shot and felt reality shift.

The last three photos clearly showed a man at my limo, one hand on Daisy's shoulder, the other caressing her neck. I knew those strong hands. Unlike Sorovsky, I couldn't mistake the moment for a lover's embrace.

The man in the photo was Grey.

"Why wasn't it me?" Sorovsky's voice brought me out of my thoughts. I handed him the camera and managed a smile.

"Wrong question," I told him. "The real one is, why wasn't it me?" I left him brooding in the chair, still clutching Daisy's underwear. Sorovsky had caught her killer. If he could bear to share those three photos, he'd make millions off her death. Somehow, I didn't think he would. Daisy owed him the undies.

I got back into the limo and checked the time. Half an hour until Code Yellow expired. It would take at least twenty minutes to get to Robbie's. It'd be close. I understood now why Grey had wanted to go to Code Red right away. It left the team more vulnerable, but the garage intact. Also, the rules were clear. We all melted into the night, left each other and everything else behind. While the rest of us were hopping the next plane, train and automobile out of LA, Grey would have swooped in. Not only would the Ferrari have been his for the taking, but tomorrow's entire shipment, all my contacts, all my deals...

My calling a Code Yellow had delayed him and Grey lived for speed. He'd be counting the seconds until the Code Yellow expired. I went for broke and hit the gas, making it back to Robbie's with only minutes to spare. I did what I had to do there and made the call.

Frankie answered. "Code Red," I told him. "Let the others know. The Hong Kong shipment is compromised but the last payment from our Kenyan client came through. Your share cleared this morning. Get it and get out."

There was a pause. I could tell he was trying to hold it together. "I'll miss you guys," he said.

"Me, too." But I didn't mean it. I didn't know if Grey had acted alone. Suspicion tainted every memory of the last two years, when I was building what I'd thought of as my team. The easy camaraderie with Russell, the late nights working on engines with Linc, it all suddenly seemed fake and forced, a long con with me as the mark. As I hung up with Frankie, I realized that my Nanny Joyce had given me love, but it was my bitter grand-mere who had taught me how to survive.

I hid the limo on a side street and waited for Grey. Half an hour later, Robbie's Ferrari was his. I watched him pull out of the gates and vanish into the night.

Back in my livery, I walked over to Robbie's estate, unlocked the door with Daisy's key and started screaming.

It took a few minutes to rouse him. Robbie had sobered up enough to panic when I got him to understand that someone had kidnapped Daisy and stolen his car. He called Daisy's manager first—this was Hollywood—but within minutes he was on with 911. It was time for me to disappear.

I went home to pack. Nothing, not even the limo, had been registered in my real name, but however safe I might be, I'd be safer out of town. Barely an hour after I'd sounded the alarm, I was ready to go. I couldn't wait any longer. I took out my burner phone and dialed Grey's number for the last time. I wasn't sure he would answer.

I wasn't sure I wanted him to.

He picked up on the first ring. Some things are hardwired.

"I thought you were the one who wanted no goodbyes," Grey said by way of hello. "Or are you changing the rules?"

"How does the Italia drive?" I asked. "I've never been at the wheel of one myself."

Grey laughed. "You can't blame a guy for nabbing the consolation prize," he said. "So did you find out who killed your boss?"

"She was my client," I corrected. "I'm my own boss. And, yes, I know you killed her."

"I'm impressed. I should start calling you Sherlock. I will, if I ever see you again."

"So why wasn't it me?" I asked, echoing Sorovsky. "With me dead, you could've taken over the team." It was amazing how detached I felt. We might have been discussing the dinner menu or a Kings game. "It would have been simpler."

"For you, maybe," Grey chuckled. "But if I killed you, how long would it take the police to discover your set-up? What would be the point of killing you if I lost the infrastructure you'd so painstakingly built? God, you were slow. Do you have any idea how hard it was these last six months, with you insisting on test runs and safety measures, blah, blah, blah..."

I'd been afraid that Grey would pretend he had loved me and couldn't hurt me. It was comforting to discover that I was just a business venture.

"Besides," he continued, "the rest of the crew adored you. They only tolerate me. Even if I could've somehow made you disappear without them wondering, they never would've stayed with me." Grey was right. He was respected, but he wasn't loved. The others would have followed him for a few weeks out of habit then they would have drifted away. "Plus now, I don't have to share."

"No," I agreed. "It's all yours. Everything you deserve." Over the phone, I could hear sirens approaching. Grey started swearing.

"Is that highway patrol?" I asked innocently. "You really shouldn't talk on your cell phone while driving." I could picture him, behind the wheel, torn between believing he could talk his way out of anything and a pure desire to floor it to the border.

"Damnit, woman! What did you do?"

"Did you check the trunk?" I asked. There was a heartbeat of silence. He hadn't, of course. I had known he wouldn't. It was my policy to check backseat, side pockets and trunk before lifting a vehicle. I did not want to be caught with someone's oxygen machine, sleeping toddler or coke stash, but I knew Grey privately sneered at my thoroughness. He valued speed. Stashing Daisy's petite body, as well as her very traceable phone, in the trunk of Robbie's Ferrari had been a risk, but a calculated one.

"Bitch!" Grey exhaled. I heard him hit the gas. I hung up quickly. I knew what would come next. The police chase, the media circus, the final mad acceleration off a bridge or into a wall. And in the wreckage, Grey's vibrant body finally stilled, red blood seeping into the bright cheerful awful yellow of a sunflower purse.

I expected nightmares that night or certainly the next, but they never came. I guess in my heart I was a killer, after all.

The Last Joy Ride

Julie G. Beers

The gun felt unexpectedly heavy in Emily's handbag. She snapped her purse shut and set it on the bed. Then she opened her jewelry box and the little ballerina inside twirled as Emily took out her mother's wedding pearls. They were a bit old fashioned but seemed like the right touch. She took a final look around the room, picked up her purse and shut the door behind her.

Greg paced nervously outside. Sunlight glinted in his hair as he turned and his breath caught in his throat when Emily stepped onto the patio. He couldn't believe how nervous he suddenly was. "You look... pretty in pink," he stammered, then grimaced. How lame could he be? But Emily just blushed and giggled slightly. "Ready?" he held out his hand.

"Are you sure?"

"I am."

"Okay, then." She took his hand and held it tight.

He pulled her into his arms. "I know you're scared, Em, and I am too, but..." He hugged her close.

"I love you." She reached up and kissed him, passion silencing doubts.

Reluctantly they broke their embrace but she clung firmly to his hand as they left the yard. Adrenaline coursed through their veins as they strolled down the street, desperately trying to seem casual. It was a short journey to the crossroads of Cumberland and Merriman.

He stopped. "This is it. No turning back."

"No turning back," she agreed and shouldered her purse with its added weight.

The house at 2787 Merriman Drive waited quietly as they knew it would. The owners worked until six and neighbors were rarely to be found during daytime hours. Still, Emily and Greg approached slowly, carefully. Emily had never been so nervous in her life. She'd practically stopped breathing so she stopped moving. "Do you think he suspects?"

"No."

"You sure?"

Greg forced a smile. "Well, if he's waiting inside, we'll know I was wrong."

"That'd be messy." She shuddered.

"So let's hope I'm right."

She nodded, then looked up and down the empty street. "Okay, let's get it over with."

They hurried down the drive to the backyard. Emily laughed when he let go of her hand, raced to the garage window and eagerly peered inside. "She's here!" Greg was overjoyed.

"Now I know for sure *she's* the real love of your life."

Greg grinned. "You know you love her, too."

Emily joined him at the window and looked at the '66 red Mustang convertible waiting inside. "Well, I will admit it's a cool way to escape."

"A classic way. She is so my car."

"Our car."

He kissed her. "Our chariot awaits." He grinned like a little kid.

"You are so corny, but I do love it. And you."

His smile, impossibly, grew wider. Weeks of careful observation and planning yielded quick results. The garden troll by the rain spout hid the house key. Greg unlocked the side door and they stepped inside. Emily hit the switch and the garage door opened. Sunlight revealed the car in all its classic glory. Greg was mesmerized, Emily was practical. She snagged the spare keys hanging by the door and dangled them teasingly. "Should I drive?"

"No way! You don't even have a license."

"Neither do you."

"A technicality. I've got plenty of experience."

"Prove it." She tossed him the keys. "Just don't get stopped for speeding or anything like that."

"Yeah," he laughed as he opened the door for her, "last thing we need is a cop on our tail." Greg slipped into the driver's seat and knew he was at home. This car fit him like a glove. He smiled at Em and leaned over for another kiss. "This is my perfect day—you, this car and freedom." He turned the key in the ignition and backed slowly, almost reverentially, out of the garage.

"Honey, I know I said don't get a speeding ticket, but at this rate, we'll die of old age before we hit the street."

"Oh, yeah? Watch this!" The car flew backwards down the drive and screeched to a halt as he stopped to check the road. Then Greg channeled his inner race car champion and the car took off like the wild Mustang she truly was.

Greg cruised down Merriman onto Kenneth and took a left onto Pacific. They were stopped at the lights at Glenoaks when a police siren startled them. Both looked around frantically for the source of the sound. "No way we could be found out this soon," Greg declared with a definite lack of certainty.

An SUV tore across the street and Emily giggled with relief. She pointed at its rear window where a homemade "Senior Ditch Day" banner was plastered. "It's not us, it's them." And indeed, the police car was only seconds behind.

"Why would you advertise? It's just asking for trouble." Greg shook his head.

"Especially if you're going eighty down Glenoaks!" She looked sternly at Greg. "Wait until we get on the freeway for that kind of speed."

"Uh huh," Greg agreed as the light changed. Within a minute they were on the 134 headed west but eighty miles per hour wasn't an option. Eight miles per hour was the top speed in this congested corner of the California freeway system. Once they cleared the 5 interchange, traffic lightened a little, but Greg kept it near the speed limit. He wasn't going to take any undue chances until they were well out of Glendale.

Toluca Lake came up quickly and Greg looked longingly at the Hollywood Way exit. "Wish we could stop at Bob's Big Boy."

She nodded. He had a thing for those Big Boy combos. "It's a little early for lunch and someone could recognize this car..."

"I know, we can't risk it." They left Toluca Lake behind and moved onto the 101 Freeway. It wasn't the race track he wanted, but at least it wasn't a complete parking lot and Greg was loving every moment behind the wheel.

It wasn't too long before they reached the Topanga Canyon exit and headed down the twisty passageway to the beach. Greg maneuvered happily through every curve. It seemed as if no time passed and suddenly they were at the Pacific Ocean.

"What first?"

"I'm a little hungry," she admitted. "I was too nervous to eat breakfast."

"Me, too." Greg turned onto the Pacific Coast Highway. "A quick stop at Starbucks?"

Emily nodded and they cruised into Malibu, feeling like celebrities in their convertible. Greg pulled into the Malibu shopping center and parked ever so carefully and they strolled to Starbucks. She decided on a Chai tea latte and a zucchini walnut muffin. He went for a mocha with extra whipped cream and a blueberry scone. They found an outside table where they could enjoy the cool ocean air and the equally cool view of the Mustang.

"We did it!" She raised her cup to toast.

"We're free and clear!" He agreed as they clinked cardboard. "I knew they couldn't stop us."

"Well, it was a good plan."

"Thank you." He grinned and took a big chug of his mocha.

They finished their breakfast and strolled hand in hand back to the Mustang. They were fueled, the car was full and Pacific Coast Highway waited. He opened her car door. "Ferris wheel first?"

"I like that idea." She slid back into the car.

It was a picture perfect Southern California day and they were almost carefree as the Mustang sped down PCH toward

Santa Monica. Greg found a radio station playing "California Dreamin'" and they sang along, living the dream.

The Santa Monica pier bustled with its usual energy. The couple climbed onto the Ferris wheel and held hands as they rose high into the sky. They reached the peak and Emily smiled as she took in the magnificent vista. "I love the view from up here."

"Me, too." But Greg was only looking at her and their kiss lasted a full revolution of the wheel. The ride was over too quickly but the arcade beckoned. They stepped inside and Greg grinned slyly. "How about some shooting games? For practice."

"Not funny!" She lightly smacked him on the arm.

"Come on, it was a little funny."

She shook her head and tears threatened.

Greg immediately put his arms around her. "Sorry, Em. I didn't mean to upset you."

She clung to him for a moment. "I know you're just trying to keep it light, but..."

"But you don't need any practice."

"Exactly." She forced a smile, "So that remark will cost you a ride on the carousel."

"No way."

"You owe me. And merry-go-rounds are good for your soul."

"In that case, let's go," he laughed. After a spin on the carousel's ponies, they wandered the pier for a while, then jumped back into the classic Mustang. The radio blared the Beach Boys' "Surfin' Safari" and they simultaneously shouted, "Duke's!"

Duke's restaurant, celebrating the fabled surfer, sat at water's edge in Malibu. They were ushered to a window table where the water crashed onto the rocks outside. "Keep an eye out for dolphins," Emily ordered before excusing herself to the ladies room.

Greg watched the restroom door close behind her and quickly fished an envelope out of his pocket. His eyes nervously darted around to make sure he wasn't watched as he shook out two pills and swallowed them. He slipped the envelope back into his pocket, closed his eyes and took a deep breath.

Greg's eyes were still shut when Emily returned. She touched his hand. "You okay?"

"Yup," he said, a little too quickly.

She stood there, staring at him. "You sure?"

"Really, I'm fine. But I'm starving so let's eat."

"Okay." She sat down and although no dolphins swam outside their window, lunch was still great. They ate and talked for a couple of hours, then retrieved the Mustang.

"How about one more spin before Paradise?"

"Whatever you want." She smiled, leaned back, and absorbed the sunshine.

Traffic was lighter than usual and the Mustang cruised easily up to Zuma Beach. Greg banged a U-turn and headed south again, stopping here and there to watch the surfers.

As the magic hour of sunset approached, he pulled into Paradise Cove and parked. "I promised you paradise."

"And you delivered." She kissed him.

Greg's hands caressed the steering wheel. "She's quite a car."

"The best get-away vehicle anyone could have."

Greg took a deep breath and looked at Emily. "Ready?"

"Not really." She turned and looked him straight in the eye. "Are you absolutely sure?"

"I am."

Emily sat for a long moment, then picked up her purse. "Okay, let's do it."

Greg got out and opened her door. His hand lingered on the Mustang for a moment, then he took Emily's hand and they strolled onto the picturesque beach.

"Do you want to walk down the pier?" asked Emily.

"No, too public."

They meandered down the beach to a quiet spot, settled against the rocks and waited for sunset. After a few moments of silence, Greg turned to her. "I love you." He kissed her again and as always, their hearts beat a little faster. She leaned her head on his shoulder and they held hands as the sun made its descent in a wash of pinks and blues.

"Amazing," she sighed.

His grip tightened on her hand. He looked at her again, suddenly uncertain. "Do you think... Will it be...?"

"Yes," she said firmly, sitting up. "Even more beautiful."

He nodded, smiled at her and returned his gaze to the water. "Thanks. For everything."

Emily nodded but tears slipped from her eyes and she couldn't talk anymore. She leaned her head back on his shoulder and they sat quietly, hand in hand, watching until the sun hit the edge of the water.

"I love you." Greg squeezed her hand reassuringly.

"I love you, too." Emily let go of his hand. She quietly reached into her purse and pulled out the gun.

Greg's eyes never left the sunset as Emily put the gun to his temple and pulled the trigger.

Emily contemplated the gun for a long moment, then shook her head and tossed it in the sand. She didn't look beside her as she pulled the cell phone out of her purse. Her hands shook uncontrollably and tears made it difficult to see the numbers. Emily barely recognized her own voice as she whispered, "Tommy, it's Mom."

Tom Peters arrived at the hospital within an hour. He nodded to the police officer standing guard outside his mother's room, took a deep breath and stepped inside. He stopped, shocked at how frail his Mom looked in the hospital bed. She was only seventy-five but suddenly looked decades older. "Mom?"

Emily opened her eyes. She was pale and her hands still trembled, but she managed a smile for her son. "Tommy." She reached for his hand.

He hugged her close. "Why?"

"Honey, you know Dad only had a few months left."

"But..."

"The pain was getting pretty bad and the... deterioration... it's not what he wanted."

"Why didn't you come to me? I could've done something."

Emily gently patted his hand. "We couldn't do that to you. You have a family and a life to live."

"You, too. What about you? You could go to jail."

"Well, that's a risk I'm willing to take. I know I didn't commit a crime. Dad was at death's door and he chose how and when to step through." Emily wiped away a tear, "Of course, I did think of joining him."

"Mom!"

"I didn't because *that* would be a crime since I'm not terminally ill." She squeezed her son's hand. "But Dad and I felt bad about the other crime."

"The other crime?" Tom's face paled and he didn't look as if he could take any more.

"Sweetie, I meant the car. We stole your car."

"Oh Mom." Tom's relief was palpable. "It's Dad's car anyway."

"No. He gave it to you when he lost his license."

"It will always be Dad's car."

"He wanted you to have it." Emily hugged her son close. "We just needed one last joy ride."

Kill Joy

Laurie Stevens

Hector knew Sabrina. He had seen her plenty of times at the car wash. Sabrina knew that even if Hector was busy washing another car, he would ask one of his coworkers to take over so he could personally attend to her Ford Explorer. Sabrina drove a soccer mom's SUV, a Limited edition, one of the more deluxe models. Subjected to the daily abuse of her three children, the white Explorer with tan interior was always in need of a wash.

Hector was consistently friendly, calling her by name as if he enjoyed the way *Sabrina* sounded on his tongue. He had a very fine Hispanic accent, so when he said her name, it sounded tempting and exotic. Because they were friendly, Sabrina wasn't the least bit surprised to find him hovering over her as she read her book in the patio waiting area of the carwash.

"You wan' a wax today, Sabrina?"

She shook her head politely. "Not today."

He nodded and was about to begin work on her vehicle, when Sabrina called after him, "Hector!"

He turned.

"Do you know of a good handyman? My son ran his skateboard into the wall and left a gouge. I tried to patch it myself, but I didn't do a very good job."

Hector shrugged. "I can fix it for you. I can fix anything. I used to work construction. Now, with this economy..." He looked pensively back at the men cleaning the cars.

"Oh?" she said, pleasantly surprised. "I didn't know you knew construction. When are you available?"

"I could come over tonight," he said. "But later, because I have another job after this one. Is that okay?"

"That's terrific."

Sabrina wrote her address and phone number on a piece of paper and handed it to Hector.

He nodded and returned to her car. Sabrina observed him as he wiped the hood of the Explorer with a towel. Hector was sincere and hard working. What a shame that such a good-looking man had a menial job. Two jobs, apparently. Sighing, Sabrina turned her attention back to her book.

It was a morbid tale, about the wife of John Wayne Gacy. This unfortunate creature had no idea her husband was butchering young boys and burying them in the basement of her home. How could she have been so blind to her husband's murderous double life? Sabrina was truly engrossed in the book and nearly jumped in fright when Hector's shadow fell over her once more.

"Sabrina," he said, a bit admonishingly. "You don' want to lose this."

Hector was perspiring slightly over his bronzed skin; his black hair damp against his neck. His brown eyes were friendly as he held out his hand to her. Sabrina smiled.

Another place, another set of circumstances, Sabrina might have fantasized about jumping into bed with Hector. He radiated a sensual heat that quickened her heart. It's not that she didn't have a good sex life with her husband Wayne; it's just that lately she felt more of a mother and less of a wife. Thinking about it, Sabrina couldn't remember the last time she and her husband had relations and that surprised her. She lifted up her hand to meet Hector's.

She expected him to drop into her palm something that belonged to one of her kids. How thoughtful of Hector to help her avoid a whining fit later on when her child discovered a treasured toy had gone missing. Then again, Sabrina thought with a wider smile, maybe Hector just wanted an excuse to talk to her.

He opened his fist and let fall a necklace.

"It look valuable," Hector told her. "I didn't wan' you to worry."

A fine gold chain holding a golden pendant fell into her waiting palm. The letter "J" was engraved in the middle and was encrusted in diamonds. Not simply diamond chips, but small, individual diamonds, which caught the filtered sunlight and sparkled. Sabrina regarded the necklace curiously. It didn't belong to her.

"Where did you find this?"

Hector wiped the back of his hand across his moist brow. "Under the back seat. I saw it when I got underneath with the vacuum."

Thorough Hector, thought Sabrina.

"Thanks," she told him, but she wasn't smiling anymore. Someone had lost a valuable piece of jewelry, a personal keepsake, for sure. Was it one of the kids in carpool? Had a child taken a piece of mommy's jewelry for show and tell? That parent was most likely having a panic attack by now. "Thanks, Hector," she repeated absently.

"And I was able to get out a lot of those spots in the back, but they were no' easy."

Sabrina lifted her eyes from the necklace. "What?"

"Those *manchas,* those stains on the backseat carpet. You didn't see them?"

"No."

"You wan' me to show you?"

She stood up as her reply, pocketed the necklace and followed him to her car, on top of which lay Hector's towels.

"See?" He crouched down and pointed to some faded blotches.

Sabrina leaned next to him and she could see spots, some large, some small, in a spray pattern on the carpeted floor mats.

"With kids," Hector suggested, "maybe is better to have rubber mats, huh?"

Of course it was better, Sabrina thought tersely. She had just liked the plush mats because they matched the rest of the Explorer's carpeting. Besides, her children knew better than to eat or drink in the car.

Sabrina distractedly stared at the spots as Hector moved away and grabbed one of his towels. He brought it over for her to inspect. Although the towel itself was orange, it had been stained a deep red where it had cleaned the spots.

Juice, Sabrina imagined. Or punch of some sort. She blew out a big breath. She'd only had this car for three months and already it was damaged.

"I used some spot cleaner." Hector smiled at her with his white teeth. "Don' tell the boss. We're supposed to charge extra for that."

Sabrina nodded and went back to the bench and her book. She dug in her wallet for a five-dollar bill and then replaced it with a ten, knowing it was a generous tip, but Hector deserved it. After all, he'd gone the extra mile to keep her car clean and then there was his comment about the economy. She was so lucky with her nice home, her new car, her husband and children.

Sabrina kept the ten-dollar bill folded in her hand so she wouldn't forget to give it to Hector. Of course, Wayne would tell her she was being a sucker. Never tip them more than a couple of bucks, he would say. Then again, Wayne could be cheap sometimes. He was always fretting over finances. Sabrina didn't know why. Her own father had plenty of money and had always been generous to his daughter. Wayne told Sabrina she was naïve, a "daddy's girl." Did naïve mean stupid? Sabrina sometimes wondered if that's what her husband really meant to say.

To get her thoughts off her marriage, Sabrina reached into her jeans and pulled out the necklace. She dangled the chain in front of her. The pendant twisted lazily in the warm air and the diamond "J" glittered. Sabrina noticed for the first time that the two strands of gold chain were broken. She fingered a torn link and then noticed the time.

"Oh, crud..."

She was late picking up the kids from school.

The suburbs of Los Angeles didn't quite escape the congestion of the city and the traffic on the boulevard crawled. As she drove toward the school, Sabrina called the Farmingtons and the Meyers. Those were the parents of her carpool kids. She wanted to see if either mother was missing a necklace. Sabrina was sure that Mrs. Farmington's first name was Jill. Neither mother, however, answered the phone.

One of the aides stood outside the elementary school with her arms crossed and her lips pursed in a firm line of anger. Next to the aide stood Sabrina's twins Nelly and Jason, a neighbor, Tommy Meyers and little Jade Farmington. Jade looked very upset, holding her lunch box protectively against her small body.

"We wait until all children are accounted for," the aide reminded Sabrina as she pulled up.

"I know and I'm sorry," Sabrina told her.

"You're late!" Tommy scolded.

"My mommy is worried about me!" Jade complained as she hopped into her booster seat.

Your mommy isn't even home yet, Sabrina thought as she buckled in the little girl and then attended to Tommy. Her twins knew how to cinch their own seatbelts over their boosters.

"Jade," Sabrina began as she pulled out of the school parking lot. "Did you leave one of your mommy's necklaces in my car?"

The little blonde girl gave her a strange look. Sabrina eyed her in the rearview mirror.

"Did you take this necklace from your mommy?" Sabrina held up the necklace.

Jade shook her head.

Nelly immediately reached out her hand. "Ooh, that's pretty! Can I have it?"

Sabrina ignored her request and said, "Which of you had a juice box in here? You know the rules, only water. Someone spilled juice all over the car."

"Not me!" Jade yelled out.

"I never had a juice box!" Tommy protested.

Jade shook her head while Nelly and Jason defended themselves and told their mother they knew the rules because it was their Ford.

Sabrina put the necklace in the cup holder and inserted a DVD into the stereo. Instantly, the sounds of a Disney movie filled the car. The rooftop monitor lowered and the kids ceased their noisy chatter and watched the movie. Sabrina moved into traffic. Her cell phone rang and she used her Bluetooth to answer.

"Hi, honey." It was Wayne.

"Hi," Sabrina answered. "I've just picked up the kids."

"A little late..."

"I know. I was getting the car washed."

"Oh," Wayne murmured. "Listen, I'm not going to be home until late tonight. I've got a meeting, so don't hold dinner, okay?"

"Okay."

They said their goodbyes. Dinner... she hadn't planned any dinner. Good thing Wayne wasn't going to be home. She'd just cook up some pasta for the kids. Her older boy, Chris, had karate later tonight and now with Wayne being late, Sabrina would have to drag the twins along with her. That would not go pleasantly because Nelly and Jason never liked to tag along, especially close to their bedtime.

Maybe Sabrina could get Joy Woods to drive Chris. Joy had a son in the same karate class and the Woods lived in the neighborhood. Surely the other woman would do her a favor since they lived so close. Of course, Sabrina would have to find Joy's phone number. Where had she put that class directory?

The Explorer parked in front of the Farmington home and Sabrina walked Jade to the door. Jill Farmington answered the bell and thanked Sabrina.

"Jill, is this yours?" Sabrina held out the necklace.

"No," Jill answered, inspecting it. "But I wish it was. I like it."

Sabrina was surprised. She had been sure the necklace belonged to Jill. Sabrina crossed her arms, confused. "I don't know who it belongs to. The carwash guy found it under the seat."

"Maybe it's been there since the previous owner."

Honestly, thought Sabrina with some annoyance, couldn't Jill tell that the SUV was new?

"Who have you driven lately that could have lost the necklace?" Jill Farmington asked "Nobody other than the kids," Sabrina replied, mystified. "I mean, I drove a couple of friends to the spa in Ojai, but that was two months ago."

"Anyone with the initial J?"

Again, Sabrina shook her head. Jill shrugged, apparently out of ideas.

Sabrina returned to her car and pondered the mystery of the necklace. No one else had driven her car except her husband and that had been for only one day. Who else could have been in her car? Sabrina dropped off Tommy and then drove toward her own home. She eventually comes to that conclusion

The Masons lived in a cookie-cutter neighborhood, where all the houses looked alike. Sabrina's model was a mid-range plan, not the most deluxe, but not the cheapest either. Sabrina's sister Angie was a magazine editor who lived in Manhattan and she often teased Sabrina about her suburban life. She would ask Sabrina if she was ever bored. How could Sabrina be bored with three kids under the age of eleven?

As if I'd like to live in your studio apartment above a store in Chinatown.

It was noisy and crowded where her sister lived. Sabrina considered herself blessed to be in the rarefied air of suburbia. And if she did get bored, if she ever got bored... well, she didn't. Sometimes though, especially when she was annoyed, like by the stains in her car, Sabrina got a little stressed out. Like when Chris ran his skateboard into the wall. Sabrina hadn't meant to yell so loud, but now she had a hole in the plaster to deal with and she hated, simply *hated* to see things out of order. Order gave her joy in life. And in the master bathroom, a little piece of wallpaper was coming off the wall. She was sure the damage was from steam because Wayne took exceedingly long showers, especially when he came home from a long workday. How that errant piece of wallpaper drove her crazy! What she needed to do was call a handyman. She would talk to Hector about everything that was out of order. He said he could fix anything.

While the noodles boiled on the stove, Sabrina turned her attention to the necklace. There was no other engraving on it, nothing to give her a clue as to the owner. It had broken and obviously slipped off someone's neck. And how did those stains get in her car? The kids probably tracked something in. It was simply impossible for her house, clothing and her car to stay clean with three kids coming and going!

When the pasta was ready, Sabrina dumped the water, added butter, garlic powder and salt and stirred the pot. She tried to think of anyone she knew with a name starting with the letter J. Other than Jill Farmington, and little Jade of course, no other "J's" surfaced in her mind.

Her ten-year-old son Chris entered the kitchen.

"Do Nelly and Jason really have to come to karate with us tonight?"

"Yes," Sabrina answered. "Now go get your uniform I laid out so you can put it on right before we leave."

Chris rolled his eyes like a preteen and retreated to his room.

"And call the twins for dinner!" his mother ordered.

After they ate, Sabrina went into the garage and flipped on the light. She opened the backseat door of the Explorer and shook her head at the stains on the carpet. Unable to see very well, she plucked a flashlight from the toolbox and returned to the SUV.

Although Hector had tried his best, the blotches were still there—dark spots against the beige carpeting. Again, they didn't appear to have been dropped or dripped, they seemed to have been sprayed, as if some liquid had shaken violently all over her car. Who did this? And when did it happen? Her eyes traveled over the leather interior. She removed the twins' booster seats and ran the flashlight beam over the backseat. Nothing stained the leather, but on the door nearest the spots, there was a small red stain on the carpeting covering the car's interior door.

Sabrina swallowed. Suddenly, her car didn't feel like hers anymore. Something had spilled without her knowledge and someone had lost a necklace. Someone had infiltrated her car! Had she locked the Explorer at the market yesterday? Perhaps she didn't and some filthy vagrant had taken a nap in her car.

A vagrant wearing a diamond necklace?

"Mom!" Chris yelled from the doorway into the house. He wore his karate uniform. "We've got to go."

Nelly and Jason, as predicted, refused to accompany their brother to karate and began to whine. Sabrina hated when the twins pitched a fit, which was doubly loud. Thinking of Joy Woods again, Sabrina frenetically searched for the karate class directory. She finally found it in the study, sitting on Wayne's desk. Sabrina flipped through the pages and found the listing, "Woods, Joy and Phillip."

Strange, the name "Joy" had been circled by a heavy pen and the paper had been doodled upon, as if someone had sat absently contemplating the page while drawing boxes and circles. Sabrina knew she had never had any reason to use the directory before and she had certainly never looked up the Woods's phone number. So why was the listing circled?

Not the listing, just the name "Joy."

She could hear the twins arguing with Chris and Sabrina quickly called the number next to the name.

The message machine answered and Sabrina hung up.

Sighing, Sabrina prodded her protesting twins into the car along with their brother and she drove them to karate.

The class was located in a strip mall next to a nail salon and a Baskin Robbins. She placated the twins with ice cream while she waited for Chris to finish his class. Sabrina noticed that the Woods boy was not present.

"Where's the Woods kid?" she asked another mother who was sitting nearby.

"At home, I guess," the mother replied. Her name was Penny and she had a daughter who was one belt higher than Chris.

"I tried calling Mrs. Woods," Sabrina said, "hoping I could get her to take Chris tonight, but nobody answered their phone." Sabrina gestured to the two younger children, who were busily lapping at their ice cream cones while trying to kick each other under the table.

"I'm not surprised," Penny said, shaking her head. "The whole family is upside down over her disappearance."

Sabrina turned away from the twins and looked at Penny. "What do you mean, her disappearance?"

"Joy Woods is gone. That's what I heard! Phillip, her husband, is sick with worry."

Sabrina sat back and absorbed the news. *She's gone.*

On the way home, Sabrina asked Chris if he had ever used the directory to call the Woods boy.

"You mean Daniel?"

Sabrina shrugged.

"No," Chris told her and yawned. "Why would I call him?"

"Did you ever use the directory?"

Chris leaned against the headrest and closed his eyes. "What are you talking about, Mom?"

When they got home, Sabrina bathed the twins and then tucked them into bed. They wanted a story, so Sabrina read them *Three Billy Goats Gruff.* She sugarcoated the part about the evil ogre who lived under the bridge because Nelly was still prone to night terrors.

After giving Chris a kiss goodnight, Sabrina went downstairs and made three lunches. She drew a heart on three napkins, folded them in a precise manner and tucked one neatly into each brown bag. She then retrieved the diamond necklace and returned to the study.

She sat at Wayne's desk and opened the karate class directory. Once again her eyes were drawn to the heavy circle around the name Joy. She looked at the pendant in her hand.

Joy begins with a "J."

Sabrina shook her head. Too weird, that's all.

She's gone...

Sabrina picked up the phone and called Joy's phone number. The message machine answered again.

"You have reached the Woods residence," a boy's polite voice recited.

Daniel...

"Please leave a message and we will call you back."

"Hi, this is Sabrina Mason. We—I have a son, Chris, in karate with Daniel. We live in the neighborhood. I got your number from the class directory. Could you call me back, please?"

Sabrina left her phone number and then ended the call. She gazed at the phone with a frown. Why did she call Joy and Phillip Woods? She didn't know them. She had no reason to call them.

Her husband is sick with worry...

Sabrina studied the broken gold chain. She saw the torn link, as if it had been yanked hard. Yanked off of someone's neck...

Sabrina's eyes scanned Wayne's desk. Her eyes came to rest upon a pad of notepaper. She reached out a hand and dragged the pad toward her. On the top page she saw circles and squares—random doodles. Just like in the directory.

Wayne.

He'd drawn circles and squares on the directory's page. He was the one who had circled Joy's name. Why?

Again, it occurred to Sabrina that her husband was the only other adult who had had access to the Explorer recently. They'd traded cars two days ago because the SUV needed its first oil change.

Wayne had driven her car!

He'd circled Joy's name.

She's gone.

Joy begins with a "J."

Frightened, Sabrina began rifling through Wayne's desk, unsure of what she was looking for, but determined to find something anyhow. She dug through a stack of bills—cable, insurance, mortgage, more insurance, car payments—nothing unusual stood out. Thrumming her fingers frantically on Wayne's desk, Sabrina finally jumped up and jogged down the steps. She moved into the kitchen, grabbed the flashlight again and went out into the garage.

She wanted to inspect the cargo area more carefully. Sabrina pressed the garage door opener and marched to the back of the Explorer. The garage door lifted with a mechanized rolling. Standing directly outside was a man.

Sabrina saw him out of the corner of her eye and gave a squeak of surprise. She quickly trained the flashlight beam on him and the light wavered in her shaking hand.

He was wild-eyed and tense. He wrung his hands and yelled, "I know you know! You must know! Tell me!"

Sabrina could only gape at the man as he entered the garage and pointed at her. Gripping the flashlight in her hand like a club, she raised her arm menacingly. "Don't come any closer!"

The man faltered and stared at her miserably.

"Who are you?" Sabrina demanded.

"Phillip Woods," the man answered and his voice cracked. "I'm desperate to know where she is!"

"Phil!" another man came running up the driveway and he grabbed Phillip's arm.

"I'm sorry," he said to Sabrina. "I'm Larry, his brother. He's just a wreck over his wife. He's bothering all the neighbors. He's—he's not himself. I'm so sorry."

Sabrina could only stare at the spectacle of the man being led away. As soon as the two men were down the driveway, she raised a trembling finger and pushed the button to close the garage door. For a few minutes, Sabrina stood with her breath whistling through her nose. That was Phillip Woods!

She's gone.

"I'm desperate to know where she is!"

Sabrina dragged her eyes toward the Explorer. Still in shock from the exchange with Phillip Woods, she deposited the flashlight in the toolbox and headed toward the door that led into the house. She froze in mid-step and then turned back toward the toolbox.

Next to the toolbox stood a can of gasoline. Sabrina narrowed her eyes at it. When she'd tried to patch that hole in Chris's room a few days ago this gas can had not been here. Wayne must have bought it. What did he need extra gasoline for? The filling station was just down the block. Sabrina sighed. She hated when things were out of place. What was with Wayne these days? It was as if she no longer knew her husband.

She's gone.

Wayne! He'd been acting strange lately, a little more distant, a little angrier. Wayne! He took her car. Sabrina covered her mouth with her hand. The stains—they were bloodstains, of course. The spray pattern—the ugly spot on the carpet. It was red and it was blood. He'd circled Joy's name... What did that mean? What did he do to Joy Woods? What other women's names had he circled?

Sabrina looked desperately toward the kitchen door. She'd have to wake the kids. She'd have to get them out of the house. They could go to her parents' house until she could figure out what to do. Panicked, Sabrina reentered her home and was halfway up the stairs when the front door swung open and her husband walked inside.

"Hi, honey," he said. Wayne seemed tired, spent. He walked past her up the stairs, giving her a peck on the cheek. His clothes were disheveled. His hair was mussed.

Sabrina's jaw dropped as she stared after him. She looked down. In her palm, the diamond necklace glistened. She followed Wayne into the bedroom. She had to know.

Wayne had his shoes off and he was removing his tie. He yawned widely.

"Kids asleep?"

Sabrina said nothing. She tossed the necklace onto the bed where it landed with a soft plop. Wayne Mason froze, his fist still pulled at his tie, his eyes settled on the necklace, which lay coiled like a snake on their bed.

After a moment, he sighed and looked at his wife. "Where did you find it?"

"Whose is it?" she demanded.

"It belongs to Joy Woods."

Sabrina felt her knees go weak. Was it relief? Was it horror?

"My God, Wayne. Why did you do it?"

"It's complicated, Sabrina," he answered, almost apologetically. "These things just happen. I didn't plan on it. But now that it's out in the open..."

"You didn't plan on it?" Sabrina cried. "How could you do something like this? You are not the man I married!"

"I know, I know."

"You killed her!"

Wayne looked at Sabrina in astonishment. "What?"

"The blood—it's all over the carpet. Right near where her necklace was found. Why did you do it, Wayne? Why?"

He narrowed his eyes at her and appeared confused. "Wait a minute..."

"Did she lose the necklace as she fought you? Is that how it went down?"

"Not exactly."

His matter-of-fact reply startled Sabrina and she stared at him in silence.

"It wasn't a struggle, per se." Wayne licked his lips and then said, "I didn't kill Joy. I'm having an affair with her."

Sabrina shook her head, not quite comprehending. "She's alive?"

"Very much so."

'But the blood!"

"That wasn't blood, Sabrina. We got a little randy in the back of the car while we were guzzling red wine. It must have spilled. I wasn't aware."

Sabrina shook her head in bewilderment. "I don't understand."

Wayne spoke to her as if she were a child. "Joy has left her husband and she's waiting for me to start a new a life with her. She's at the Holiday Inn downtown. Her husband is a bit of a screwball so we both thought she would be better off keeping her distance from him until things got settled."

"You both thought... You and Joy Woods?"

He nodded.

Sabrina looked from the necklace back to her husband. "You're leaving me?"

He shook his head. "No, Sabrina. You're leaving me." Wayne began to wind the tie around his fist. "Please don't scream and upset the kids. I would have divorced you, except I've been paying on a hefty life insurance for you, a million dollar policy. I could use that money, Sabrina."

"What? Wayne..."

Her husband slowly approached her and pulled the tie taut between his hands. "If we divorced, you'd have your dad to take care of you, but what would I have? There are a lot of debts and... well, this is a better plan."

Sabrina wildly shook her head, trying to clear it.

"You're going to have a fiery accident in the Explorer," Wayne told her. "But don't worry, I will never stop being a father to our kids."

"N-No," Sabrina stammered and willed her leaden feet to move.

He was almost at her and Sabrina gave a cry of fright. She turned and bolted for the stairwell. Wayne chased her down the carpeted steps and caught her by her shirt. She tripped and the two of them spilled onto the entry room floor. Wayne twisted the tie around her neck and began to pull as Sabrina clawed at his face and clutched at his hair. Suddenly, she couldn't breathe. Her hands went to her neck and her frantic fingers scrabbled to pull the tie from her throat.

Out of nowhere, a shovel came whizzing down and caught Wayne Mason on the side of the head. He was flung over as Sabrina choked and struggled with the tie. Her vision cleared and Sabrina saw Hector, holding the shovel and breathing heavily. He stood over Wayne's inert body.

"You okay, Sabrina?" Hector asked gently.

She nodded and stared fixedly at the blood escaping from her husband's head.

"I came to fix the hole in the wall."

Sabrina made no reply.

Hector quietly laid the shovel down and knelt next to her. He took the tie from her hands and dropped it unceremoniously onto Wayne. He cupped Sabrina's chin in his hand and searched her eyes with concern.

"Why don' you go upstairs?" he suggested. "Take a bath, maybe. Don' worry about this. Remember, I can fix anything."

In a half-daze, Sabrina wandered upstairs to the master bathroom, undressed and drew a bath for herself. While she waited for the tub to fill, she noticed the tiny edge of wallpaper lifting from the wall. Sabrina pinched it hard between her thumb and forefinger and began to pull. She tore a long, slow, satisfying swath from the wall. She then moved to the bathtub. As she slowly descended into the warm, scented bubbles, Sabrina decided that she would call Phillip

Woods tomorrow. They would commiserate over how their spouses had abandoned them.

Although the hour was late, Sabrina would place a call to the Holiday Inn and leave a message for Joy Woods. The message would be from Wayne saying that he desperately needed to meet Joy tonight—had they already met this evening?

Of course, they had. That would explain Wayne's disheveled look. Maybe they had been "guzzling" red wine to get "randy." Sabrina smiled and let her hair fan across the hot water. Yes, Wayne needed to meet Joy tonight. After all, they were starting a new life together.

Sabrina held up the pendant in her wet fingers. She was sure that Joy would want her necklace back. Sabrina would give it to her. That and more.

And Sabrina would not stress over any mess. After all, Hector was a pro at cleaning. Look how well he took care of her car.

Dark Nights at the Deluxe Drive-In

Sally Carpenter

"You'll build a mall here over my dead body."

The white-haired man extended a pair of long-handled tongs to snatch a wadded-up Snickers bar wrapper from the asphalt. He deposited the debris into a plastic trash bag held in his other hand. In the days before his back went out, he could stoop over and pick up rubbish with his hands.

With his shoulders hunched, Chester now trudged through the ten-acre lot, dragging the half-filled trash bag on the ground beside him, collecting the rubbish and ignoring the thirty-something man keeping pace beside him. Years ago Chester would easily have outrun this pipsqueak, but ever since his stroke he had trouble keeping up with the intruder in the business suit.

"The city needs a new business here, pops. Crowds like this won't pay your bills."

The unwanted guest gestured at two sedans and an SUV, each parked beside a metal post planted in the lot. From each post ran a wire connected to a small metal speaker that was clipped on a rolled-down car window. Ten rows of similar speaker-topped poles filled the otherwise empty drive-in theater.

"It's only Wednesday, Nathan. Business picks up on the weekends."

"Uh huh." The businessman gazed at the images flickering across the sixty-foot outdoor movie screen. "What kind of crap are you showing this week?"

Chester stopped and leaned against a speaker pole to catch his breath. He sniffled in the cool night air, pulled a handkerchief from the pocket of his twill pants and wiped his runny nose. His watery blue eyes narrowed at Nathan. One eye was developing a cataract so the man looked a little out of focus, which was fine with Chester. Lately he'd seen far more of this irritant than he wanted.

"Nathan, you wouldn't recognize a good movie if it bit your butt." He gazed at the screen. "Couple of good hot rod movies tonight. First film was *The Gumball Rally* from 1976. This is *Two-Lane Blacktop* from '71. Lots of action, pretty girls. Great stuff."

On the screen a '55 Chevy and a '70 GTO raced silently. A muted audio track peeped out from the pole speakers.

Nathan chuckled. "Movies from the '70s? Get with the times, pops. The public wants IMAX, special effects. You ever see a real 3-D movie, pops? I don't mean those silly '50s horror flicks with the cardboard glasses; I mean the new 3-D movies. They'll take your breath away. So realistic. You'd think the characters were in the room with you." He tapped one of the pole speakers. "And audiences want great audio, well mixed, not this tinny noise."

"The audio will sound better. I'm putting in new speakers."

"When?"

"Real soon."

"That's what you said two years ago about replacing the playground equipment."

They stopped beside the kiddie amusement area set up directly beneath the screen. Chester didn't have to clean this area because the children hadn't played here in months.

Nathan tugged on a rusty swing chain holding a cracked plastic seat. "What if a kid sits here and the seat breaks? Kid goes flying and lands on a Beemer. The lawsuit would kill you, pops."

"Stop calling me 'pops.' I'm not your father—thank God."

"All right, Uncle Chester. Don't you want the property to stay in the family?"

"You're not family. You're some kind of deranged mutant. What's wrong with you? Wanting to tear down a man's life's work just to build a bunch of prissy overpriced stores so rich folk can buy more stuff that they don't need."

They walked past a dirt-covered slide and jungle gym pipes turned green from corrosion. "Soon as I have the money, I'm putting in a whole new kiddie section," said Chester.

"Brand-new swings, little go-karts, maybe one of those bouncy things. That'll bring back the families. I remember back when the playground was full of those little tykes running around while their parents watched the movies. The rascals had to stand in line to go down the slide. The best family entertainment in the Valley. Only five bucks a carload back then."

"Face it, Uncle, those days are gone. The kiddies play video games on their iPads while their parents—if they're still married to each other—watch an R-rated movie on their flat-screen TV. If they want to sit in a car to watch a movie, their SUV has a built-in DVD player. Drive-ins are dinosaurs, Uncle. They're as dead as the Edsel."

Chester blinked at the screen. "Last reel's started. Gotta head back so I can close up."

At the other end of the property stood a two-story building covered in corrugated metal. From a second floor window a stream of light stabbed through the night to light the screen. The two men headed for the building, walking along the lot's perimeter so as not to disturb the movie watchers. Nearby, crickets chirped. From beyond the high wooden fence surrounding the theater, the highway traffic zoomed by.

"When they started building the 118 Freeway back in the '70s," said Chester, "I thought I'd get more patrons—they'd take the Topanga Canyon exit south and drive right in. But all those lanes just made everyone want to drive faster. Everyone's in a hurry these days. No time to stop and watch a movie. Nowhere special to go but they're all in a rush to get there."

They passed by the front gate where the patrons entered and a retro neon sign advertised the Deluxe Drive-In. Several of the neon bulbs had shorted out and the rest burned dimly. Even if Chester could find a neon dealer still in business, he couldn't afford the expensive bulbs.

"I remember when this lot was full just about every night. Mostly families on weekends. That's when I showed the comedies. Good, clean fun, not the toilet garbage you see nowadays. On weeknights I had the high school, college crowd. That's when I ran the monster flicks and the beach films. The boys came to show off their cars. Back in '50, '60, that's when the kids really loved their cars. They'd buy these old junkers and fix 'em up, souped-up engines, real fine paint jobs, custom work. Some nights I had more classic cars parked here than the Petersen Museum. Stop yapping on your cell phone while I'm talking."

Nathan scowled at the old man but dutifully terminated the call and returned the phone to his inside jacket pocket.

"What's the matter, did I stop you from earning another million? Who the hell are you talking to this time of night?"

"Uncle, you can be so infuriating."

Chester stopped beside a dumpster at the side of the concession stand. He handed the tongs to Nathan so he could tie the bag's drawstring into a neat bow and drop the bag into the dumpster. Chester wiped his hands on his plaid shirt, stepped over to the side door and removed a metal ring full of keys from his pocket. A chrome chain attached to the key ring held it securely to his brown leather belt. Chester picked through the keys to find the right one, then unlocked the door, entered the concession stand and flipped on the light switch.

The snack stand was already shuttered for the night. A roll-down metal window closed off the serving area from the outside. A long fluorescent tube, embedded in the ceiling, hummed softly as it lit the long, narrow room. Worn vintage Coca-Cola posters covered the fading paint on the walls. The air reeked of popcorn butter and Pine-Sol Cleaner. Years ago Chester kept the stand open late for those who wanted to take home a nighttime snack. Nowadays he didn't have the patrons or staff to keep the concessions going after intermission. His traditional workforce of high school boys had abandoned him for AP classes, community service projects, internships and jobs at Best Buy, Hot Topic or the Apple Store.

"Put the tongs away," Chester ordered. "You know where they go."

"I don't work for you anymore, Uncle, not since high school." Nathan eyed the empty corn popping machine, the half-full metal canisters of soda, the hot dog warmer and the locked cabinets holding a few boxes of Junior Mints and Hershey bars. "Audiences today don't want stale popcorn, flat cola, greasy hot dogs. Multiplexes sell hot pretzels, ice cream, gourmet foods. How are you going to compete against that, Uncle?"

Chester took out his handkerchief and wiped a small puddle of spilled soda off the Formica counter. "What do you know about concessions? When you worked here, you were too busy stealing from the till to mind the store. If your mother wasn't my sister, I would have called the police."

"I wasn't stealing. I was making up for the slave wages you paid me occasionally."

"Why should I pay you for harassing the girls and goofing off?"

"I worked like a dog for you, Uncle, only you were too busy criticizing to notice. Everything I did was wrong. You didn't even like the way I mopped the floor. You choked the life out of me."

At the far end of the room, Chester opened a door to a staircase that led to the second floor. The old man wheezed and his knees hurt as he climbed the squeaky wooden stairs to the projection room. Nathan followed. The tiny upstairs room was dark save for a gooseneck metal lamp atop a wooden table, light from one of two projectors and the glowing screen of a laptop operated by the room's lone occupant. The table held the splicing and rewinding machines. Beside the table stood a metal rack for storing film reels. A small electric fan bolted in one corner of the ceiling vainly tried to cool down the heat generated by the projectors. As the celluloid strip of film nosily clacked through the projection gate, the audio track boomed through a small speaker placed high on the wall.

A skinny young woman with glasses and tousled hair sat in an armless chair beside the table. She wore blue jeans, sandals and a California State University Northridge sweatshirt. She typed on a laptop set up on the table. When the men entered the room, she stood and turned a knob on the speaker to muffle the noise.

Chester made introductions. "Nathan, this is Edie Woods, my employee. Edie, my nephew, Nathan Montgomery."

The woman held out her hand. "Hi, Mr. Montgomery, nice to meet you. Chester talks about you all the time."

Nathan set the tongs on the table and warily gave her hand a perfunctory squeeze. "I'm sure he does."

"Edie's a film student at CSUN. Sharp as they come. Mark my words, she'll be the next Spielberg."

"Chester, you're too kind." She gestured at the second projector. "The closing slide is all ready to go."

The uncle smiled at Nathan. "What did I tell you? Always a step ahead of me."

Nathan glared at the woman. "Why don't you scram? Your boss and I have some business to discuss."

"But I have to help Chester close up—"

"That's okay, Edie," said Chester. "You go on home and finish writing your movie history paper. I'll take care of things tonight."

"Are you sure you can handle lock-up on your own?"

"Yeah, I'll be fine, Edie. I'll clock you out at the usual time so you won't lose any wages."

"Thanks, Chester. That's sweet of you." Edie closed down her laptop, stuffed the computer into a backpack, and flung the sack over her shoulder. "I'll see you tomorrow night then." She glanced at the nephew. "'Bye, Mr. Montgomery." She hurried out the door and down the stairs.

As her footsteps receded, Chester said, "I told Edie I'd run her student movies between the pictures."

"Sure, a hokey amateur film with bad acting and atrocious writing will certainly draw in the crowds." Nathan eased himself into the just-emptied chair. "Still using those old thirty-five-millimeter projectors, Uncle? Those things went out with high button shoes and buggy whips. Everyone uses platters these days. No reel changes, no rewinding. You wouldn't need to pay that kid to sit here and babysit the machines. And soon even platters will be obsolete. The wave of the future is digital. The film beams down from a satellite and onto the screen. No bulky cans to haul around, no film breaking or jamming."

"Computers! They're only as smart as the idiots who program them."

"You should have sold the theater years ago, Uncle. The business itself is worthless and the land value tanked in the recession."

Chester checked the film cans in the rack. "This weekend is a Disney double feature. *The Love Bug* and *Herbie Rides Again*. Couple of fun car flicks. The kids love Herbie."

"Uncle, why are you knocking yourself out for a few measly customers? Why don't you retire?"

The old man glowered at his nephew. "And do what? Sit in some old farts' home and listen to the geezers whine about their ailments? So I got three patrons tonight. Maybe tomorrow night I'll have ten or twenty or a hundred. I like showing movies. I'm making people happy. How many people come home from their jobs at night and say they made somebody happy that day? Can you?"

Nathan pushed back his sleeve, checked his Rolex and stood up. "Look, Uncle Chester, I don't have time to sit in this stuffy room all night arguing with you. I have a developer who's ready to go, but he'll pull out if I can't hand over the property immediately. Look, I'll pay you more than market value for the land. You can take the money and I don't know, buy a DVD player and watch all the old movies you want at home."

"Nephew, if your money is burning a hole in your pocket, then help me fix up the Deluxe. Let's spruce her up, make her nice and shiny, like she was in the old days. I'll even let you put in one of those new platter things. We'll fill up the lot again and make people happy."

"You just don't get it, do you, Uncle? The old days are never coming back. Now, get over it and move on."

"What's so bad about the old days? Why is something better just because it's newfangled and high tech? What's wrong with old-fashioned fun?"

Chester's eyes began to mist over. He gazed fondly out the projection window as Nathan checked his text messages.

"Back in the '60s this great state had more than two hundred and twenty drive-ins. People packed them every weekend. Then those damned indoor movie houses moved in and the grand old theaters died out, one by one. The Thousand Oaks drive-in closed in 1982. Theaters in Simi Valley and Ventura, both gone in 2001. Azusa Foothill is now a parking lot. The Carson, Gardena, Reseda drive-ins, no more. I watched them all go dark and I swore I'd keep this grand old lady open until my last breath."

Nathan turned off his cell and pocketed it. "Uncle, your old lady is losing money. I've seen the figures. You're barely covering expenses. Do you know what I can earn from a multiplex showing the latest blockbusters?"

"Money!" Chester snorted and wiped his nose with his handkerchief. "Don't you ever think about anything else? The way you run after money, Nathan, it'll kill you. Now you may as well calm down and finish watching the film. If I ever sell the Deluxe, it won't be to you."

Nathan's eyes burned and his cheeks flushed. "Look, Uncle, nobody tells me no. Not my mother, not my business partners, not the developers. You sell me this property right now or you'll regret it."

"Regrets? I only have one regret in life, nephew, that I didn't call the police when I caught you stealing from me. Once a thief, always a thief. Now get the hell out of here. You ever step foot in the Deluxe again, I'll call the cops and have you hauled off for trespassing."

Nathan punched the old man in the face. Chester staggered back and fell against the film rack. As he slid to the ground, the rack tilted forward and dumped the cans on him. A few cans clattered to the floor. The nephew continued to pummel his uncle's face with quick, vicious jabs. Chester screamed and swung his arms in a vain attempt to stop the attack. Nathan shouted at the old man to shut up. He picked up an empty film can and beat his uncle on the head.

But instead of quieting down, Chester moaned loudly and gasped for air. He clutched at his chest and his limbs jerked. The music from the film's closing credits boomed over the speaker. Nathan straightened up and stepped back. Blood trickled from the cuts in the old man's face. He gave a final convulsion. His head and eyes rolled back. His arms flopped down and he lay still.

Panting, Nathan stared at the body. He leaned over, shook the old man by the shoulders and shouted at him to get up. No response. Sweat ran down Nathan's face and his heart beat a quick staccato. Outside, the parked cars started up. Nathan stared at the projection window. He'd forgotten about the patrons. He gripped the edge of the window and peered out. Had the people in the cars below heard the screaming? Were they calling the police on their cell phones?

The closing credits ended and the room fell silent except for the tail end of film flapping on the take-up reel. Nathan stared at the blank screen outside and caught his breath. The closing slide! His crazy old uncle had always run a closing slide at the end of each night's show. If the message didn't appear, the patrons might grow suspicious.

Frantic, he thought back when he worked at the Deluxe. That girl who was in the room earlier said the closing slide was in place. The second projector was loaded with a small reel. Was this the right piece of film? Nathan had no time to check it out. He tried to remember how the projectors worked. Biting his lip, he pressed buttons and flipped switches randomly in an attempt to turn one projection off and the other one on. After what seemed like an eternity, the second projection came to life and a message appeared on the outdoor screen: THANK YOU FOR YOUR PATRONAGE. PLEASE COME AGAIN. DRIVE SAFELY.

Nathan watched the patrons as they replaced the speakers onto the poles, accelerated and drove off the lot. He switched off the projectors, sank in the chair, took a deep breath and closed his eyes. In his career he'd stolen, embezzled and scammed, but he'd never killed before. His body shook and his mouth went dry. He opened his eyes and stared at the body.

"This is all your fault, Uncle," he yelled. "If you hadn't been so stubborn, this wouldn't have happened. Now I have to clean up the mess. Even in death, you're a damned nuisance."

Nathan steepled his index fingers and pressed them to his chin as his rational brain kicked in, mulling over his next step just as he would with any business deal gone awry. He weighed his options and made a plan. He guessed that the old man had suffered a heart attack, typical for a man his age. But the bruises and wounds on Chester's face and head would look suspicious—so the best solution was to make him disappear.

First he had to shut down the theater so the motorists driving by wouldn't notice anything amiss or even worse, try to come in. Nathan pushed the film cans off the body, fumbled in the old man's pants pocket and pulled out the key ring. He unlatched the safety catch and palmed the key ring. He hurried down the stairs and across the lot to the entrance. Nathan pulled the main gates shut and locked them, switched off the neon sign and dimmed the lot lights.

Back in the projection room, he pulled off his tie and stuffed it into a jacket pocket. Then he removed his suit jacket and draped it across the back of the chair. He found a pair of white cotton gloves on the table. Chester had lectured him to always wear gloves before splicing film to keep the celluloid clean. Now he needed the gloves to keep from leaving fingerprints. He pulled on the gloves, picked up a cleaning rag and wiped all the surfaces he had previously touched.

The old man was meticulous in making everything tidy before leaving each night. Nathan set up the film rack and replaced the cans. He picked up the dented film can he used in the attack and set it beside his jacket to dispose of later. He removed the take-up reel of the feature film from the projector, placed it on the rewinding machine, threaded the tail of the film into an empty reel and flipped the "on" switch.

The phone rang.

Nathan stared at the black rotary wall phone as the persistent ring shattering the stillness. Who would be calling at this hour? The police? Was that girl checking up on the old man?

His hand shook as he picked up the receiver. He cleared his throat and spoke calmly. "Deluxe Drive-in Theater." He listened. "Sorry, you have the wrong number."

Nathan replaced the receiver and let out a sigh of relief. Hopefully the caller would assume the old man had answered and was still alive. Nathan ran down the stairs to the office, a tiny cramped room just behind the concession stand with only a desk, swivel chair and file cabinets stuffed full of receipts and film catalogues. He switched on the answering machine on the desk. Now anyone calling would hear Chester's recorded message about the upcoming shows.

Nathan opened a closet full of cleaning supplies. He headed back upstairs with a bucket of water, a bottle of bleach, rags and a pile of plastic trash bags. He placed the rewound film reel back in the can and on the rack. He likewise rewound the closing slide reel. Nathan got on his knees and thoroughly scoured the floor to remove any possible trace of blood or hair. There! Spotless! Good enough to pass the old man's white-glove test.

Nathan wrapped up the body with the trash bags. He turned off the fan, closed the shutter on the projection window and gave a last look around. He replaced the cleaning supplies and the tongs in the downstairs closet, then one last trip upstairs to fetch the body and the dented film can. Good thing Nathan had worked out in the gym so he had the stamina for this chore.

He draped his jacket over one arm, tucked the film can under the other arm and lifted the body over his shoulder. Nathan turned out the table lamp and left the room. With the old man's key he locked the door behind him and walked down the stairs, careful that the body didn't rub against the walls and leave a mark. He turned out the lights in the concession stand and locked that door as well. He headed to the shed to fetch the shovel, stored right where Nathan remembered. In all these years the old man hadn't changed a thing.

He set the bundle beside the kiddie pool, hung his jacket over a bar on the jungle gym and placed the dented film can on the ground nearby. Nathan began digging beside the concrete pool by the light of a full moon. His heart pounded with each shovel of dirt and he kept glancing over his shoulder, fearful that a cop might appear. The tall wooden fence surrounding the lot kept passers-by from watching the dirty deed. When the hole was finished, Nathan buried the body and carefully replaced the dirt, packing the sod to remove signs of digging. He cleaned off the shovel with a rag, grabbed his jacket and returned to the shed to replace the shovel and lock the shed door. No wonder the old man had so many keys on the heavy ring.

Now he had to figure out which key started the old man's truck, the Chevy pickup he'd driven for years. The truck was parked behind the concession stand. Nathan had some trouble with the stick shift, but managed to drive the clunker through the back gate and onto a deserted surface street.

He drove the few blocks to the Chatsworth Metrolink Park 'N' Ride train station where Nathan parked the truck. He put on his jacket, stripped off the gloves, tucked them into his suit pocket and walked back to the theater along the city sidewalks, turning his face away from any passing cars. He didn't dare take a taxi and risk having the cabbie identify him.

Back at the drive-in Nathan retrieved the dented film can and walked to his Lexus. He had parked beside the old man's truck, so the patrons would not have seen his car. He unlocked his car and hid the film can in the truck. He got in, started up, drove through the back gate and stopped the car so he could close up the Deluxe for the last time.

But he didn't get out to shut the gate just yet. Nathan remembered his cell. He should have turned it off earlier as not to attract attention in case someone called. Nathan reached into the empty pocket where he always kept his cell.

Where was it?

For a moment he panicked. Did he leave the phone in the locked projection room? Did it fall into the pit with the body? Worse yet, did he leave it in his uncle's truck? Did it drop out of his pocket during his walk from the station? Frantic, he drove his car back onto the lot and meticulously retraced his steps from the building to the playground. A cloud slid over the moon, reducing visibility. In the darkness he got down on his knees and groped around on the ground. There! He felt it! Nathan picked up the phone and sat back on his knees. Apparently, it had fallen out when he hung his jacket on the jungle gym. He gave a sigh of relief, stood, dusted off his knees and firmly stuffed the cell into the pocket. Back in the Lexus he pulled out of the lot, set the car in park and stepped out.

Now, he was ready to leave. He pulled shut the heavy iron back gate that creaked on its hinges and locked it. He used his handkerchief to wipe his prints off the latch. There. All done. Everything spic and span, just the way the old man would have closed up for the night. Nathan pocketed the stolen keys and drove. He stayed within the speed limit and obeyed the traffic lights so a cop wouldn't pull him over and start asking questions.

He found a dive where the people didn't know him so he could establish an alibi. Nathan sat at the bar, ordered a gin and tonic and loudly complained about working late at the office. After nursing his drink for a while, he paid in cash and left.

He swung around to the old man's house, a two-bedroom bungalow on a quiet side street north of Ventura Boulevard in Winnetka. He parked his car in the shadows two blocks away, walked to the house, put the gloves on again and unlocked the back door. He left his dirty shoes on the back stoop to avoid leaving footprints. The house was crammed with framed movie posters and bookcases full of movies on videocassettes. Nathan found an old brown leather suitcase and filled it with clothes and toiletries. He closed up the house and placed the suitcase and the dirty gloves in the trunk of the Lexus. In the morning he'd drive out to his boat docked in the marina. He'd put the film can, the keys, the gloves and heavy rocks in the suitcase, sail out a mile or two and chuck the evidence into the ocean.

At his house in Malibu, Nathan took a long, hot shower and put on his pajamas. He lit the fireplace and burned his suit. He couldn't risk having someone at the dry cleaners wonder why the clothes were so dirty.

As he watched the crackling flames, he thought about the girl in the projection booth—what was her name? Edie Woods. Would she connect him with the old man's disappearance? Should he try to silence her? Tracking down a student at the large, crowded university campus would be difficult and risky. Covering up one murder was hard enough; besides, with no evidence or body, the girl couldn't prove anything. Nathan could deny that he was at the drive-in. He'd claim that the girl couldn't identify his uncle's visitor in the dark projection room.

Nathan poured himself a drink and tried to relax. He couldn't. Around 4 a.m. he took a sleeping pill and drifted into a dreamless sleep.

"I wish the old man could see this. He'd have a fit."

Nathan took a deep breath, taking in the smell of the new leather seats in Screening Room No. 13. He held out his arms and spun around on his heels for another view of his masterpiece—a two hundred eighty-five seat indoor theater with retro styling, chandeliers, stadium seating with cup holders and tables for the gourmet hors d'oeuvres available at the concession stand. The CinemaLux offered twenty-four screening rooms, the largest movie house in the San Fernando Valley.

A mere two years ago, patrons were puzzled when they arrived for an evening show at the Deluxe Drive-In and found the front gate locked. Edie filed a missing persons report with the police, who found no signs of violence at either the theater or Chester's home. Sometime later Chester's truck was found at the Park 'N' Ride station and the police closed the case, stating that the old man had simply taken a train to Union Station and left town.

With Chester out of the way, Nathan's battery of lawyers quickly seized ownership of the Deluxe. He ordered the building bulldozed, the speaker poles uprooted, the rusted playground equipment removed and the kiddie pool filled in with cement. After the edifice went up, Nathan noticed that the screen of Room No. 13 hung directly over the site of the kiddie pool. Ah, such irony.

The lobby door opened and Edie stepped into the room, smiling at him. She held a pair of plastic 3-D glasses. The young woman looked quite attractive in the CinemaLux employee uniform—tight black pants, white shirt, maroon vest and black bow tie. Far more stylish than jeans and sweatshirts.

"I appreciate you giving me a job, Mr. Montgomery. I needed the money to finish my film projects for school."

"Don't expect any pampering. I'm not a pushover like my uncle. Don't expect me to let you out early so you can do homework. I only pay for actual hours worked, not for chatting with your buddies or taking smoke breaks." Edie started to sit in an aisle chair. "Don't do that, you'll get the seat dirty."

"I'm sorry." She stood up and brushed the leather cushion. "These are nice seats, Mr. Montgomery. They look expensive."

"Too bad my uncle isn't here to see this. This is how movies were meant for viewing, in comfortable seats and fine surroundings, not by looking through a bug-spattered windshield and listening to tinny mono speakers. The grand opening tomorrow will be fantastic. The Chamber of Commerce will be here, City Council, the neighborhood association, everyone who's anyone."

"Whatever happened to your Uncle Chester? Did he ever come back?"

"No, he didn't," Nathan snapped.

"That's weird. Chester never missed opening the Deluxe on a show night. He even came in one week when he had the flu. He sat in the projection room wrapped up in a blanket and shivered while the films ran."

"My uncle had dementia. The last time I saw him, he was talking nonsense. Working so hard on a losing business made him tired and crazy." Nathan smiled. "He sends me postcards from New York City. He says he's happy there and he's never coming back. He's glad I took that old money pit off his hands. But that's enough about my uncle. Go start the film. I want to see how it looks and check out the sound system."

Edie handed him the plastic glasses. "It's a 3-D movie, Mr. Montgomery. You'll need these."

Nathan took the glasses and Edie left through the lobby doors. He slid down into one of the high-back chairs in back row center, slipped on the glasses and grinned. He'd use the profits from CinemaLux to add more stores to the new shopping center. Montgomery Square would be the premium retail complex of the Valley, better than the aging Northridge Fashion Center or the Burbank Town Center.

The house lights dimmed and the darkness enveloped Nathan like a shroud. The screen lit up with the opening credits of *Zombie Hell*, an R-rated slasher film geared for the lucrative teen-to-young-male-adult demographic. Nathan thought back to the nights he worked at the Deluxe when he was forced to screen such dreck as *Robot Monster*, *Attack of the 50-Foot Woman*, and *Plan 9 From Outer Space*. Not even a five-year-old would find those films scary.

The eerie Dolby soundtrack music thumped through the quad speaker system. On the screen the camera panned through a nighttime graveyard as the zombies came out of their tombs. A close-up on one grave—the ground shook and the earth collapsed into the hole. A man struggled to climb out of the trench. Nathan laughed. The shot reminded him of a similar scene in *Plan 9* in which the obese Tor Johnson groped his way out of a grave. No doubt an inside joke by the filmmaker.

The zombie stood erect on the ground and stared at the audience. The white-haired man with the decomposed face and torn clothing lurched forward. He raised his hands straight out as he lumbered along, legs locked at the knee. The 3-D effect was fantastic—the zombie's hands seemed to reach out into the audience, ready to grab his next victim. Nathan mentally computed how many tickets he could sell with repeat business. The kids would eat this up. Then the smile fell off Nathan's face and his eyes grew wide. He sat straight up in the chair.

The zombie looked exactly like Uncle Chester.

Even with the rotted-flesh make-up, the resemblance was incredible. The same watery blue eyes, tight lips, bad haircut. The zombie wore a plaid shirt and twill pants, the same color and style as the clothing Chester wore on his last night alive. No, just a coincidence, Nathan thought. All elderly actors look alike and plenty of old men wear plaid shirts and twill pants. The movie was playing tricks on his mind.

A chrome keychain, hanging from the zombie's brown leather belt, swung in a wide arc with each clumsy step. The chain had an empty hook on the end with no keys on it.

With the 3-D effect the zombie seemed to step off the screen. The body hovered over the front row seats, then headed straight toward the lone viewer. The arms reached out and the boney fingers flexed with anticipation.

Nathan jumped from his seat and stood in the aisle. He called to the projection booth, "Edie! You can turn it off now. I've seen enough." The light kept streaming from the small window. "Edie! Did you hear me? I said turn it off!" The zombie kept coming. "Is this some kind of a joke? It's not funny! Stop the movie!"

Nathan faced the screen. The larger-than-life zombie stood only a few feet from him. The decayed fingers grabbed at his face. Nathan slapped at the image but his hands only swung through the air, striking nothing. He grabbed the earpieces and tried to pull off the glasses, but the eyewear was stuck to his face. Nathan stepped back from the zombie image until he reached the lobby door. He pushed the panic bar as hard as he could but the door was locked tight.

"Edie! Unlock this door!" He pounded on the door with both fists. "Edie! Open the hell up!"

The sound of a heartbeat pulsed over the speakers, growing louder and louder. Nathan turned and stared at the image that filled the room. Shreds of putrid flesh hung from the face of the late Uncle Chester. The image smiled, revealing rows of rotted teeth. The mouth moved in a silent laugh. Nathan stepped back until his spine pressed against the lobby door.

"Go away! Leave me alone!" Nathan screamed at the image. "You're dead! I buried you under the kiddie pool! Go back to your grave!"

The fingers encircled his neck. Nathan grabbed at the zombie's arms but his hands clutched nothing. "Stop it, Uncle! Stop choking me! The Deluxe is gone! Drive-ins are dead! They'll never come back to life! This is my theater now!

You're trespassing! Get out of my theater!" Tears ran down the nephew's cheeks. "Please, Uncle! Leave me alone! I'm sorry I killed you. Just leave me alone. Please?"

The zombie's face filled the room. The nephew's heart raced and he couldn't breathe. The heartbeat pounded at full volume. Nathan slid down the door to the floor, clutching his throat and sobbing. The old man's voice boomed over the speakers from every corner of the room.

"You'll build a mall here over my dead body!"

Inside the booth, Edie switched off the projector. The house lights came on inside the theater, bathing the room in a warm friendly glow and the zombie disappeared. On the screening room floor, Nathan lay curled up in a heap, shaking. Edie swiveled around in her chair and faced her invited guests—a homicide detective and the faculty advisor for her senior film project.

"I knew something was wrong the night I showed up for work and Chester didn't have the back gate open for me. Chester loved the Deluxe too much to ever leave it. He had told me that his nephew was trying to take the property from him. The police refused to investigate, so I took matters into my own hands and made this little film."

"Very nice work, Edie," said the professor. "Definitely 'A' material. Who's the actor?"

"Someone I found through the SAG roster. I held auditions and searched for several months to find someone with just the right look. Of course the makeup and clothes helped create the illusion."

"The special effects are especially creative."

"Thank you. I wanted to make sure Mr. Montgomery saw the entire film, so I placed Super Glue on the earpieces of his glasses."

"The zombie voice was a nice touch," said the professor. "Made the film come alive."

Edie frowned at the blank screen. "That's a mystery. I shot the film without sound. I have no idea how that voice got onto the audio track."

ABOUT THE CONTRIBUTORS

(Editor and Author Bios (in story order))

Darrell James is the author of both short stories and novels. His short stories have appeared in numerous mystery magazines and book anthologies, and have garnered a number of awards, to include his latest story in the Lee Child anthology, *Vengeance*, with Lee Child, Michael Connelly, Dennis Lehane, Alafair Burke, Karin Slaughter and other notable authors. His Del Shannon series of novels include: *Nazareth Child*, winner of the Left Coast Crime Eureka! Award for Best First Novel and *Sonora Crossing*, released in Sept. 2012. Book three in the series, *Purgatory Key,* is forthcoming in August 2013. www.darrelljames.com.

Linda O. Johnston's first published fiction appeared in *Ellery Queen's Mystery Magazine* and won the Robert L. Fish Memorial Award for Best First Mystery Short Story of the year. Since then, Linda has published more short stories, plus 33 romance and mystery novels, including Harlequin Romantic Suspense as well as the Alpha Force paranormal romance miniseries for Harlequin Nocturne. Linda's Pet Rescue Mysteries, a spinoff from her Kendra Ballantyne, Pet-Sitter mysteries for Berkley Prime Crime, feature Lauren Vancouver, a determined pet rescuer who runs a no-kill shelter. In this cozy series, "no-kill" refers to pets, not people! Website: www.lindaojohnston.com.

Tammy Kaehler's career in marketing and technical writing landed her in the world of automobile racing, which inspired her with its blend of drama, competition, and welcoming people. Her debut, *Dead Man's Switch,* was praised by mystery fans as well as racing insiders, and she took readers back behind the wheel in *Braking Points,* the second Kate Reilly Racing Mystery. Tammy works as a technical writer in the Los Angeles area, where she lives with her husband and many cars. Website: www.tammykaehler.com.

Gary Phillips' latest is the *Essex Man: 10 Seconds to Death*, a homage to '70s era paperback vigilante series. He also edited the anthology *Scoundrels: Tales of Greed, Murder and Financial Crimes* for Down & Out Books, and has *The Perpetrators* in ebook from the publisher. One of his proudest times was rebuilding a '58 Ford Fairlane Interceptor with his mechanic father, Dikes. Website: www.gdphillips.com.

L.H. Dillman lives in Southern California, has a teenage son and detests mini-vans. Any other coincidences with the fiction in "Cam The Man" are purely accidental. The author is working on a legal mystery novel set in Los Angeles.

Donna May is a native of Boston. Her first short story, "The Acquisition," appeared in the anthology, *Murder in LaLa Land.* If it weren't for her work on a variety of television shows, including *Heroes, The West Wing, ER* and currently *Switched at Birth,* she would be hard at work on her latest novel, *Lucy Who,* a fast-paced thriller about self-reinvention.

Dr. Beverly J. Graf teaches film studies at Pepperdine University and UCLA Extension, and is the former VP of Development for Abilene Pictures (*Primal Fear, Frequency, Fracture*). She has just completed the manuscript for her first mystery novel, also set in 2020 LA and featuring the same Detectives Eddie Piedmont and Shin Miyaguchi as seen in "Shikata Ga Nai." This is her first short story to be published.

Andrew Jetarski works as a television motion picture editor in Southern California. Fellow writers and his loving wife have encouraged his literary endeavors. This is his first published story. Having thrived in the shallows of reality TV, he is nevertheless drawn by deeper-flowing currents of the past. Los Angeles in the 1930s is a great well of inspiration. He works his day job under the name on his Social Security card; as a fiction writer he uses an Americanized version of his grandfather's birth name.

Paul D. Marks is the author of over thirty published short stories in a variety of genres, ranging from noir to straight mystery, satire to serious fiction, including several award winners. A former script doctor, his award-winning mystery-thriller *White Heat* has received favorable reviews from Publishers Weekly, Midwest Book Review, etc. and was chosen one of the Best Fiction Books of 2012 by Rosa St. Claire of Examiner.com. Paul also has the distinction, dubious though it might be, of being the last person to film on the famed MGM backlot before it bit the dust to make way for housing. Website: www.pauldmarks.com.

Lynn Allyson was born in San Francisco and grew up in the heart of Silicon Valley. After completing her MBA she worked as a healthcare administrator for a number of years before starting a second career in real estate. Lynn has written non-fiction articles for *Los Angeles Family* magazine and worked as a contributing writer for an online lifestyle magazine. "Identity Crisis" is her first published short story. She is currently working on her second novel.

Bonnie J. Cardone is a writer, editor, photographer and scuba diver with two nonfiction books and about 1,000 nonfiction articles to her credit. She is also the author of the Cinnamon Greene Adventure Mysteries, whose characters appear in her short story in this anthology. The first book in the Greene series is scheduled for publication this year. Bonnie served as editor of the Sisters in Crime national newsletter for nine years and is a former president of the Central Coast

Chapter of Sisters in Crime. A long time California resident and SinC/LA member, she grew up in Arizona, Chicago and Michigan. Website: www.bonniejcardone.com.

Stephen Buehler grew up in Flourtown, a suburb of Philadelphia but headed west to Hollywood with the ambition of being a writer for film and TV. Finding only production jobs in television, he changed paths and worked in advertising for many years. These days Stephen is a Script/Story Consultant for his own business, ReWriteDr, helping other writers achieve their goals and dreams. His short fiction has been published in numerous on-line publications but "Not My Day" is Stephen's first traditionally published short story. He is currently working on a mystery/comedy novel, *Detective Rules*. Email: stephen@rewritedr.com.

Miko Johnson "By Anonymous" is the first published work of fiction by Miko Johnston, a former television and freelance print journalist. She is currently completing a series of historical novels which follow a troubled heroine from childhood to middle age, set against the turmoil of early 20th century Europe. Miko lives in Glendale, California with her rocket scientist husband. Website: www.mikojohnston.com.

Nena Jover Kelty, born in the UK, uses her life experiences in her writing. Her books include a memoir, *My Father was Carmen Miranda*. It tells of working in show business with her family during WWII. She was also a feature writer for the *Glendale News Press* and is a regular contributor for the UK magazine, *Best of British*. News that her entry had been accepted for *Last Exit to Murder*, her first venture into fiction, arrived just before her 90th birthday. Nena wishes to thank Sisters in Crime/Los Angeles for this great honor.

Eric Stone worked for many years as a writer, reporter, photographer, editor and publisher in the U.S. and Asia, covering everything from economics to crime; politics to sex, drugs and rock & roll. He is the author of the four Ray Sharp novels: *Shanghaied*, *Flight of the Hornbill*, *Grave Imports* and *The Living Room of the Dead.* The books are set in Asia and based on stories that Eric covered as a journalist. He is also the author of the true crime / sports biography, *Wrong Side of the Wall*, and the upcoming *Los Angeles Trilogy: The Avenue, The River & The Valley.* Website: www.ericstone.com.

Avril Adams is a first-time contributor to Sisters in Crime/Los Angeles publications. She has, however, been writing short stories for a number of years in various genres. Currently she is working on a crime novel with a female African-American protagonist that takes on all kinds of shadowy figures in high places. Her background is in English literature and agricultural science, which may seem a strange combination for some but fuels her passion for both legs of literature, the abstract and the real world. She is delighted her short story, "The Low Riders," has been accepted for this anthology.

Laura Brennan's career includes theater, news, television and the web. She was a founding member of The Open Door Theater Company before going on to write and produce for PBS. Laura then lopped off heads and played with dinosaurs on such action-adventure series as *Highlander: The Raven, The Lost World* and *The Invisible Man.* She consults as a pitching coach and is co-creator of the web series *Faux Baby*, available on Hulu. Her short stories have appeared in the anthologies *An Evening at Joe's* and *Hell Comes to Hollywood,* a Bram Stoker Award nominee. Check her out at www.PitchingPerfectly.com.

Julie G. Beers has written for multiple television series including *Walker, Texas Ranger*, *Renegade* and *Gene Roddenberry's Earth: Final Conflict.* She is a freelance writer and editor, and currently works as a researcher at AFI (American Film Institute) on the AFI Catalog of Feature Films. "The Last Joy Ride" is Julie's first mystery short story and she is thrilled to have been selected alongside her dear friend, Nena Jover Kelty, a fellow member of the Burbank Barnes & Noble Writers Group.

Laurie Stevens is a novelist, screenwriter and playwright. Her articles and short fiction have appeared in numerous publications. Her debut novel *The Dark Before Dawn* is the first in a psychological suspense series. The novel earned the Kirkus Star and was named to Kirkus Review's "Best of 2011/Indie." The second in the series *Deep into Dusk* is due out Spring 2013. Laurie lives in the hills near Los Angeles with her husband and two children. To learn more about the author, visit her at http://www.lauriestevensbooks.com.

Sally Carpenter, a native Hoosier, now lives in Moorpark, California. Carpenter, a black belt in tae kwon do, has a master's degree in theater from Indiana State University. Her plays *Star Collector* and *Common Ground* were American College Theater Festival One-Act Playwrighting Competition finalists. Now employed at a community newspaper, she's worked as an actress, writing instructor, jail chaplain and movie studio tour guide/page. She writes the Sandy Fairfax Teen Idol mystery series. *The Baffled Beatlemaniac Caper* was a Eureka! Award finalist for best first mystery novel. *Sinister Sitcom Caper*, book two of the series, is close to completion. Blog: http://sandyfairfaxauthor.com.

OTHER TITLES FROM DOWN AND OUT BOOKS

By J. L. Abramo
Catching Water in a Net
Clutching at Straws
Counting to Infinity
Gravesend
Chasing Charlie Chan
Circling the Runway (*)

By Trey R. Barker
2,000 Miles to Open Road
Road Gig: A Novella
Exit Blood

By Richard Barre
The Innocents
Bearing Secrets
Christmas Stories
The Ghosts of Morning
Blackheart Highway
Burning Moon
Echo Bay (*)
Lost (*)

By Milton T. Burton
Texas Noir

By Reed Farrel Coleman
The Brooklyn Rules

By Tom Crowley
Viper' Tail(*)

By Frank De Blase
Pine Box for a Pin-Up (*)

By Jack Getze
Big Numbers (*)
Big Money (*)
Big Mojo (*)

By Keith Gilman
Bad Habits (*)

By Darrel James, Linda O. Johsonton & Tammy Kaehler (editors)
Last Exit to Murder

By David Housewright & Renée Valois
The Devil and the Diva

By David Housewright
Finders Keepers

By Jon Jordan
Interrogations

By Jon Jordan & Ruth Jordan
Murder and Mayhem in Muskego (Editors)

By Bill Moody
Czechmate: The Spy Who Played Jazz
The Man in Red Square
Solo Hand (*)
The Death of a Tenor Man (*)
The Sound of the Trumpet (*)
Bird Lives! (*)

By Gary Phillips
The Perpetrators
Scoundrels: Tales of Greed, Murder and Financial Crimes (Editor)

By Lono Waiwaiole
Wiley's Lament
Wiley's Shuffle
Wiley's Refrain
Dark Paradise

(*)—Coming Soon

Made in the USA
Charleston, SC
27 July 2013